KILLER
RESEARCH

By Ilana S. Lehmann

Other Works by Ilana Lehmann

All You Need to Know about Disability is on Star Trek

Dear Student: Inside the Twisted Mind of an Exasperated Professor

The Completely Useless Dictionary of Higher Education

Cheryl Locke Mysteries

Book One: Killer Research

Book Two: Pain Killers (coming soon)

KILLER RESEARCH

Book One of the

Cheryl Locke Mysteries

By Ilana S. Lehmann

Cover design by Elizabyth Harrington at 4 Monkeys Design, LLC.

Edited by Susan Frager

Printed on acid free paper.

Library of Congress Control Number: 2020909721

Lehmann, Ilana S., 1961 -

Killer Research / Ilana Lehmann -1ˢ edition p. cm

ISBN 978-0-9904540-6-9

For Rachel,
my daughter,
my superhero,
and my inspiration for Emily Locke

Chapter 1
"To Begin at the Beginning"

As I sat down for Sunday breakfast, I listened to my news stream. The death of Dr. Rolando Hernandez, professor of computer programming, caught my attention. I had met Dr. Hernandez when his wife, Dr. Alisha Patel, became dean of the College of Cybernetics. My five years at the University of New England were a closed chapter in my life. Even though tenure had been abolished the following year, I knew that since I had not been granted tenure, I could never go back there. I did not know why I had yet to delete UNE from my newsfeed.

No sooner had the report story, when my *intelligent domestic*, iDom for short, announced I had an incoming call from Dr. Malka Goldberg.

"Watson, pause newsfeed," I requested; I had named my iDom Watson. Dr. Malka Goldberg was probably instructing her intelligent domestic to match the bandwidth.

I glanced at my reflection in the food dispenser's glass and said, "Watson, answer call, voice only."

No makeup, no video. I really should look into getting my freckles removed.

"Hello Malka, how are you doing? How long has it been?" I tried to sound happy to hear from her.

Malka was old enough to be my mother. However, our relationship was either a balance of opposites or symbiosis. Where she was affluent and led a conventional life, my background was . . . not.

I appreciated how kind Malka had been to me at the university. She had invited me to co-author a book, in an attempt to strengthen my tenure application. We worked on several research projects together. Malka invited me out to lunch on my birthday every year that I taught at UNE. When my daughter Emily came to visit, Malka invited us to her beachfront home on Cape Cod. After serving us a marvelous luncheon, she and her husband provided us a personal tour of the Cape. I was surprised that such a famous surgeon as Martin Goldberg would be so knowledgeable about the history of the Cape.

Malka was personally generous, but professionally demanding. Her voice, complete with Cape Cod accent, came through without video as well.

Perhaps we have more in common than I realize.

"The last time I heard from you was when we finally published our last article in–"

Malka cut me off. "Cheryl, I wanted to let you know Sara is being dethroned. Don't believe what's reported aun the Internet. Sara lost ha funding because she was unethical and got caught. I thought you'd want ta know she's almost out, especially aftah the way she treated you."

This was news. *Sara–on her way out? Unbelievable.* She had been hired as a distinguished professor; a title not often given to professors at any university. Firing a full professor and department chair would take a great deal of misconduct. Add "distinguished professor" to the mix and it would probably take a homicide charge.

"You said not to believe the reports," I repeated. "What reports?"

"I'll call you later. Someone's coming," Malka said softly, and quickly ended the call.

One of the disadvantages of wireless communications in smart-homes was that unless you were in a communication closet, anyone in the room could hear your conversation. Malka's iDom, Hilary, could be recording the call, depending on the programming.

As much as I admired Malka, she could be annoying on occasion. When she communicated the old-fashioned way, sending texts or emails, she would forego proper punctuation and even spelling. Calling me and ending the call before telling me the entire story was another irritating trait. As I thought about the conversation, Holmes made a "errr-hufff" sound which was his way of saying he needed to go for a walk.

My father had been a devoted Sherlock Holmes fan. As a child, my daddy would read Sherlock Holmes books to me, but only the ones written before 1924. In homage to my father's memory, I had named my dog 'Holmes,' my cat 'Professor Moriarty,' and my iDom 'Watson.'

I grabbed both the LEESH (Limiting Electronic Exercise Sports Harness) and the Pooperizer (dog-waste vaporizer). The LEESH emitted a force field which kept my corgi from running off.

I felt a buzz on my wrist and looked at my wearable to see if Malka had called me back. I did not recognize the origin, so I assumed it was from one of my students and let the call go to voicemail. I refused to answer any questions about the course or grant an extension to an assignment, while vaporizing dog poo on a Sunday. Even though I was a lowly adjunct instructor and no longer a professor, I was not required to tolerate unscheduled calls.

After our walk, I turned off the LEESH as Holmes and I entered the front door. I was wondering who to contact for the rest of the story about Sara, when Watson announced, "Dr. Frank Covington is calling."

Calls from two former colleagues in one day; this is a red-letter event.

Watson connected us without video on my side.

"Hello Frank. You are the second person from my untenured past to call me today. What is going on?"

"Hello Cher, so you've heard the news 'bout ole Sara?" Frank's soft-spoken manner of talking was comforting.

Listening to his voice reminded me of my loving daddy who would caress my long hair as he tucked me into bed for the night. Frank was the only other person, besides my dad, who I allowed to call me Cher. Mom called me 'Ginger' because of my red hair. To everyone else, I was Cheryl.

"Malka called to tell me Sara is on her way out, but she provided no other details. How did you hear about this so fast? I thought you were in Georgia these days?"

"Yes ma'am. Georgia's my stompin' grounds these days," Frank said. "You should move down here. You'd love the cuisine."

"Do not let your clan back in South Carolina hear you talk like that, or they will brand you a traitor. No, I think I belong on the West Coast. So, are you going to tell me what happened, or do I need to call Leonardo?"

"Believe it or not," Frank said, "Leonardo is prancing around like a cat on a hot tin roof 'bout Sara. Besides, Leonardo never tells the truth. You, of all people, know that."

I chuckled. Leonardo had taken his turn as department chair within weeks of my arrival at UNE. A few months before I left, he had been awarded full professorship after a little shenanigan on his part.

"Sara lost her research grant, and the Institutional Review Board is chargin' her with misconduct," Frank revealed. "According to the IRB, one of her graduate assistants reported she intentionally falsified her data. Do you have any idea what that'll mean?"

"Of course. I sat on the IRB. Remember?"

My terms on the board were some of my fondest assistant professor memories.

"She resigned her position as department chair today," Frank added. "She is as nervous as a long-tailed cat in a room full of rocking chairs."

"That is a long way from a confession. She was probably told to resign by the Dean."

"No, that order came from the provost," Frank corrected me. "The Dean is on administrative leave while the police are investigatin' her husband's death."

For the first time since I heard the news story about Dr. Hernandez, I realized there was probably more to the death than I had previously considered.

"What do you think, Frank?" I asked. "You spent considerably more time working with Sara than I did. The difference being, you already had tenure before she was hired."

"I think Sara could lie to a saint, if it suits her interests," Frank said. "At the same time, it's not like her to be caught with her pants down."

"Agreed. It would be more Sara-like to blame someone else for the misconduct than simply claim she is innocent," I said, and after a pause added, "I hope the grant was not from the Department of Defense this time."

"Yep, the DoD," Frank said, with a little horror in his voice.

"No wonder Leonardo is upset. He is probably worried about keeping his preposterous salary if the DoD stops funding his UNE research. He might even have to lower himself to teaching students again."

Frank's white hair and Van Dyke beard always reminded me of the Colonel Sanders from around 100 years ago. When he disapproved of something, Frank's face would contort into an expression somewhere between disgust and mortification—an expression he frequently wore during department meetings. I doubted Frank played much poker.

"But, Frank, you have not said how you know about Sara. Who told you?" I asked.

"Sara called me. She is going to contact you." His words bypassed my brain and went straight to my stomach. I felt sick.

"Why in the HELL would Sara call me? She knows how I feel about her." The words left my mouth before I realized I had yelled at Frank. I softened my voice. "I am sorry, Frank."

"Good Lord, Cher, you're probably going to yell at me again when I tell ya that I'm the one who told her to call you."

"WHAT?"

"Don't get all riled up. I'll explain everything," Frank said.

He started with how Sara needed someone with expertise in cybernetic implants. I was a former cybernetics implant researcher and expert cybernetic programmer. My five years on the IRB had given me a reputation for integrity and fairness. That same reputation had led to my current work as an investigator of researcher misconduct. Ironically, federal reviewers were paid more and worked less than assistant professors. Frank added that my experience with the faculty might be useful. His explanation followed the same deductive reasoning as Sherlock Holmes. The Department of Defense quickly accepted Frank's suggestion to have me investigate.

In other words, I know where the bodies are buried.

As I ended the call, I realized Frank had told me why Sara would be calling, while carefully omitting the details of the allegations against her.

Why is a former professor at UNE in charge of making the arrangements?

* * *

I settled into my home office and my zero-gravity chair. Uncle Walter had left his Seattle home to me in his will the year before I was denied tenure at UNE. I had always enjoyed visiting my uncle, with his wild hair and even wilder ideas. At the same time, I was surprised when the executor to his estate contacted me about my inheritance.

Without tenure, I had to decide my next career move. I decided to take possession of the house so I could be closer to my daughter, Emily, who lived in Portland, Oregon. I felt like a boomerang, returning to the West coast.

Comfortably surrounded by windows and Uncle Walter's art glass collection, I responded to requests for my consulting services. Most of the requests came from the Worldwide Science Federation, but a few were from private institutions seeking approval of computer-controlled medical equipment. When I was between WSF investigations, I worked as an independent consultant. I also taught as an adjunct instructor because I wanted to shape the ethics of the next generation of researchers.

Ethics had become a religion of our time. Unfortunately, like other religions of the past, the tenets were only honored when they were convenient. My articles on research ethics were one of the reasons the Worldwide Science Federation hired me to investigate allegations of researcher misconduct. They put a high value on my refusal to compromise.

Halfway through my emails, I decided to see if Sara had made the news. I searched for her name on the Internet news channels. Sure enough, Sara Sheppard was national news—at least on the higher education news feeds.

Sara Sheppard, distinguished professor of cybernetics at the University of New England, resigned her position as chair of the Medical Device Engineering Department effective immediately after researcher misconduct charges were filed by the Institutional Review Board. Among other allegations, Dr. Sheppard is charged with falsification of her research data. In a press release, the IRB stated the university has frozen her research funding and will be sending the results of their investigation to the Federal Register. In a written response, Dr. Sheppard denied any wrongdoing and declared that the investigation will prove she never engaged in any misconduct . . ..

I thought back to the IRB procedures that were followed when I caught a professor falsifying his research data. He had been so arrogant he never considered the possibility anyone else would ever crunch his numbers. When I did, I discovered he was a fraud. Although there was no public record of his misdeeds, his tenure was stripped. To prevent a scandal, he was allowed to resign. He grumbled his way into obscurity. Sara, however, clearly would not leave her position without a fight.

Like me, Sara had been denied tenure at the first university where she taught. The similarities stopped there. Sara had failed to earn tenure at North Atlantic State University because she had prioritized mainstream publications over scholarly journals. I had failed at UNE because I did not hold a board position at a national organization related to my work. The ratio between the number of open positions in national organizations to the number of researchers seeking those roles was abysmal. There had been little hope of securing a position unless someone was fired, retired, or died.

Sara went on to secure another professorship at Lucy Flucker

University, a small private university, where she earned tenure the following year. Tenure was easier to obtain at private schools, because there were fewer scholarship and service requirements. Sara left the school when Dr. Les Gregson was elected department chair for the third time in a row. His election was less than amicable.

Sara was ambitious and probably wanted to work her way up to dean or provost somewhere. Who knows, she may have envisioned herself as a college president or chancellor. When she came to UNE, she brought her previously awarded tenure with her.

Disillusioned with higher education, I left academia. Adjunct instructors were not considered academics.

Even though tenure had been abolished the following year, Sara's appointment under the old system meant the university would need a vote from the Board of Regents to fire a tenured, let alone "distinguished" full professor.

I scanned down the higher education news report to the last paragraph. The reporter stated that an emergency meeting of the Board of Regents would be held on Friday. Sara would need to establish her innocence within the next five days to avoid termination. Being fired for research misconduct would mean Dr. Sara Sheppard would never work in academia again.

Karma can be a bitch.

A couple of hours before lunch, I logged on to the virtual course room and began answering the questions my students had posted. Teaching research methods had been difficult enough in a traditional brick-and-mortar classroom; teaching them online was a royal pain in the arse. The school required that I answer questions every day–including weekends.

For the one-millionth time, I thought about quitting. I was in the eighth week of a ten-week quarter, and my students were dropping like the Seattle rain. Almost two-thirds of the students who started my course had bailed. The upside of being an adjunct was I no longer had to endure the politics of the department, the vicious competition of fellow faculty, or the endless meetings over minutia. The downside was that adjunct pay meant teaching was more a hobby than a job.

When Watson announced the incoming call from Dr. Sara Sheppard, I considered requesting a text exchange instead. If anyone other than Frank had told her to call me, I never would have answered her call. I did not enable video.

"Good afternoon, Cheryl," Sara began. "I hope now is a good time to talk?"

It is never a good time to talk to Sara.

"Now is fine," I lied.

"Frank said he'd call and tell you about my . . . er . . . situation."

I could have been more welcoming. I could have said things to put Sara at ease. At the same time, I enjoyed listening to Sara grovel.

"He said he told you to call me."

"Well, will you help me?" Sara blurted out. The roughness of her voice betrayed the fact she had been crying. Crying hard.

I softened my voice to comfort the woman who had made me cry on multiple occasions. "I am not sure what I can do."

"Cheryl, you don't owe me anything. Frank thinks," she paused, "Frank says" she paused again, "you're the only one I can trust in this nightmare."

"Sara, please start at the beginning," I said. "I need to know the entire story."

"I don't have time for that now," Sara's voice was getting louder. "If you'll help me, I will tell you everything after you get here. I know you're at home, but I don't trust these wireless communications. When can you leave?"

"I have two weeks left in my term," I explained.

"But the Regents meet in a few days. Aren't you teaching virtually?" Sara asked.

"Yes," I said.

"Then you can finish your class while you are consulting with the IRB to get to the bottom of this craziness. Frank arranged everything with the IRB. You will receive a WSF appointment as the investigator into my misconduct charges. The IRB trusts your integrity."

My head began to spin. The same university who considered me unworthy of tenure was willing to pay me to investigate the misconduct charges against their beloved, distinguished professor. It was unfathomable. Either the IRB thought I was objective, or they thought I would secure my revenge and help them by burning Sara at the stake. If I were a gambler, I would have bet on the latter.

"Sara, have you considered why the IRB would hire me after UNE rejected my application for tenure?" I asked.

"Cheryl, for good or evil, tenure has been abolished," Sara said. "Besides, the IRB had nothing to do with your tenure decision. The members of the IRB think you're highly ethical and competent."

Should I grab a wash cloth to clean Sara's nose print off my derrière?

Sara added, "Frank was the one to suggest the IRB hire you as the reviewer, not me."

"Be that as it may, what do you expect me to do with my pets?" I asked.

Sara sighed—loudly. "You'll bring Holmes with you, of course. I've already arranged for a dog nanny."

I decided Frank must have told Sara that I usually left Mori at home when I traveled on WSF business. Mori, short for Professor Moriarty, was not as dependent on me as Holmes. Mori only needed me to put food in her bowl. Holmes slept in my bed.

Dogs have masters and cats have staff.

At the same time, I knew that Sara's concern for others was a sham. Sara consistently demonstrated she was oblivious of other people's feelings. A case in point was the incident when we traded offices. I had willingly agreed to switch offices with her. My office was one of the largest in the department suite. I never felt comfortable with the setup, because my research did not require the space I was given. Not concerned with the artificial prestige of a large office, I was more than happy to trade with Sara. After all, Sara was the department chair, and she had a research assistant as well as a graduate assistant working with her. She needed to set up another desk.

After I agreed to trade offices, Sara decided my office needed painting before we made the move. Throwing me a bone, she requested both offices be painted. We agreed to wait until the winter break so our belongings could be moved into the conference room while the offices were painted. Sara offered to have her graduate assistant box my belongings. For personal reasons, I told her I did not want anyone, including her GA, to move my books or things.

I was not informed that the facilities department had told her painting could not be done during winter break. Without saying a word to me, Sara scheduled the workers to paint my office three weeks before the end of the semester. To make matters worse, Sara boxed up my belongings and put them in the middle of the room. On my way to school that day, Sara called me to tell me the painting was underway, and she had boxed my belongings—as if I should be grateful. The students who came to see me that day took one look at my office and assumed I had been sacked.

As humiliating as that was, the worst part was that I had no idea where to find anything. Before Sara's intrusion, I knew where everything was—based on its position in my office. Now, three weeks before final exams, I no longer could find a damn thing. Dealing with questions from the students had been equally distressing.

"No, I have not been fired."

"Yes, I will be teaching next semester; I am only trading offices."

The experience added to the trust issues I developed during my divorce.

Sara interrupted my silent reminiscences.

"Frank booked your flight. You leave at five this evening. You'll be flying first class with a seat for your dog."

Before I could voice any objections, Sara added, "In first class, Holmes can stay with you without the need for vet certification."

Only Sara would assume I would drop everything to come to her rescue. She was wrong.

"You presume a lot," I said softly. "Frank should not have made reservations without consulting me first. I will not be on that flight."

I could hear Sara breathing slowly, as though she was holding back more tears.

"Frank said you'd help me," Sara said, whimpering like a kicked puppy.

"I am going to a birthday party tonight."

"I'm sure I need you more than the birthday person." Sara sounded angry and no longer on the verge of tears. Her tone raised my hackles.

"You better tell that to Frank," I said, and tapped on a control that signaled Watson to disconnect the call.

I knew Sara would call Frank and complain about how I treated her. Frank would inform her that he had forgotten today was my daughter's birthday. I could only hope Sara would feel guilty for being so self-centered. At the same time, I knew that was a long shot. I wanted Sara to get used to the fact that I no longer sought her endorsement.

Although I was making a good living as a consultant, being denied tenure had come as a blow. When I had started working on my doctorate degree there were ten other students in my cohort. At graduation only two of us had secured university positions. Five years later, my former classmate was promoted and I left the ivory towers. It had been . . . humbling.

*　　*　　*

Throughout her childhood, Emily's birthday parties had themes. For her first birthday, I dressed Emily as a squirrel, and I wore a tree costume. Her party guests wore forest creature costumes. As Emily grew up, she took over choosing the themes. Her friends would always wear costumes supporting her themes. Everything was coordinated down to the cake and games.

Even though Emily was turning twenty-four, she still enjoyed the tradition. Emily had picked a robotics theme this year. She decided to be a peacekeeper, complete with an old-fashioned exoskeleton. The peacekeeper uniform was easy enough to find. She had many friends who had been in the peacekeeper forces. The exoskeleton was made by my full-sized 3-D printer, minus the motors of course.

The birthday party was a blast. I had not realized how much pop music included robot references. Emily's friends went all out on their costumes. They wore robot costumes from the last 150 years of science fiction movies, books, and comics. I was especially entertained by a dude wearing a 'Robbie the Robot' costume. My costume was simple.

I went as a television show android. The costume only required me to change my skin and eye color to a yellowish one. I replicated the uniform from the old show.

After the party, I was so tired I was happy that cars had been replaced by electric self-driving vehicles. As I turned on my SDV to go home, my forward screen displayed a message from Frank. He had booked me and Holmes on an overnight flight. Most of the time, I traveled by hyperloop. Traveling coast-to-coast or overseas still meant using an airline. I redirected my SDV to take me to the airport.

I hope the other passengers will recognize I am wearing a costume.

The screen displayed a letter of appointment, signed by the chair of the IRB and co-signed by the provost. I would be staying in visiting professor housing. They would provide me with an assistant. Better still, I would be paid handsomely for my consulting.

Frank had thought of everything. He used the access code I had given him to allow the young man he hired to retrieve Holmes and my emergency suitcase. More intriguing was how, within a few short hours, he had secured my appointment letter.

Did Frank fly to Boston and get the provost out of bed on a Sunday?

Although Frank was no longer a faculty member of UNE, his involvement in the proceedings must have been the result of calling in favors. He had held most academic positions including professor, chair, dean and provost at UNE, before he became professor emeritus. I was mystified as to why Frank was helping Sara.

Just inside the terminal doors, a young man walked up to me. His smile reminded me I was still dressed as an android, which made me easy to identify. He turned off his "Dr. Locke" light projector as soon as I walked in the door. Holmes waited patiently by his side. I took the LEESH from the young man, relieving him of his furry charge. He informed me that my suitcase had already cleared security and was in my cabin.

All I had to do was walk to the gate with Holmes and board the flight. The last-minute change in the reservations meant I was flying in a sleeper suite, not just first class. I tried to estimate how much this flight had cost the IRB. Holmes jumped on the bed as soon as I opened the door. I closed the door and returned my appearance to normal. An android may have boarded this flight, but a human would disembark. I crawled into bed and Holmes and I were asleep before the plane took off.

With the air travel speed limits, the fastest planes traveled at the same speed as their 50-year-old counterparts. When we arrived at the Leonard Nimoy International Airport, it was going to take some time for over two hundred passengers to disembark. After a few minutes, I joined the herd of humanity trying to get off the plane. My furry companion enjoyed the attention and frequent behind-the-ear scratches he received. Holmes acted as though "It's a corgi" was just another nickname.

I was astonished to see Malka in the reception area. She was not a fan of Sara's. Still, she looked happy to see me.

"Malka, I did not expect you to be here."

"Frank called and asked if I could help him with the arrangements for your stay," Malka said. "You look good. Have you lost weight?"

I ignored her comment on my appearance. Malka was petite, well-dressed, and dripping in diamonds. I was none of the above.

"You'll be staying in one of the university's visiting professor homes. I've arranged for Eliana to be your assistant—and nanny for your dog." Malka smiled at me, and added, "You remember Ellie, don't you?"

"Of course I do," I replied. "I thought she had joined a think tank in Maryland."

I had remained in contact with my former graduate assistant after I left the university. Ellie, short for Eliana, had been my first and best GA. She was a Russian who married a Greek jeweler. Ellie was fluent in six different languages. I relied on earbud translation devices.

"Frank must have told her about the investigation." Malka explained. "He was the one who told me she was taking a leave of absence to be your assistant. Frank said you would need someone you could trust."

Malka and I talked about Ellie as we walked over to her limo. Leave it to Malka to have a chauffeur-driven limousine in the age of SDVs.

"I can never thank you enough for helping Ellie, after the shocking accident," I said. "I wished I could have been here to help with her husband's funeral and all."

"You should not feel bad," Malka said. "I had connections you didn't. The result was that Ellie received the most advanced exo-skeleton evah constructed. You forget how much I relied on her aftah you left."

The compassion in her voice made me want to hug her. Up until that moment, I had struggled with being jealous of Malka. I had never considered that Malka's friendship with Ellie was equal to my own.

Once inside the limo, Malka presented me with an early morning snack. The iced tea was especially refreshing after last night's party. I was served a bagel with cream cheese and lox. Malka knew I always ate breakfast. I thanked her for the food, but she put up her hand.

"The meal is from Sara," Malka said. She looked at me sympathetically and added, "I think this is supposed to be an apology for how she talked to you on the phone."

I seriously doubted Sara would ever say she was sorry, let alone admit she was wrong. Still, I appreciated the food, and told Malka to thank Sara for me.

When we arrived at the house, Malka directed her chauffeur to unload my things, and take them to the bedroom upstairs. When Malka got ready to leave, she said, "You'll be meeting the IRB chairman in Sara's lab at 9 a.m. I will send an SDV for you, but not my limo." Malka grinned as though she had told a joke.

"Here, let me get you the keycard for the lab," Malka said, as she got back in the limo to take the card out of her purse.

Keycards? You might as well leave the door unlocked!

She rolled down the window and handed the card to me, saying in a low voice, "I hope your trust issues will keep you safe."

Without time to say another word, the limo pulled into the quiet street.

Chapter 2
Meetings on Monday

The house for visiting professors was an artifact from the past. Wood paneling lined the interior, and the furniture was at least 75, if not 100, years old. I walked upstairs to the master bedroom and changed into some comfortable clothes. I felt too keyed-up to sleep right away, so I began exploring the downstairs.

I was pleased to find a room with real books. Paper and leather covers! In another era, this room would have been called the library. Most people these days kept their books as files on the smarthome's computer.

From the bookshelf I selected "The Study in Scarlet" and settled into a comfortable soft chair. A few minutes later, Ellie came into the room with Holmes. My corgi's face betrayed his instant adoration for his nanny. Ellie had long dark-brown hair, exotic eyes, and an olive skin complexion. Before avatars began walking virtual runways, she could have been a super model.

Holmes joined me on the chair. Ellie momentarily left the room and returned carrying two glasses of Russian red wine. She took a seat on the sofa and my loyal companion immediately deserted me to join her, head on her lap. I was happy to see Holmes would be in good hands during my stay, but I knew my dog's vices.

"You will need two coasters if you plan to drink your wine," I told Ellie. "Holmes is a boozehound and will drink anything but white wine. If you leave your glass unattended, you should put a coaster on top of it."

"In other words, your dog takes after you," Ellie said with a chuckle.

"I drink white wine," I protested. "Sometimes."

* * *

The time difference between the two coasts challenged my sleep-wake cycle. Thank heavens the world had abandoned the biannual time change my grandmother called "Daylight Savings" time. Although the flight only took a little more than five hours, the change in time zones meant I had lost an additional three hours. I knew I needed a few more hours of sleep. Chances were, I would be taken out to dinner that evening at one of Boston's famous restaurants. Dinner would be formal, expensive, and damn late.

"Ellie, am I right to assume you were given instructions not to talk about Sara until after my briefing in the morning?"

Ellie bowed her head to avoid eye contact. She looked as though she was checking to make sure she was wearing shoes. "I am sorry, Dr. Locke. You're right."

"Dr. Locke?" I repeated emphatically. "Dr. Locke?" I was taken aback by the formality in her tone. "You are no longer my grad student. What happened to 'Cheryl'?"

Ellie blushed. "I had no trouble calling you Cheryl when you were no longer at the university. Now that you're back, calling you Cheryl feels . . . I don't know. . . a little . . . disrespectful."

"Ellie, for heaven's sake. You either call me Cheryl or I will start calling you Dr. Eliana Zelyonaya!" My exaggerated offended tone let her know I was joking.

Ellie nodded in understanding and added, "You probably need to get a few more hours of slumber before going to the lab. I'll have Irene wake you in four hours."

"Noteworthy name choice for the iDom. Irene."

"I wondered if the name was selected on your account," Ellie mused.

Just as I had named my iDom for a male character, someone had named this iDom after a woman. An important woman to Sherlock Holmes. Irene's sole appearance was in "Scandal in Bohemia," yet she was considered Sherlock's only love interest.

I agreed with Ellie's suggestion that I needed a few more hours of sleep. I set the book on the table next to the chair and called for Holmes to join me. My furry friend walked up the stairs with me to the bedroom. As I got into bed, Holmes joined me by climbing the ramp Ellie had thoughtfully provided for my short-legged companion.

"Irene, lights off please," I said, and quickly fell asleep.

*   *   *

True to Ellie's word, Irene woke me an hour before my first appointment by slowly turning up the lights and playing classical music. I enjoyed waking up to "Feeling Groovy" and wondered if Irene or Ellie had been the one to quiz Watson about my morning rituals.

Holmes had abandoned me sometime in the early morning. He probably preferred Ellie's company to my snoring. I was well aware my dog was an attention seeker.

I showered and dressed. My meeting with the IRB chair called for more impression management than I could accomplish wearing jeans and a T-shirt. After all, they had probably paid a king's ransom for my flight. I donned my power suit, a 1940s style navy blue skirt with a matching jacket. To complete the look of that era, I wore a red hat and my single strand of pearls.

After putting on my makeup, it was time to choose my shoes. Since I was out of practice wearing high heels all day, my low heels would ensure I did not fall on my face. On my way downstairs, I caught my reflection in a large mirror on the landing.

If anyone calls me today, I will definitely enable video.

Ellie had my favorite breakfast waiting for me, along with iced tea.

"Did you find Holmes' food?" I asked, over a bite of eggs.

"I fed him about an hour ago."

Holmes was asleep on a rug in front of the sliding glass doors. He appeared to be enjoying his food coma.

"You look amazing," Ellie added. "That outfit definitely shows off your bright blue eyes."

"Thank you," I said. "And thank you for the wakeup song. Whose idea was that?"

Ellie looked at me with a slightly bewildered expression. "I have no idea," she said.

I heard an SDV pull into the drive. I had not heard motor noises for such a long time, that at first, I was puzzled by the sound. Then I realized those engine noises were probably generated by Irene. Electrical and hydrogen powered SDVs were almost silent.

I grabbed my microcomputer and notebook. Ellie and Holmes joined me on the large back seat. True to Malka's statement, the SDV was not a limo, but it was almost as big.

On the ride to UNE, Ellie talked about all the changes in faculty since I had left.

No, since I was fired.

Silently, I reassured myself that I was the expert this time and not a lowly candidate for a position seeking approval. I was in charge.

Malka should have sent the limo.

When we arrived at the campus, the SDV dropped the three of us off by the door to the cybernetics building. It was a short walk to the lab. At the door, Ellie put her hand on my arm.

"I'll take Holmes on a walk around campus while you're in the meeting," she said. Apparently, she had not been invited.

She took over Holmes' LEESH and whispered in my ear, "Be careful."

In the center of the lab was the hub where the cybernetic limbs were modified and tested. Surrounding the hub was a circle of five workstations. In place of a sixth, stood a gate to the hub. Each work-station had a black surface which controlled the computers and multiple display screens. Around the walls were cabinets both above and below another set of polished black work surfaces which doubled as display screens and remote controls. To the right side of the door was a desk with a dozen drawers. Next to a desk were heavy metal lockers. I could not tell if they still housed cybernetic limbs. A few pieces of cast-off equipment were piled in the far corner and covered with dust cloths. Comfortable rolling chairs with powered footrests dotted the room. Sara's team evidently liked to work in comfort.

The University of New England had originally hired me because of my research into the development and programming of cybernetic implants, which were a considerable improvement over the previous generation of motorized exoskeletons. Whereas exoskeletons were a wearable machine, my cybernetic implants replaced absent limbs with as much function as the real body part. The implants were sensitive enough to allow someone to play a violin or ice skate. Even the most sophisticated exoskeletons could not deliver such fine motor movements.

Three other people were in the lab when I entered. Sara wore one of her long, full skirts with a flowing blouse and a scarf over her head. She looked more like a fortune teller than a researcher. She barely acknowledged my arrival. Her discomfort was evident from the insincere smile on her face.

Dr. Kim Yong-Chun rose from his chair and walked across the room to greet me with a handshake. The chair of the IRB looked happy to see me again. Dr. Kim refused to Americanize his name. His given name was Yong-Chun, and his surname was Kim. In traditional Korean fashion, he was Dr. Kim Yong-Chun. When he was appointed to UNE, he decided renouncing his Korean citizenship was the limit to the concessions he would make. The increasing tensions between the U.S. and the Korean Empire made his adherence to tradition less than popular.

I sat in the chair he offered, next to a desk. Yong-Chun gestured toward the third person in the room. "Cheryl, may I introduce you to our new Provost, Robaire Brown."

Provost Brown rose slowly. He stepped unsteadily toward me and offered his hand in greeting. He looked about twice the age of the previous administrator who had held this post during my assistant professorship.

"Thank you for coming," Provost Brown said with a crisp Jamaican accent. He was wearing a cream linen suit, with a white shirt and black bowtie. His personal dignity made him appear as though he was wearing imperial robes.

Dr. Kim took command of the room. He began reading from a display on his wearable as if he were a town crier. "Dr. Sheppard is accused of multiple counts of scientific misconduct, not the least of which is that she intentionally falsified data in three of her published papers. She is accused of plagiarizing another researcher's study. She is accused of inappropriate requests of her research assistant. Finally, Dr. Sheppard is accused of violating conflict of interest regulations and financially gaining from her misconduct. Dr. Sara Sheppard, do you deny these charges?"

Sara looked aghast. "Yes, all of them."

The expression on the provost's face was pure loathing. Yong-Chun appeared bored.

"Given the serious nature of these accusations," I said, "I believe Dr. Sheppard has a right to know her accuser."

"Conrad Joe Hatfield," Yong-Chun responded, "her research assistant."

Of course. No one else is going to accuse her of inappropriate requests of a research assistant.

Sara did not look the least bit surprised at the name. She was either using her best poker face, or she already knew the identity of her accuser.

"Dr. Locke," Provost Brown began, "I have arranged for you to work out of an office in the administration building. We have already granted you access to the university's files."

"Thank you," I said, and turned to Sara. "I need you to provide me with your personal field journals, code books, and rough data. All handwritten notes should be included."

Sara flinched. Surely, she knew I would ask for these files. The request was a standard procedure for any investigation of misconduct. *Why the surprise act? What is she expecting to gain?*

Sara fiddled with her scarf before answering. "Since I no longer have anyone to assist me, I will have to bring them to you myself. I rarely used handwritten notes, but I will try to find the few notes I kept."

She stood up, looked around the room, and then headed for the door. The hardship of bringing her notes to me was clear. She no longer had a serf.

"Sara," I said loudly, and she paused at the door without looking at me. "I am to report to the Board of Regents on Friday. I will need those materials before the end of the day."

Sara left the room without saying a word–only a flip of her skirt.

Yong-Chun stood up and bowed, "Please excuse me, the meeting of the Cybernetics Overseers starts in a few minutes." As he exited the lab, he added, "Cheryl, please let me know if I can help you with your investigation in any way."

"See you later, Dr. Kim," Provost Brown said.

"One more thing," I said to Provost Brown after Yong-Chun had left. "Please secure this lab. If anyone tries to gain access, I want to know."

"Consider it done. Our system records the card owner every time the door is opened."

"This cardkey must be the only one with access," I said, and held up the card. "That includes administration members as well."

Provost Brown nodded in agreement. I contacted Ellie to let her know I was on my way to the administration building to see what kind of office I had been given.

As I left the lab, I noticed a container marked *Cybermuscle* on the desk. Shortly before I left UNE, I had submitted a proposal to develop an artificial muscle tissue. The sample was probably left here by the researcher who had taken over my work.

* * *

The office provided by the provost rivaled offices I had seen occupied by deans and vice presidents. Near the center of the room was a rich-looking leather sofa facing a floor-to-ceiling window. Leather recliners were placed near the sofa's arm rests, making the U-shaped furniture arrangement a good conversation space. A coffee table provided a place for refreshments or belongings.

I moved to the soft leather office chair behind the elaborate mahogany desk. From the chair I could see both the center of the room, and beyond to the huge window. A small chair sat facing the desk. The heavy desk may have been necessary back when professors and administrators worked on what they called "hard copies." Paper was rarely used these days, yet the desk remained as a symbol of power and authority. No one could sit behind that desk without feeling superior to the person on the other side.

As I sat in the leather chair, I was startled by the voice of a British male.

"Dr. Locke, please scan your eye into the reader to validate your identity and access the computer."

I submitted to the iris scan which determined my access level. A large screen came down from the ceiling. The display showed hundreds of files in a folder named Sara Sheppard.

"Dr. Locke, you may call me 'Mycroft'." The British voice sounded quite proper.

Did someone named this iAdmin "Mycroft" because of my affection for Sherlock Holmes?

"Mycroft, please show me the report from Conrad Joe Hatfield to the IRB."

"Do you want them in chronological order going backwards or forwards?" Mycroft asked.

"I did not realize there was more than one. Show me the file where Hatfield accuses Dr. Sheppard of misconduct."

Mycroft reported, "There are seventeen reports to the IRB by Mr. Hatfield alleging misconduct. The oldest report was filed two years ago. The most recent was 3 weeks ago."

"Show them in chronological order. Oldest first," I instructed.

I read page after page of accusations Hatfield had sent to the IRB while working as Sara's research assistant. He signed them all "C. J. Hatfield." Most of the accusations could be categorized as whiny rants about how the poor research assistant was being mistreated by Sara.

"I was forced to work all night on her research proposal to meet the grantor's deadline."

"Dr. Sheppard refused to give me second authorship of the article, even though I was the one who did the literature review and cleaned up the lab every night."

"Dr. Sheppard has me running around like her personal assistant–not a research colleague. Today I watered the plants in her office and took her SDV in to be serviced."

"Dr. Sheppard refuses to share her communications with the Department of Defense. The file is encrypted with a password."

"I was given a B in "Cybernetic Mechanics" because my assignments were late. Dr. Sheppard knew they would be late because I was working on HER research."

The final report contained the allegations which set the current investigation in motion. The report stood out by both the details provided, and the voice of the writer.

My stomach growled as I finished with the last report.

"Dr. Locke, may I let Dr. Eliana Zelyonaya into your office? She has food with her."

"Of course," I said.

"Dr. Locke, a short-legged animal is with her. May I let the animal in as well?"

"Yes. Mycroft, the animal is my dog Holmes. Both of them are always to be allowed into this office during my stay."

"Understood," Mycroft replied.

I heard locks click as Ellie came into the office with a tray of food in one hand, and a pitcher of iced tea in the other. On the tray was a green salad, a roast beef sandwich, and a bowl of berries. Holmes was walking right next to her, a prisoner more to the smell of the roast beef than the LEESH.

"Thank you, Ellie. I was wondering how I was going to get lunch."

"Cheryl, have you heard about dinner?" Ellie asked, with a mischievous grin on her face.

"No, what do you know?" I asked.

"Malka told me that dinner will be at The Union Oyster House at eight tonight."

"I am lucky you brought me lunch. I never would have survived until dinner," I said.

The look on Ellie's face told me she had not finished telling me about dinner.

"Go on," I encouraged.

"I've been invited too. I'm sure Holmes will be fine for a few hours," Ellie said.

"I am sure he will be. And…?" I was getting impatient.

Ellie's eyes were twinkling. "Oh, did I mention that Frank will be there?" Her voice was filled with delight.

I laughed as she winked at me. We agreed to go back to the house around 6 p.m. to freshen up and change clothes. I suddenly realized nothing in my valise was suitable for such an important dinner.

"Oh, no!" I exclaimed. "Frank had my emergency suitcase delivered to me at the airport. I doubt there is anything classy enough to wear for a formal dinner."

"I'll find you something," Ellie offered.

Ellie told Mycroft to send instructions to the SDV to pick her up in front of the administration building. I leaned back in the leather chair and enjoyed my lunch. The office provided a beautiful view of the harbor. Holmes took up a position by the floor-to-ceiling window as I began my file review. I wondered what secrets about UNE I would uncover.

I never knew this office existed when I was teaching here.

* * *

I finished my lunch, and said, "Mycroft, show me a list of the most recently accessed files."

"Dr. Locke, most of the files have been recently accessed. Could you be more specific?"

Am I imagining things, or does Mycroft sound a little embarrassed?

I should have guessed others had already been digging in the files. "Okay, Mycroft, how many files have been accessed more than average within the last three months?"

"There are eight files which meet your criteria—unless you want to include hidden files or passworded files."

I was stunned by the iAdmin volunteering information, rather than simply responding to a request.

What other services can Mycroft provide?

"How many hidden and passworded files fit my criteria?" I inquired.

Holmes let out a snore as he slept in the warmth provided by the sunrays filtering through the window.

"Dr. Locke, there are three hidden files and one of those files is both encrypted and passworded," Mycroft explained. "Do you need help decrypting the file or getting past the password?"

"That would be most welcome, Mycroft," I said.

I realized this was likely one of the communications between Professor Sara Sheppard and the Department of Defense.

Is this the file Mr. Hatfield feels is so important?

Since my eyes were already fatigued, I had Mycroft read the file to me. At face value, the file sounded like two people negotiating the purchase of a condo. The negotiations included prices for several versions including the numbers of windows, doors, front and back yards, etc. The seller, who sounded like Sara, always signed her communications "Felicity."

The buyer was a bigger puzzle. Over time the writing style of the buyer changed. In my experience, this meant more than one author was writing. But all the messages were signed "Gerald."

As Mycroft continued to read the file to me, I had a sense that something important was missing, but I could not put my finger on it. Suddenly Holmes jumped up and barked as an alarm sounded.

"Mycroft, what is going on?" I asked, with more irritation than panic in my voice.

"Dr. Sheppard has transmitted her files, but there is a virus in the transmission. I have, of course, blocked the virus."

Does Sara know about the virus or is she ignorant of having sent it?

"Dr. Locke, the file with the virus is now safe for viewing," Mycroft said. "What would you like me to do?"

"Put it on the viewscreen," I said.

The data analyses in this file were standard for this type of research, with one glaring exception. There were only five data points per trial, yet her research had involved at least fifty observations per trial.

I was jolted out of my contemplation when Mycroft announced the time had come to return to the house and get ready for dinner.

Holmes and I exited the building through the grand double doors. The overly ornate doors symbolized the prestige of the University of New England's administration building. The SDV was already at the curb. Once inside the vehicle, Holmes immediately put his head in my lap. He was snoring before we arrived at the house.

* * *

Ellie had procured the most elegant little black dress I had seen in years. The chiffon dress had a jewel neckline with a fitted bodice and a slightly flared skirt which hit me just above my knees. Beads hung from the capped sleeves. A sexy deep scoop in the back almost went down to my waist.

My single-strand pearl necklace with matching earrings were the perfect accessories. They made any outfit more elegant, so I always kept them packed. Since I would not be doing much walking, I opted to wear my high-heeled shoes. I arranged my long red hair in an up-do. My clutch purse would carry my physician-issued nutrition card.

When I met Ellie downstairs, she looked equally elegant in a silky, midnight-blue pantsuit with wide legs and a boxy jacket. She was wearing flats rather than heels. The plunging V-neckline of the jacket showed off her dragonfly necklace. The colored stones on the dragonfly's body were set in pavé style, giving the impression of the iridescent colors of the real thing. The wings were made of opal cut so thin as to be transparent, with fine wire holding the stones to the thorax.

*   *   *

The last time I dined with so many professors was at my faculty search committee dinner years ago. My mentor had told me that this dinner was as important, if not more, than the formal interview. I could only remember the anxiety, not the food. Tonight, I no longer had anything to prove. I would be dining as a well-respected expert in the fields of cybernetic programming and researcher ethics.

During the drive to the restaurant, Ellie brought my attention to her dragonfly necklace.

"Cheryl, do you remember I told you I was creating a line of jewelry?"

I nodded.

"My pendants incorporate the same technology as the micromotors we engineered for the exoskeletons."

I looked closer at her dragonfly necklace. "Oh, is that one of them? It is so beautiful. How small is the motor? What does it do?" I pelted her with questions faster than she could answer.

"Since these motors are only moving tiny articulated pendants, I was able to reduce them to the size of a large nanite. The motors are powered by bacteria. Put the dragonfly in your hand," she instructed.

As soon as I put the pendant in my hand, the wings of the dragonfly began to flutter and the tail moved. The dragonfly appeared to come to life. Startled by the movements, I dropped the pendant and Ellie laughed.

"Can it fly?" I asked.

"Of course," Ellie said, "but controlling it in the air can be tricky. My ladybugs don't fly, but they will crawl onto someone's hand when held. Most of my other creations move, but don't leave the chain."

"Ellie, when you are ready to go to market with your jewelry line, I hope you will let me be your first customer."

Her smile was non-committal. I had a sneaking suspicion Malka had already beaten me to that position.

The SDV took us to the entrance of the Union Oyster House. As I got out of the vehicle, my mouth moistened in response to the smells from the wood-burning oven. As we entered the restaurant, I was amused by the sign which identified this was *not* a family-friendly place.

WELL-BEHAVED CHILDREN OVER THE AGE OF 12 ARE WELCOME. POORLY-BEHAVED CHILDREN WILL BE ASKED TO LEAVE WITH THEIR INCOMPETENT PARENTS. IF YOUR CHILDREN ARE UNDER 12, WE WOULD BE HAPPY TO PREPARE YOUR MEAL TO GO.

The Union Oyster House enjoyed the distinction of being America's oldest restaurant. The building dated back to pre-revolutionary days, and the restaurant started serving food in 1826. The owners claimed Daniel Webster had been a regular customer. The historic location was a stark contrast to the faculty of the high-tech Medical Device Engineering Department.

As we approached the table, I noticed more seats than I had expected. Three chairs were still unoccupied, but they were not together. Ellie was not going to be sitting next to me. I was sure the seating arrangements were not random.

Frank motioned me toward the vacant chair on his left. As I approached, he rose and greeted me with a hug. He was wearing a dark blue suit with a raspberry-colored button-down shirt and white bow tie. I doubted he could button the jacket owing to the extra twenty pounds he carried. With all the medical regulations these days, people rarely gained more than five pounds without having their nutrition cards restrict their caloric intake. The regulations naturally led to a black-market of clearance cards for individuals who cared more for prime rib, scotch, and cheesecake than their BMI.

Frank must have spent a small fortune on his card.

Malka was seated on Frank's right. She was wearing a dazzling white pantsuit with sparkling accents. The artistic elegance likely meant the outfit was one of a kind. She gestured to Ellie with her white fur wrap, and my assistant glided into the empty chair between Malka and Leonardo. Malka, adorned with more diamonds than a monarch, sat nearly opposite Priscilla.

Priscilla sat on my left. Both Malka and Priscilla tried to appear casual, while at the same time ignoring each other's existence. I had never learned the cause of the estrangement in their friendship. Their struggle was palpable.

The way Ellie greeted Leonardo was worthy of an Academy Award. I made a mental note to congratulate her later for not laughing at his scarf. Leonardo's traditional Venezuelan scarf might not have appeared ridiculous if the man wearing it had been a little less pretentious. Leonardo had been born in Hollister, Missouri, and had never met his Venezuelan father. Everything Leonardo wore, from his crazy-expensive glasses to his duster-length Italian leather coat, were part of a scheme to impress the right people.

Leonardo Gonzales was a master strategist. Shortly before he applied for tenure, he filed a discrimination complaint against the university, claiming his research was less respected because of his father's political exile in Cuba. Granting him tenure was the only way for the school to avoid the appearance of retaliating against him for the complaint.

As soon as I sat down, Priscilla leaned toward me and began to whisper. While I believed she meant to whisper in my ear, she was actually talking to my chin.

"Yaw know, I supported yaws tenurah . . . .."

I found it difficult to tell if Priscilla had given up trying to hide her Boston accent or if she had consumed so many cocktails, she could no longer muster the effort. Apparently, her Cosmopolitan consumption obliterated her memory of the lies in her report about my faculty senate participation.

If she supported my tenure, I am lucky she was not against me.

Priscilla and I had been hired as new faculty during the same semester. About a month after being hired at UNE, she published an article exposing another researcher's conflicts of interest. Priscilla had been to a cocktail party where she overheard an academic bragging about how their new treatment protocol was being adopted in hospitals around the world. After the party, she made some inquiries. She discovered the protocol required the administration of one pharmaceutical company's newest drug. Using the freedom of information act, she went on to find that the researcher had purchased stock in the company before releasing his protocol. A few months later, the pharmaceutical company awarded a multimillion-dollar research grant to the professor. When she reported his behavior to the ethics board, not only did the investigator go to prison, but Priscilla became an academic celebrity.

Her path to tenure had been strewn with interviews by mainstream media regarding how society could be protected from these kinds of conflicts of interest. When Dr. Abagail Ball retired, Dr. Priscilla Kennedy became the new neuroimplant program coordinator.

To fill the open faculty position created by Abby's retirement, Priscilla campaigned for her old chum, Sara Sheppard, to be hired as a researcher in her program. She reminded the dean that her implant had been developed by Sara. As Dean, Alisha was able to bulldoze Sara's approval up the food chain. Once the offer was made, Sara had the chutzpah to refuse the position unless the university would grant her the title of "distinguished professor."

Dr. Bruce Nigel was the last dinner guest to arrive. For most of my career at UNE, Bruce had been a puzzle to me. Sometimes I thought he respected my work; at other times, I felt he thought of me as a kindergartener pretending to be a scientist.

When Sara ran for department chair, Bruce decided I should help him count the votes. Neither of us wanted Sara to be elected, but we both felt ethically bound to admit she won. I apparently impressed

Bruce when I told him we should declare Sara the winner, but never let the rest of the department know she had won by only one vote. As far as I knew, that secret remained.

As soon as Bruce took his seat, the rustic wooden table revealed The Oyster House no longer operated on Revolutionary War technology. Menus glowed from the tabletop for a few moments, and then vanished. Frank tapped his water glass with a knife.

"Y'all are in for a treat," he said. "I've made for us to be served by professional wait staff. We'll be placing our orders and be served by living, breathing people."

A middle-aged man wearing a tuxedo appeared with leather-bound menus. Two younger men quickly filled everyone's water glasses. I accepted my menu and began considering my options.

I leaned close to Frank and whispered. "I have no idea whether my nutrition card will allow me to order here. There was no time to get it updated."

"Cher, nutrition cards are no longer used in New England. The cards led to a black market. The commonwealth invested in new tech which reads your health status from health monitorin' implants. As someone from the West Coast, ya'll be allowed to order anything you want, but limited alcohol, for the next 14 days."

As the waiters took our food and drink orders, they appeared to be reading something on the back of each diner's chair. Frank smiled at me as I stared at the chairs.

"They call it 'MOM.' Medically Ordered Meals. There is one system for purchasing groceries, and another for eating at restaurants. Both systems use the same implants."

"Whoever came up with that name must love puns," I said. "Obviously, there are ways around the system," I added and conspicuously looked at Frank's unbuttoned jacket.

"Well, if one doesn't have an implant, one cannot be bossed around by MOM," Frank said, and laughed at his own joke. "As a person with dual citizenship, I'm exempt."

Frank was so much a quintessential Southern gentleman; it was easy to forget his mother was an Egyptian who had married an Army intelligence officer. The family moved to South Carolina while Frank was still a baby. Out of respect for his father, Frank had attended a military institution in Charleston, before attending graduate school at Duke. He earned his doctorate at ETH Zürich in Switzerland.

"Have you heard the latest news about the dean?" Leonardo asked no one in particular. "The dean is going to be charged with her husband's murder." All other conversations stopped instantly, and we turned our attention to Leonardo.

Well-played, Leonardo, well-played.

"Hernandez's murder was recorded by their iDom. There's no doubt what happened," Leonardo continued.

"How do you know?" I asked.

"I overheard a police officer interviewing the dean's assistant," Leonardo said.

"Well, that means the murdah didn't take place in the bedroom," Malka said.

Malka is right. Most people programmed their iDom not to record bedroom activity.

Frank poured boredom into his tone. "Did you overhear anything we don't already know?" He was not one to give into Leonardo's grandstanding.

Trying to ignore Frank, Leonardo began to resemble a peacock. "The provost will announce tomorrow that I have been appointed as the acting dean. The university can't start to look for a new dean until Patel is convicted."

"If there's a trial, that could take years," Bruce said.

"But if there is a video of her killing her husband, she might as well plead guilty," I offered.

Suddenly, Malka shouted, "Oy vey!"

We looked in her direction to see Ellie's dragonfly pendant take flight. The dragonfly seemed so real the way it flapped both sets of wings together. The sparkling insect hovered over the table and landed on Ellie's lapel. The jeweled insect walked backwards over to the chain around her neck and stopped. Once in contact with the chain, the dragonfly ceased to look alive and appeared as a jeweled pendant again.

Frank clapped. "Eliana, I applaud your attention to detail. Many people don't know that dragonflies can only walk backwards."

Leonardo's face betrayed his anger at Ellie for stealing his audience.

Bruce and Priscilla began asking Ellie questions about the power supply and flight controls. I considered Leonardo's announcement. Luck was smiling on Leonardo. If not for the charges against Sara, she would have been appointed acting dean.

Or is it luck?

The food arrived, and the conversation at the table became small talk. My braised lamb with the caramelized onions was the best dinner I had eaten in some time. The wine the waiter recommended was exceptional, but I was allowed only two glasses owing to my lack of MOM permissions.

"Cheryl, I know you can't talk about your current investigation, but can you tell us about the methods you use to investigate misconduct?" Bruce asked.

Before I had a chance to answer, Frank jumped in and said, "If she tells you, she'll have to kill you, Bruce."

My fellow diners exploded with nervous laughter. Bruce had come close to violating an unwritten rule among researchers. No one ever talked about *their* research–to anyone. Not even lovers. The competition to produce cutting-edge research was beyond vicious. During my service on the IRB I had seen tactics including false accusations of unethical conduct, denying tenure to professors in order to steal their research agenda, fabricating data, and even violence. My appointment to the IRB was largely due to the trust I had earned by having a robust research portfolio, which meant I would be less tempted to steal research ideas from the proposals I reviewed.

Bruce looked mortified.

I smiled at Bruce. "Frank's almost right. If I talk about my methods, I may reveal how to avoid getting caught."

"Cheryl, where are you going on vacation this year?" Malka asked, deliberately diverting the conversation away from all discussions of research.

"I remain undecided," I said. "I will entertain any suggestions from the table."

"Even though Casablanca has changed from that movie you love, the sunsets are still the most spectacular in the world," Frank advised. He knew about my affection for classic Humphrey Bogart movies.

"If you want to see true beauty, you should go to Brazil," Leonardo recommended.

"I went to Iceland last yeah," Malka said. "The place was lovely. If you go during the winta, you'll see the Aurora Borealis. But if you go in the summa, be prepared fah twenty hours auf sunlight."

"I highly recommend Key West," Bruce said. "That is where we went on our honeymoon last year."

"I am sorry to have missed your wedding, Bruce. Do you have any pictures?" I asked. Within seconds, holographic images of Bruce and Richard exchanging vows appeared in the middle of the table.

"Yaw hader ask," Priscilla slurred.

Priscilla must be drinking something from her purse when she goes into the restroom.

The waiter had been serving her only water.

"Australia has become the most pet-friendly country on the planet," Ellie suggested. "I'm sure Holmes would have a great time walking on the beaches. We could go together."

"Well, that may be the best suggestion I have had all night," I said, smiling at my doggy-advocate.

"Frank, do you know if Sara is skilled with hacking computers?" Ellie asked.

I was stunned as much by her question as by the abrupt change in topic. Not only had Ellie mentioned Sara, the "elephant in the room," but I had not told her about the virus Mycroft had intercepted.

"I am not sure," Frank said.

"You should ask C. J. Hatfield," Leonardo said. "He frequently compares himself to the famous white hat hackers, Robert Tappan Morris and Kevin Mitnik."

Malka's face betrayed her dislike of Hatfield. "I'm not shurah I'd trust anything Mr. Hatfield has to say on any subject."

"Leonardo, do you think Sara capable of hacking into another computer?" Ellie asked.

"Maybe," Leonardo said. "I don't know much about her programming skills."

"Wouldn't that be out of charactah for the chawman of the Cybernetic Research Ethics Council?" Priscilla asked.

Leonardo nearly choked on his water. "Does everyone remember that faculty meeting when Sara insinuated that I wanted to seduce a faculty candidate?"

"Who could forget that meeting?" I asked rhetorically. Everyone bobbed their heads up and down in agreement. Everybody but Malka, who had been on her sabbatical.

"Consider that my answer to your question about her ethics," Leonardo said, once again enjoying the attention of everyone at the table.

"Speaking of ethics," Malka said, "Sara has been in trouble with the Dean many times."

"Did she ever get sanctioned?" I asked.

"*Plenneer* times," Priscilla slurred.

"The IRB sanctioned her more than once," Frank said.

I guess those confidential proceedings are not all that confidential.

Ellie and I were the first to leave. I offered time zones rather than age as my excuse.

On the drive back to the house, I asked, "Ellie, why did you ask about Sara's hacking abilities?"

"There are a few things that just don't feel right," Ellie began.

"Please, tell me what you have found."

"Cheryl, it's nothing more than a feeling. I'm afraid I'll sound paranoid. I promise to tell you if I find something more substantial than a creepy feeling."

"I frequently rely on my feelings. Gut instincts are often accurate," I said.

She agreed to let me know if anything further aroused her suspicions.

Back at the house, Ellie walked Holmes. I went to bed with little fanfare.

Around 1 a.m. I was awoken by a priority message from campus security. Sara Sheppard's keycard had been used in an attempt to enter her lab.

Chapter 3
Treachery on Tuesday

*T*uesday morning, I was up before the sun. In spite of the fact that I needed to report to the Board of Regents on Friday, I had yet to receive any handwritten notes or research journals from Sara. Although I seriously doubted there would be anything incriminating in Sara's field journals, the request had paid off more than once in the past. Rather than get into a power struggle with Sara, I sent a message to Yong-Chun that her notes had not yet been delivered. Sara might ignore requests from former junior faculty, but to ignore the chairman of the IRB was another thing entirely. I took the opportunity to ask for access to IRB files where she had been sanctioned or accused of wrongdoing on other projects.

Holmes and I had just finished breakfast when Ellie joined us downstairs.

"Shall we walk Holmes together?" I suggested. "I could use the exercise."

"That would be lovely, but are you sure you want to walk in this rain?"

"No problem," I said. "Corgis may come from Wales, but Holmes is a rain wimp, so I modified the LEESH to keep it off us when we walk. In Seattle, that is more than half the year."

"Genius," Ellie said.

"I will expand the field to keep you dry as well."

As we walked, Ellie and I began discussing how she could assist me with my investigation. "Ellie, I need to talk to Mr. Hatfield. Would you arrange for an interview?"

"Face to face or virtual?"

"Face to face, if possible. I still believe I can best evaluate people when I am in the same room as them," I said.

Ellie laughed. Holmes stopped abruptly and twitched his nose in a familiar fashion.

I sniffed the air and smelled the faint scent of cheap aftershave.

Leaning close to Ellie I whispered, "Someone is following us. Holmes smells him as well."

Ellie nodded. We increased our stride and returned to the house quickly. Holmes looked disappointed that his morning walk had been cut short.

"Irene, contact Security," I instructed, as I walked through the front door.

"Campus Security," a voice said, "How may I help you?"

"I think I am being followed," I began. "Can you send me the video from the cameras on the 600 block of Springfield Street?"

"Are you in fear for your safety?" The artificial intelligence officer had no emotion in its voice.

"Not at the moment," I said.

"Are you being stalked?"

The A.I. officer seemed to be following a protocol of questions. My red-headed short temper was getting the better of me.

"Please connect me to someone with a pulse!" I ordered.

Admittedly, my request sounded more like a rude demand.

Following a series of clicks, another voice came on the line. "Dr. Locke, this is Officer Bradstreet, how may I help you?"

"I believe I was followed this morning and want to see the video from the camera which would have captured the man."

"Did you see him?" Bradstreet asked.

"No, I did not. That is why I want to see the video." I tried not to sound exasperated.

"Then how do you know it was a man?"

"Because I smelled him," I said, before realizing the odd nature of my statement. "He smelled of cheap aftershave probably covering poor personal hygiene."

Bradstreet chuckled. "Are you a detective as well as a Worldwide Science Federation investigator?"

"There is little difference between the two," I said.

"We only release video to law enforcement," he said. "Have you filed a police report?"

"I am short on time," I complained.

"If you want to see the video, you'll need to file a police report," Bradstreet said. "I would suggest that you talk with Detective Yano Johnson. He handles most cases involving UNE, and I can send *him* the video."

The conversation ended with niceties, and I called the police station straight away.

"May I speak to Detective Johnson?" I asked, when the A.I. officer answered the call.

"Johnson here. How may I help you?" the detective asked.

I quickly relayed an account of the events and my conversation with Officer Bradstreet.

"Why would anyone be following *you*?"

I was only slightly offended. After all, I could hardly expect anyone outside the field of cybernetics to recognize my name. Unlike campus security, it was doubtful the local police had been informed of my arrival or purpose.

"I have been assigned to investigate researcher misconduct allegations against Dr. Sheppard," I said. "There are always people who are threatened by my investigations."

"Yes, I remember hearing about those charges," Johnson said. "But if memory serves me correctly, Professor Sheppard is a woman. You say you were being followed by a man."

"In these kinds of investigations, rarely is only one person's future at risk," I offered.

"Right. I'll call Bradstreet and ask him to send me the video," Johnson said. "I will need to show it to you in person. Regulations, you understand?"

I did not want to spend time going down to the police station. I asked, pleaded, and then begged for the detective to meet me at my UNE office. Then I remembered a boy from grade school also named Yano. His family was from the Czech Republic. I gambled on knowing the detective's weakness. I promised him a MOM-defying lunch of roast duck with dumplings and braised red cabbage, followed by kolaches for dessert.

As I ended the call, Ellie looked at me as if I had become an extra-terrestrial. "Have you lost your mind? Where in the world do you plan to get all that Czech food? You have no medical clearances and this is really short notice."

"I will leave that in your capable, dual-citizenship hands," I said, unable to resist the impulse to smirk. "Maybe Frank can help. From my experience, the man can do anything short of dividing the Red Sea. But then again, maybe he has not been asked to part the Red Sea."

Ellie and Holmes joined me on the SDV ride to my UNE office. I insisted Ellie work from there because the admin building had more security than the house. As my assistant, she might likewise be in danger. Holmes could defend himself with his eardrum-piercing bark and never-ending demands for belly rubs.

As Ellie set about her tasks, I asked Mycroft for an analysis of all the emails Sara had sent and received.

"That will take several hours," Mycroft said.

"Mycroft, I am expecting a visitor this afternoon." I said. I thought about how unexpectedly helpful Mycroft had been yesterday with the encrypted file. On an impulse, I asked, "Mycroft, who do you need to inform?"

"Provost Robaire Brown, Dr. Frank Covington, Dr. Kim Yong-Chun, Dr. Leonardo Gonzales, and Dr. Bruce Nigel."

I could feel the heat rise in my face. "Connect me to Provost Brown, holographic interface, force video."

Mycroft projected the image of Provost Brown in front of me.

"Provost, I have called to inform you that I will be making departure arrangements within the hour. I am obligated to notify you that I will be alerting the Department of Defense and the Worldwide Science Federation that I cannot perform my investigation under the current conditions."

The provost appeared visibly shaken.

"What conditions are you referring to?"

"Provost Brown, Mycroft has informed me that my activities are being reported to you as well as to others."

The provost's countenance betrayed his embarrassment.

"I see," Brown said. "You are aware that such a report will bring an end to all DoD and WSF funded research at UNE for years to come. The impact will go beyond Dr. Sheppard's research."

"Be that as it may, my report will point out that due to these irregularities, I am unable to verify the guilt or innocence of Dr. Sheppard. Good day, sir."

I ended the call. Within seconds, Provost Brown called me back.

"Wait," Provost Brown interjected, "How can I convince you to continue your investigation?"

"To begin with, the office iAdmin needs to be reprogrammed. All instructions to report my activities to others must be deleted. Is Mycroft also equipped with video surveillance?"

Smarthomes had video recording as home security. Offices usually only had one camera in the entryway to display a person wanting admittance.

"No," Provost Brown said. He seemed offended that I would suggest such an invasion of privacy.

"I require twenty-four-hour security for myself, Ellie, and Holmes, from Pinkerton's. Other considerations as they come up during my investigation."

I waited for objections or requests for compromises. None were offered.

"Agreed," the provost said.

"One more thing," I said. "You will provide Ellie with everything she needs to assist me with this investigation."

"Agreed," the provost said again.

I ended the call.

"Well, emergency suitcase packing has been avoided," I said to Ellie. "We should get to work."

"Rather than asking Frank for assistance with that extravagant lunch," Ellie said, "I think I should ask Provost Brown." Ellie's grin may have been broader than the Cheshire cat's.

"Good idea. After all, I have already softened him up."

Ellie nearly fell out of her chair laughing.

"Mycroft, connect me to Dr. Frank Covington," I instructed.

Frank answered the phone with a cheery "Howdy."

"Frank, to quote Sherlock Holmes, 'the game is afoot,'" I said, and ended the call.

During my days at UNE, Frank and I had created this secret code. Any time I quoted anything from Sherlock Holmes, it meant I wanted Frank to meet me at the lighthouse. I took Holmes with me. If anyone was watching, it would appear I was simply taking him for a walk. Holmes started barking as soon as he detected Frank. Holmes's sense of smell and hearing were his superpowers. No sooner had Frank kissed me on the forehead, then Holmes offered him a belly to rub.

"I see that Holmes would not make a good guard dog," Frank said with a laugh.

Frank and I sat on a large slab of granite. I expanded the LEESH to allow Holmes to chase the seagulls. The green light which emitted from my round handheld communication scrambler made it look like a glowing turtle. The lighthouse protected us from the summer sun as well as security cameras, while the turtle thwarted eavesdroppers.

"You have got some 'splaining to do," I said, by way of greeting.

"Cher, what's wrong? What do I need to explain?" Frank asked.

"Let us start with why has Mycroft been reporting my actions to a cluster of people? Including you."

"Your investigation has more repercussions than you've considered," Frank said. "Did Mycroft reveal the names of the others?"

I told Frank the names of the other four people Mycroft had identified.

"Have you asked Mycroft who programmed him to reveal he was a snitch?" Frank asked.

"Frank, are you saying you programmed Mycroft?" I asked.

"Cher, the DoD has the utmost confidence in you," Frank explained. "At the same time, they don't trust some people in the university administration."

Once again, Frank had eluded my question.

"Answer the damn question, Frank," I demanded. "Did you program Mycroft?"

Frank took my hand, and said, "I only added a subroutine into Mycroft's programming. The others must have employed hackers."

His voice was so soft I wondered if Frank was talking to himself or to me. His eyes looked out toward the bay. "My program must have interacted with theirs, otherwise Mycroft would not have revealed their names."

"Did you employ someone to follow Ellie and me this morning?" I asked.

"What?" Frank shouted, as he was jerked out of his reverie. "What happened?"

"Avoiding my questions is getting rather irritating," I said. "Did you have someone follow us this morning?"

"No," Frank said, "I did not have anyone follow you two." He lightly stroked my cheek with his hand and looked me in the eyes. "Please. Tell me what happened."

The softness of Frank's voice reminded me of how much I had relied on him after my divorce. I could not believe that anything had changed between us. So, I recited the events of my morning walk.

"I suspect Irene has been listening in on your conversations," Frank said. "When you and Eliana went for a walk, only a person equipped with eavesdropping equipment could report your conversation."

I had not considered that. "I decided on a whim to accompany Ellie this morning."

"Then your stalker must have been waiting near the house, just in case he was needed."

"I hope you are telling me the truth," I said.

"Cher, I may have held back information on occasion, but I've never lied to you," Frank said.

Am I being equally deceptive? Should I tell him about my conversations with Officer Bradstreet and Detective Johnson?

"Do you trust me?" Frank asked.

"That depends on your answer to my next question," I said. "How did you come to orchestrate so much of this investigation? You no longer work for UNE."

Frank looked around as though he suspected the seagulls were spying on us.

"I work for the Defense Department," Frank whispered. "I have since before we met."

I was stunned. Frank had always shown distaste for anything to do with the military.

Note to self, never play poker player with Frank.

"Cher, you should move out of the university house as soon as possible. I doubt Irene will confess her surveillance in the same way Mycroft did."

I nodded in agreement. Frank was right.

"Holmes, come here!" I shouted. Holmes ran to me as I dialed back the LEESH.

I left Frank sitting by the lighthouse. He was right. I needed to get home. I needed Watson.

While I walked Holmes back to the office, I sent a message to Emily. She was not only my daughter; she was an expert in cyber-security. I asked her to check on my iDom, and determine if he had caught a cold. Within seconds she texted back, "I will take his temperature, and let you know tonight."

Holmes took up his position in front of the big window as soon as we were back in the office.

"Did Holmes have a good walk?" Ellie asked.

"We both did," I said.

Now that Ellie and I knew Mycroft was reporting our activities to others, we were confined to small talk in the office. *Will Mycroft report on the class I am about to teach?*

I started the virtual classroom program and waited as each student said hello. One by one faces appeared on the view screen. I respected the five remaining students toughing out the class. Taking a research methods course was difficult enough back when it was taught in a physical classroom. In the online environment took even more dedication. The lecture was dead, may it rest in peace. My classes were conducted as a community of learning.

"Ms. Morstan, please start our discussion," I said.

"Today's assignment is to improve our understanding of outliers," Morstan said. "Outliers are observations which lie an abnormal distance from other values in a dataset. Mr. McDonald, please identify a reason a dataset may contain outliers."

"They can occur by chance," McDonald answered. "Just as it is possible, but unlikely, to have five tails in a row when flipping a coin."

"Ms. Hudson, name a reason for an outlier which is not a matter of chance," I requested.

"There could be an interaction effect," Ms. Hudson responded.

"Please elaborate," Mr. LeDoy said.

"Well, let's say we're studying the effects of alcohol on ten college students," Hudson began. "We measure the effects in terms of observable changes. Only one student's cheeks flush red and show changes in their coordination after the first drink. The reason may be a genetic lack of the enzyme that metabolizes alcohol. An interaction of genetics and treatment conditions."

"Dr. Locke, is it true that East Asians often lack this enzyme?" LeDoy asked.

"East Asians are one of the ethnic groups who are genetically predisposed to lack acetaldehyde dehydrogenase," I said.

"What about the choice of drink, Mr. LeDoy?" I probed "If the students were allowed to choose their own drinks, some students may drink a beer which has considerably less alcohol ounce-for-ounce than vodka, for example," LeDoy said.

"Mr. Greyson, what is the most common method of dealing with outliers?" Ms. Hudson asked.

"Delete the non-conformists," Greyson replied. We all laughed.

I hope all the spies who messed with Mycroft are being bored to tears.

I gave the students their next assignment. They could either write about why keeping outliers in the dataset may be appropriate, or why studying outliers aside from the dataset may be preferred.

After the class, I turned my attention to my upcoming interview with Sara's research assistant.

"Conrad Hatfield will be here in less than an hour," Ellie said. "What are you going to do about Mycroft?"

I cannot interview Hatfield in the office with Mycroft reporting my every movement.

"Is Sara's lab still shielded?" I asked.

"I would think so," Ellie answered.

"Good," I said, "Then I will conduct the interview in her lab where no one can eavesdrop." I paused and then asked, "How is lunch coming?"

"The artery-clogging food will be here at noon. Do you want to have lunch in the lab as well?"

"Definitely," I said.

I continued to review Sara's raw data up until my appointment with her whistleblower. The regularity of her outliers was most intriguing.

"Mr. Conrad Joe Hatfield is here to see you," Mycroft announced.

I picked up my notebook and left the office.

"Mr. Hatfield, I am Dr. Locke from the Worldwide Science Federation. As you know, I am investigating your charges against Dr. Sheppard."

"Please, call me C. J.," he said.

Hatfield wore a white cap with a black bill and gold braid. He sported a navy-blue blazer over a white shirt which was unbuttoned at the collar. Beneath his khaki pants were deck shoes. Even lacking epaulets on his shirt, he looked every inch a yacht captain.

"Pleased to meet such an accomplished professor," Hatfield said, oozing admiration.

Evidently, he was either unaware I was no longer called professor, or was trying to be ingratiating. The title of professor was reserved for those who had achieved tenure before it was abolished.

Faculty who conducted research without teaching classes were called 'researchers.' Those who lowered themselves to teach, and adjunct professors, were called 'Instructors.' With the death of tenure, there would be no new professors.

"I reviewed your biography after Ellie called me to schedule this meeting," Hatfield said. "Quite impressive."

This guy could be awarded a degree in smarmy without further study.

"We will talk in Dr. Sheppard's lab."

"Of course," Hatfield said. "Allow me to lead the way."

"Are you continuing your studies?" I asked, trying to make small talk.

He shook his head. "By coming forward about Sara's misconduct, I've eliminated researcher as a career. I can only hope the university and the WSF will compensate me for putting ethics ahead of my job prospects."

"Where are you working?" I asked, trying to avoid looking at his cap.

"I've been doing free-lance computer programming," Hatfield said, as we entered the cybernetics building. "My skills are in high demand."

So, if you are so highly skilled, why do you need compensation for doing the right thing?

Hatfield scanned his keycard, but the door did not open. When I scanned my card, the door slid open. He raised his eyebrows in surprise. Inside the lab, Hatfield took a seat at the desk. I pulled out a rolling chair and sat down opposite him.

"Where shall we start?" Hatfield asked.

"Please describe how you assisted Dr. Sheppard with her research."

Hatfield leaned back in his chair, resting his elbows on the arm rests and his feet on the corner of the desk. He steepled his fingers and sighed. "Would it be possible to have Ellie bring me a cold bottle of water?"

Hatfield's use of first names was getting on my nerves. "*Doctor* Zelyonaya is otherwise occupied. Besides, I know your time is limited."

Is it possible this buffoon is oblivious to how offensive he is? How in the blazes does Sara put up with him?

Hatfield got up and walked over to one of the floor level cabinets. He opened the unlocked door to reveal a small fridge and took out a bottle of water.

"I see no one has prepped the lab for the next researcher," he said.

"I see you are a pompous arse," I said.

Hatfield smiled smugly and returned to his previous position in the chair.

"Well, to begin with, I was more than an assistant. I am a researcher as well. However, because I was *her* research assistant, I wasn't allowed to be included in the authorship of the team's publications."

"I asked you what you did, not how poorly you were treated," I said.

Hatfield sighed again.

"I wrote almost all of the code for the new line of cybernetic implants," Hatfield began. "Sara is not much of a programmer, in my humble opinion."

You have never had a humble moment in your life.

"Did you work on the data collection or the data analysis?" I asked.

"Funny you should ask about that," Hatfield said. "Sara guarded the raw data and refused to let any other team member run any of the analyses."

"By team members, are you referring to Dr. Covington and Dr. Nigel?"

"Frank did very little other than lend his prestigious name to the articles," Hatfield said. "Oh, and secure the research funding."

"For all of Dr. Sheppard's research?" I asked.

"I'm not certain," Hatfield replied. "After all, he's semi-retired now."

"What was Dr. Nigel's role?"

"Bruce conducted the research trials and collected the data. I think Sara only let him join her project so she could learn more about the brain implants he was developing. The implants showed great promise for helping stroke victims regain the use of their limbs."

"Dr. Nigel never conducted any data analysis on his own?" I asked.

"I don't think so. Sara conducted the data analysis on her air-gapped computer."

"Air-gapped?"

"An air-gapped computer is one that is unable to connect to other computers or systems. Not only was her computer physically outside the network, but no other devices could connect to it," Hatfield explained.

"If she refused to let anyone see the analysis, then how is it you discovered she had faked it?"

"I told you, I'm a gifted computer programmer," Hatfield said, and winked at me.

I suppressed the desire to strangle him.

"In other words, you hacked into Dr. Nigel's computer and downloaded the raw data," I said.

Chapter 4
Outliers and Outright Liars

*T*here was a knock at the door, and I opened it. Ellie announced that Detective Johnson and our lunch had arrived. She pushed a cart with the unauthorized meal into the lab.

"You'll have to excuse me," I said to Hatfield. "I have a luncheon engagement."

Hatfield stood up and walked toward the door. His face showed surprise at the sight of the detective and the extravagant food. As Detective Johnson entered the room, Hatfield walked up to him and shook his hand.

"Hello, Mr. Hatfield," Detective Johnson said. "What a surprise to see you again."

"I still feel bad about the dean," Hatfield said. His tone oozed compassion that was not reflected in his face. "Her marriage always appeared to be so happy and loving. Like a fairy tale."

"Women in the fairy tales I've read, don't throttle their husbands," Johnson said.

"Thank you for your time, Mr. Hatfield," I said. "Obviously, you know your way out."

The way Hatfield was staring at Ellie made my skin crawl. He appeared offended that I excluded him from our lunch.

"Should we eat first," I suggested, after the pious pretender left.

"Good idea," the detective said. "Am I right to assume that you were interviewing Mr. Hatfield as part of your investigation?"

"Yes," I said. "Am I right to assume you interviewed Hatfield as part of your murder inquiry, Detective Johnson?"

Detective Johnson smiled in acknowledgement. "Please, call me Yano. Detective to investigator, it is my opinion Mr. Hatfield is incapable of telling the truth."

"You will get no arguments from me," I said.

Ellie dished up a plate of roasted duck, braised cabbage, and potato dumplings for Yano. She had brought a salad for herself. I looked for the least fattening food, and settled on the cabbage. The detective appeared to be in ecstasy over the meal.

I estimated Yano to be a few years older than me. Since most men took the prescription Elgae to prevent hair loss, I nd it difficult not to stare at his bald head. He even allowed his mustache and the fringe of his hair to show natural grey. I found him oddly attractive.

"I haven't enjoyed a meal like this since the last time I visited my grandmother," he said.

Yano had no trouble eating most of the roasted duck by himself. He ate two poppy seed kolaches and asked if he could take two more with him for later. Ellie took the remaining five kolaches and placed them in a bag.

Yano tucked the bag under his jacket. "I hope no one catches me with these kolaches, or MOM will have me on a restricted diet for weeks. I owe you one." Yano smiled like a schoolboy.

"Shall we watch the video?" I asked.

Yano took a small object out of his pocket and placed it on the table. The video from the security cameras was only two dimensional and was projected on the white wall of the lab.

"I'm afraid you won't see much," Yano explained. "The man obviously knew how to avoid being recorded by the cameras."

A figure appeared about 15 seconds after Ellie and I were seen walking past the camera. His face was hidden by the hood of his jacket. He was wearing dirty blue jeans and sneakers.

"How tall do you think he is?" I asked.

"From the video, he appears to be about five-foot ten," Yano replied. "About the same height as Mr. Hatfield."

"Can you tell anything else? Like his age?"

"Not really," Yano answered. "I can't even be certain about his ethnicity. Notice how he keeps his hands in his pockets."

"I am sorry to have wasted your time, Detective," I said.

"Are you kidding?" Yano asserted. "I won't forget that meal any time soon."

We all laughed.

"Dr. Zelyonaya, I understand that you have worked with implants and exoskeletons," Yano said.

"Yes. I was the principal engineer for the micromotors. And please, call me Ellie."

Yano nodded. Clearly, he already knew about her expertise with those motors.

"Ellie, would you be willing to watch another video?" Yano asked. "The security video of the homicide of Dr. Hernandez?"

"To what end?" Ellie queried.

"I need to know if Dr. Patel was in control of her implant when she murdered her husband," Yano said. "I will understand if you decline. It isn't easy to watch someone die."

Ellie looked at me, and I counseled, "Your decision, Ellie."

"All right," Ellie said softly.

Dr. Rolando Hernandez had been a big man. He was six-foot three, with a muscular build. I estimated he weighed about 220 pounds. His physique was in stark contrast to his petite wife.

Dr. Alisha Patel was only about five-foot four. She probably weighed a little over 100 pounds dripping wet.

The video showed the couple sitting on the sofa, drinking wine, and watching a golf tournament. Suddenly, Alisha reached over and wrapped her left hand around her husband's neck. He looked terrified. He stood up, trying to fight her off. Alisha was pulled to her feet. She could be heard yelling, "Oh my god! I can't control my arm! Fight me, Rollie!" She took her right hand and grabbed her left one. From the video, it was difficult to tell if she was trying to increase her hold or break her grip with her right arm. Within seconds Rolando dropped to the floor. Alisha was sobbing hysterically. The house iDom announced that the police had been called. Yano stopped the video.

"Dr. Patel's left arm was a cybernetic implant," Ellie said. "She lost her arm in a boating accident when she was in her twenties." Ellie's face was as white as the lab walls. "When she came to UNE, Priscilla managed to get the Cybernetic Overseers to allow Alisha to receive a cutting-edge implant prototype."

"What has not been reported by the media, is that Dr. Hernandez died from the injury to his neck, not strangulation," Yano divulged.

"How much force would it take to break a man's neck?" I asked.

"To break a someone's neck usually involves swift flexion, extension with rotation, whilst neck muscles are relaxed," Yano said, "while using only about eight pounds of force."

"But Rolando was not caught off guard," I said.

"He was a strong man," Ellie added. "He was on a rowing team."

"His neck wasn't snapped," Yano said, "his throat was crushed."

"If I had not seen the video," I declared, "I would have sworn that Dr. Patel was not strong enough to crush his throat, even with both hands."

"How is Alisha doing?" Ellie asked.

"She is on suicide watch," Yano said. "The doctors have her heavily medicated."

"Cybernetic implants do not provide superhuman strength, detective," I said.

"Maybe . . .," Ellie said as her voice trailed off. She had a faraway look in her eyes. "Remember the low-profile exoskeletons that were developed for the military?"

"Yes, but Alisha had a cybernetic implant, not an exoskeleton," I said.

"Right, but if the motors in a cybernetic implant could be boosted in the same way as with the exoskeletons . . .," Ellie speculated, sounding worried. "The combination of the motors and the titanium skeletal structure would make the person incredibly powerful."

"Noteworthy theory," I observed. "But if she boosted the motors in her implant, that means she intended to kill her husband."

Yano's green eyes looked from me to Ellie.

"Do you think she is psychotic?" Yano asked.

"I'm not a psychiatrist," Ellie answered, "but saying she can't control her arm certainly sounds crazy."

I nodded in agreement.

"Where is Holmes?" I asked.

"I left him in the office," Ellie replied. "He was getting belly rubs from our security guard."

Yano looked at me with an inquisitive expression on his face.

"Holmes is my dog," I explained. "He is the one who alerted me to my spy."

"Clever dog," Yano remarked. "Why does he need a security guard?"

"After the events of this morning, I told the provost we needed round-the-clock security for all of us."

We said our good-byes to Yano. I was about to snoop around the lab, when there was a knock at the door. On the other side of the door stood a uniformed woman stood in the hall with Holmes. As I looked at her bright red hair and freckled complexion, I wondered if she had been born in Ireland.

"'Ello Dr. Locke, I'm Molly Fitzpatrick," she said. "I was sent by Pinkerton Security Services. Dr. Sheppard brought some boxes to your office. She said she'd like to talk to you."

Holmes trotted over to the table where we had eaten our lunch. He twitched his nose. He looked at the table. He looked at me. He looked at the table again. He looked at Ellie. He looked back at the table and sighed. Telepathy was not required to know Holmes thought he should have been invited to lunch as well.

*　　*　　*

When I returned to the office, I found Frank and a young man waiting for me outside.

"I brought Bhavesh to help me re-program Mycroft," Frank said.

"I have reconsidered that request," I said. "I am afraid I may lose the parts of his program which have been helpful so far. Now that I know he is a snitch, I will simply use Sara's lab for anything I want unreported."

"Very well," Frank agreed. "If that is what you want."

I squeezed Frank's hand and smiled. He smiled back and the two men left my tattletale without deleting his spy programming.

Inside my office, Sara was seated in one of the leather recliners. Several boxes were on the floor by her feet.

"I know you will find more questions than answers in my paper docs," she declared, tossing back her long silver hair. "I have recorded more by hand than I entered in the computer."

In other words, what you told me in the lab was a lie.

"I thought I was the only one who preferred paper these days," I said. I worked to keep my face from betraying my thoughts.

Why am I not surprised?

"You used to say, 'Papers can be stolen, but they can't be hacked,'" Sara recited, as if we were old chums.

She forgot to add, "At least you will know if your papers are stolen."

"Speaking of hacking, where is your air-gapped computer?" I asked.

"The DoD took possession of it this morning. I transmitted my files to Mycroft with my UNE computer." Sara pointed toward the small device sitting in one of the boxes. She placed a slip of paper into my palm.

On the chance that someone had added a camera to Mycroft's hardware, I put both my hands in my pockets and left the paper there.

How does Sara know Mycroft cannot be trusted? Or is she simply being cautious?

"Sara, why did you hire Mr. Hatfield to be your research assistant?" I asked.

"I take it the two of you didn't get on well," Sara observed smugly.

"Answer the question."

"Very well," Sara declared. "Mr. Hatfield secured his position in his typically criminal manner. He blackmailed me."

"With what?" I asked.

"I don't care to say," Sara said in a flippant tone and raised her nose higher. "The nature of his blackmail is personal. It has nothing to do with the charges against me." She leaned forward and added, "General Westmore will be contacting you. He's DoD. He'll set everything straight."

"Why him and not you?" I asked. Sara's evasiveness was irritating.

"I'm not at liberty to discuss my research," Sara said. "Not even with the person investigating the misconduct charges against me."

Her expression was difficult to read. *Is she angry? Or demoralized?*

"Are you *at liberty* to say how Priscilla secured a prototype cybernetic implant for the dean?"

"I had nothing to do with that," Sara said, with heat in her voice. "Patel was behind the denial of my tenure at North Atlantic State University."

I knew Alisha had been interim dean at NASU, where Sara's academic career began. I had not realized Sara blamed Alisha for failing to be awarded tenure.

"Why did General Westmore neglect to contact Yong-Chun?" I asked "The general could have saved the IRB considerable time and money."

Sara's expression morphed back to unreadable. "You'll have to ask him that question. I'm not happy about how the general has treated me–after everything I've done for the DoD."

"Why does General Westmore want to talk to me instead of Yong-Chun?" I asked.

"I can't say," Sara said.

"Cannot? Or will not?" I prodded.

"Honestly, Cheryl," she proclaimed. "I have no idea. Ask him! Maybe it has to do with Dr. Kim's ties to Korea." She threw her hands up in dramatic exasperation.

In an attempt to catch her off-guard, I asked, "Why did you try to get into your lab last night?"

"I didn't," Sara protested.

"According to campus security, your keycard was used in an attempt to gain access."

"My keycard was stolen sometime last week."

"Did you report it missing?" I asked.

"I don't remember," Sara said. "Probably not. I was going to get a new one and have the missing one deactivated. The next thing I knew, I was being charged with misconduct."

Her body slouched with fatigue.

I pointed at the boxes on the floor. "Is this all you have?"

Sara nodded her head. "The general will explain everything," Sara promised, and pranced out of the office.

Does the woman always flip her skirt when she makes her exit?

I was reviewing Sara's IRB file when Ellie, Molly, and Holmes returned from the lab. Holmes took up his customary spot in front of the big window and was soon sleeping on his back. His head was straight back, his front paws bent toward his belly, and his back legs hung limp. He looked like a dead cockroach.

Sara's confidential IRB file was the reason agencies such as the WSF were created. The university IRB was touted as the watchdog for both the research and the researcher. However, if Sara's file was an example, then a slap on the wrist would have been more painful than the IRB's so-called sanctions.

One report read, "The investigation has concluded. Dr. Sheppard has agreed she will follow university policy regarding the sale of her research without university approval."

Are you kidding me?

There was no need for the privacy of Sara's lab to review her paper files. Besides, Holmes preferred the office.

I wonder if Mycroft reported that I discovered he was spying.

I pushed one box of Sara's papers toward Ellie.

"Ellie, can you look through these field journals while I review the data collection sheets?" I asked.

"You sure know how to have a good time." Sarcasm dripped from every word.

I had an eye for reviewing rough data. The first thing I noticed was there were five outliers in every dataset. Every outlier was above the mean of the rest of the observations.

"Ellie, does Sara say anything in her field notes about outliers?"

"She states the outliers were removed prior to data analysis," Ellie replied.

"If you find any other references to outliers, please let me know."

"Why the interest in the outliers?" Ellie asked.

"I find it suspicious there were exactly five outliers in every data set," I said. "That is an outlier in, and of, itself. The file with the virus was an analysis of five observations. I doubt that is a coincidence."

Our examination of the data was interrupted by Mycroft.

"Dr. Locke, my analysis of Dr. Sheppard's emails is complete," Mycroft said. "Are you ready for my report?"

"Yes, engage conversation mode," I said and took out a notepad to begin writing.

"Nine point-seven-three-one percent of her emails are of a personal nature," Mycroft said. "Exchanges with her family. Do you want any further analysis?"

"Not at the moment," I said. "Mycroft, please use whole numbers."

"Very good, Dr. Locke," Mycroft said.

Do I detect a change in his tone? Am I imagining things, or does is he offended at my request for less than exact figures?

"Seventeen percent of her emails relate to department business. Meeting dates and times, agendas, minutes of meetings, and search committee proceedings. Do you want a further breakdown?"

"No."

"Three percent were from Mr. Conrad Joe Hatfield. Sixty-seven percent of her emails are related to her research," Mycroft continued.

Now we are getting somewhere.

"Please break those down further. Identify who they are to and from," I requested.

"Seventy-eight percent of the research emails are to, or from, DoD email addresses," Mycroft explained. "Ten percent are exchanges with the comptroller's office regarding grant funds accounting, and five percent with IRB members. The remaining five percent are to, or from, the other members of the research team. Two percent are from outside researchers offering to join the team."

Only seconds after Mycroft finished his breakdown of the emails, he announced General Westmore had sent a message requesting a video call. My stomach told me the dinner hour was quickly approaching.

"Mycroft, connect me to General Westmore," I said. "Invite video."

General Westmore appeared on the view screen. He had a strong build. His muscular arms stretched the sleeves of his uniform. He wore rows and rows of ribbons.

Does the top row say "continued on other side?"

"Hello, Dr. Locke," he said. His dark skin provided a striking contrast to his white teeth as he smiled. "We need to meet regarding your investigation."

I worried that my expression would betray my attraction for the man. "Dr. Sheppard told me you would be in touch. Do you have a secure location in mind?"

"Please come to my home in Brookline for dinner," the general replied. "I'm an accomplished cook, and my home has the most advanced military-grade shielding available."

"That is the best offer I have had all day," I said. "Would it be possible for my assistant to come as well?"

I could use a chaperone.

He looked down at his hands with an expression of apology on his face. "I am afraid not. Dr. Zelyonaya does not have the necessary clearances."

"I see."

"I will send a car for you at six, if you accept my invitation."

"I accept, General," I said. "But send your car to the Brookline hyperloop station at six-thirty. The hyperloop will save me considerable travel time."

"Very good," the general said. "I look forward meeting you."

After the call ended, I noticed Ellie's inquisitive expression.

"I want to get a look at Sara's computer," I said to Ellie. She nodded in agreement.

"Mycroft, is Dr. Bruce Nigel on campus?" I asked.

"Yes," Mycroft replied. "He should be finished teaching his class in the next four minutes. His schedule is free for the next two hours."

"Good. Please invite Dr. Nigel to visit me in Sara's lab."

"As you wish, Dr. Locke," Mycroft responded.

I was certain I detected a change in his tone. *Does Mycroft know why I am spending so much time in Sara's lab? He cannot be offended. After all, he's a program . . . not a person.*

"I also need to meet with Leonardo," I said.

"Shall I invite him for coffee with us?" Ellie asked.

"Splendid idea. Invite him here for coffee, first thing in the morning."

Ellie looked surprised. I wrote on my pad, "I want to confront him about Mycroft's reporting." I pushed the pad to Ellie; she smiled as she read.

"You'll want iced tea," Ellie said. "Your dislike for coffee is one of the things which sets you apart from the rest of academia."

I walked down to Sara's lab.

What else does Ellie think makes me different from the rest of the academic world.

Chapter 5
Friends, Enemies, and Frenemies

*D*r. Bruce Nigel was waiting for me at the lab door when I arrived.

"Thank you for coming on such short notice, Bruce," I said, as I opened the door.

"I am delighted for the chance to talk with you, Cheryl," he said. "Dinner was far too public."

"I wish this was a social visit."

"Since the Board of Regents meets in three days, I realize your time is limited to conducting this investigation," Bruce said.

"I am glad you understand. Tell me about Sara's research."

"To be blunt, I think she's been cooking the data," Bruce said. "She was always so secretive about her data analysis—especially when it came to data cleaning."

"Removing the outliers?" I asked.

"Right."

Bruce fidgeted uncomfortably in his chair and smoothed his grey slacks with both hands. On his perfectly manicured left hand was a beautiful wedding ring with surprisingly large diamonds.

"Anything else?" I asked.

"I filed a grievance with the union when Sara appointed Priscilla to be the new program director for the brain implants," he added. "Sara asked *me* to be part of her research team, and then turned around and made that lush the program director."

His face flushed almost as red as the polo shirt he was wearing.

"You could have declined to work on the project," I said.

"You know the old adage, 'keep your friends close and your enemies closer.'"

When did Bruce start to consider Sara an enemy?

"Did you let Mr. Hatfield know about your suspicions?" I asked.

"C. J. probably could sense the tension between us," Bruce said. "I know C. J. comes across as an arrogant twit. At the same time, he didn't deserve to be treated like her personal toady."

"If you suspected Sara was falsifying the data, why not report her to the IRB?"

"I became suspicious *after* I filed my grievance," Bruce said. "At that point, accusations of misconduct would have been construed as retaliation for being passed over as program director."

"Did you share your suspicions with anyone else in the department?" I asked. "Did you confide in a friend outside the department?"

"No," Bruce said. "I know you consider Frank a friend, Cheryl, but personally I don't trust him."

"And why is that?" I asked.

"Ask him to tell you the story about how his father left the military after sensitive information was leaked to the Egyptian government," Bruce said. "The Egyptian Defense Department."

"How do you know that?" I tried to sound as though I already knew this story. "Did he tell you?"

"No," Bruce replied. "C. J. did."

How does Hatfield know about Frank's past?

"Do you trust anyone in the department?" I asked.

"I trusted you and Ellie," Bruce said. "I have trusted Malka."

Why is he speaking in the past tense?

"Do you have any reason not to trust Malka now?" I asked.

"No, but I don't have a reason to trust her either."

"Bruce, do you think someone is trying to sabotage your brain implants research?"

"Sabotage, no. Hijack, yes," Bruce said. "I don't want to sound paranoid, but surely you remember how fierce the competition is for research funding. With the abolishment of tenure, there are no promotions. Salary increases are solely based on the amount of research dollars we bring into the university. This environment doesn't exactly cultivate trust."

"Speaking of trust," I began, "why has Mycroft been reporting my activities to you?"

All the color drained from Bruce's face and he swayed in his seat.

"I don't know what you mean," Bruce protested.

"Come now, Bruce," I said. "Mycroft has already revealed to me that he has been reporting my actions to a number of people. Your name was on the list."

"Honestly, Cheryl, I had nothing to do with that," Bruce said.

"Then you deny getting reports on my activities?"

"Do you have any idea how much skill is involved in hacking an iAdmin?" Bruce asked.

I sat back in my chair.

"Noteworthy," I said. "I did not say Mycroft had been hacked. Until this meeting, my hypothesis had been that his reporting was part of Mycroft's original programming."

"I can't believe you are accusing me of spying on you, Cheryl!" Bruce stood up and quickly left the lab, slamming the door on his way out.

Noteworthy indeed.

I returned to the office. Ellie was studying Sara's field journals. She looked up when I sat down at the desk.

"Leonardo will be here at eight tomorrow morning for coffee," Ellie said.

"I need a walk," I said. At the word "walk" Holmes' ears perked up and he dashed toward the door. When Ellie and Molly joined us, the smile on his face widened.

Molly held my glowing green turtle as we walked.

"What's our game plan?" Ellie asked. "If we're going to play 'Good cop, bad cop' I want to be the bad cop."

All three of us laughed. After my interview with Bruce, it felt good to laugh.

"No, we are going to play 'Cat and Mouse,'" I said.

"Oh, tell me how to play that game!" Ellie requested.

"First, we let Leonardo think he is free like a mouse," I explained.

"Then you pounce on him?" Ellie asked.

"Nah, den she'll be setting her snare," Molly said.

"Right," I said. "I will ask him matter-of-factly why he did not just ask me about my investigation, rather than programming Mycroft and Irene to spy on me . . . and have us followed."

"But we don't know if Leonardo did all those things," Ellie said.

"There's the trap," Molly explained. "If the man says he didn't have anything to do with one of those things, he'll correct Dr. Locke."

"Trap sprung!" I said. "He will be admitting to the things he did, by denying what he did not do."

"Will catching him really be that easy?" Ellie asked.

"No, but that is the gist of the strategy," I said.

After our walk, we returned to the office and spent the afternoon analyzing Sara's notes. About five o'clock, we went back to the visiting professor house. I went upstairs to get ready for my dinner with General Westmore and Ellie went to her room. As I took off my slacks, the paper Sara had given me fell to the floor. I picked it up and read, "Sign on: Porkribs. Password: Alpha 5 Delta 1 Echo 9."

*   *   *

I came downstairs to find Molly had been relieved by another security officer. Of course, Molly would need to go home at some point. For the first time since meeting her, I wondered if she was married, or had children.

"Cheryl, this is Spencer Fraser," Ellie said. "He has the night duty."

The blond security guard rubbed his hands on his pant legs before reaching out to shake my hand. "Glad to meet you, Dr. Locke." Between his boyish face and wiry physique, he looked all of fourteen years old.

"Nice to meet you, Spencer," I said. "Please call me Cheryl. Will Molly be back tomorrow?"

"I think so," Spencer said with a smile.

"While you were in the shower," Ellie said, "I called Malka. We'll be having dinner at her place tonight."

"Good," I said. "I felt bad when the general would not include you in his dinner invitation."

Ellie stood in the way of Irene's camera and put her notepad in front of me. The message said, "Tonight, we are moving to Malka's summer house on Cape Cod."

I nodded. Ellie impressed me with the speed with which she had figured out a way to get out from under Irene's surveillance.

"Great idea," I said. "Malka is a fantastic cook."

I went upstairs to my bedroom and packed my suitcase. I wondered how I would get to Malka's house. I didn't want anyone, even the general, to know I had moved.

Ellie walked me to the SDV which would take me to the hyperloop. In a whisper, she told me to take an air taxi to the Cape Cod H-loop station after dinner. She would relocate our belongings and Holmes. Ellie had thought of everything. I hugged her before getting into the SDV.

*   *   *

General Westmore greeted me at the door of what could only be described as a mansion. He was wearing a dark grey suit with a pumpkin turtleneck. By his feet an elderly German Shepherd stood guard.

"Thank you for coming, Dr. Locke," he said. "Please allow Sarge to smell your hand."

I held out my hand. After a thorough inspection with his nose, Sarge granted me entry.

"Please, call me Cheryl," I said.

"Cheryl it is," he said in a friendly voice. "And you must call me Luke."

As we walked to the dining hall, we made small talk. Luke told me of the house's history. The estate had been handed down for four generations.

Luke provided names for his relatives as we passed their painted portraits on the walls. Near the end of the row the portraits became large professional photographs. The uniforms the men wore showed the era in which they served. Luke narrated an impressive family history of service and sacrifice.

He led me into a sitting room which reflected only the man standing before me. Awards and certificates displayed his achievements. I thought it was odd that Luke's diploma from the Citadel was placed higher on the wall than his diploma from West Point. His retired K9 had been awarded a Purple Heart. I walked up to Sarge's Purple Heart citation.

"Do you feel any competition with Sarge?" I asked, pointing to Sarge's commendation.

"No, ma'am," Luke replied. "But he may feel a competition with me. I have three Purple Hearts." Luke pointed to the opposite wall displaying his commendations.

I should have studied his ribbons more carefully when he called.

"I am sure you could have retired after the second one," I said.

"That was an option," Luke said. "I'm not the same man who graduated West Point."

"Not the same man . . .." I repeated.

"I have two cybernetic implants and a brain implant," Luke said.

I looked at him carefully. There was no way to tell which parts of his well-toned physique had been replaced.

"Most people with implants are reluctant to discuss them," I said.

"I have nothing to hide from you, Cheryl." Luke tenderly touched my arm. Goose bumps spread out from his touch.

Damn, this man is sexy! But his moves feel a little too well-practiced.

Luke led me to the dining room. Beautiful antique china with matching serving dishes decorated the table. Heirloom crystal wine glasses filled with red wine sat in front of each plate. The dinner was a delicious fare of jambalaya, cornbread, and roasted zucchini. Luke put more food on my plate than I could eat in a week.

"General–I mean–Luke, please tell me about Sara's research," I requested.

"Sara's research has served two purposes," Luke began. "One was for the civilian population, and the other has military applications."

"Was the IRB at UNE informed about the dual purposes?" I asked.

"No," Luke said. "That would compromise national security. Some members of the IRB have *questionable* loyalties. However, the research was reviewed by the HQ USAMRMC IRB."

"The Army's counterpart IRB," I said. "Please tell me more."

"Let's just say that Dr. Kim's ties to the Korean Empire are of concern to the DoD," Luke said.

He took a sip of his wine and then added, "The Korean Empire has come to possess some of UNE's research, without obtaining the data through regular channels. We suspect Dr. Kim is selling it."

I took a sip from my water glass to hide my smile.

Yong-Chun is probably selling research to the highest bidder regardless of citizenship.

"Cheryl, you haven't even tried your wine," Luke observed.

"I do not want to drink too much. Your glass has less wine. Would you object to trading glasses?"

"Not at all," Luke said. He placed his glass in front of me. As he reached to take my glass away, he knocked it over with his wrist.

Yes, Malka, my lack of trust serves me well.

Luke jumped up and put cloth napkins on the spill.

"I'm so sorry," Luke said. "I hope I didn't spill any on you."

"Not at all," I said, trying to hide my disappointment.

Luke placed the wine glasses on the sideboard, next to the bottle. We both drank water with the remainder of dinner.

"I need to know, was Sara was acting under the authority of the Department of Defense when she omitted the outliers from her data analysis?"

"I should probably tell you," Luke began, "I checked your background. I was surprised to find that you served in the military, and have a top-secret clearance."

I guess my military service is another way I am different from the rest of academia.

I looked at him, silently waiting for a response to my question. Waiting is an unappreciated skill.

"Yes, the outliers," Luke continued, "were integral to Sara's work for the DoD."

"Go on."

"You have apparently uncovered the DoD's agenda regarding Sara's research."

"The DoD wanted Sara to provide a means to increase the power to cybernetic implants," I postulated.

"As her team had previously done with the exoskeletons," Luke agreed. "But only for military personnel."

"Is that all?" I probed.

"The ability to boost the power of the cybernetic motors required the use of a brain implant," Luke said.

"So, those soldiers had brain implants?" I inquired.

"The implants were placed *before* the soldiers received the cybernetic limbs," Luke said. His matter-of-fact tone gave me chills. For heaven's sake, he was talking about brain surgery on perfectly healthy young people.

"Working for the DoD is not research misconduct," I said. "Sara was accused of faking her data, among other things."

"Falsifying data is a concern for all of us," Luke said. "Can you tell if any of her data was faked?"

"I need to compare the data she used in her analysis with the raw data which was collected by Dr. Nigel. In order to do that, I will need her computer."

Luke rose from the table and left the room. As soon as he left, I quickly squeezed some wine out of a cloth napkin into my clutch purse. A few moments later, Luke returned carrying a computer case.

"I will leave this in your capable and patriotic hands," Luke said smoothly as he handed me the case.

In other words, you have already tried to find evidence on this computer and failed.

As I stood up, he gallantly pulled back my chair. Then, he walked me to the SDV which would take me to the H-loop.

"I have one request," Luke said. "If you find that Sara faked any data, would you let me know ahead of the IRB?"

"As a matter of national security?" I asked, not needing the answer. Luke nodded.

Driving from Luke's Brookline house to Malka's Cape Cod cottage would have taken over eight times as long as taking the hyperloop. There was an air taxi waiting for me at the Cape Cod station. The drive to Malka's home was barely long enough to read a message from my daughter on my wearable.

Hey Mom, Watson is still healthy. There were a couple of indications someone tried to make him sick, but he recovered quickly. I gave him an extra shot of vitamins in case the bug is still going around. His immune system couldn't be stronger. Call me if you need anything. Love you, Emily. P. S. Any idea where Mori would have hidden one of my earrings?

I messaged back that she should check under the sofa, behind the bookcase, and inside the bathroom cabinet.

Mori earned her name by her criminal nature.

As soon as I exited the air taxi, I could hear laughter coming from the other side of Malka's front door. Roaring laughter.

I knocked and waited a few seconds. I tried the doorknob and was surprised when it opened. Some security guard Spencer was; he had not even checked the locks.

Malka, Ellie, Spencer, and a plush corgi sat at the dining room table behind Mah-Jongg tiles. Everyone was singing along with B.J. Thomas'

"Another Somebody Done Somebody Wrong Song." Malka stood up, and immediately grabbed the edge of the table to steady her balance.

"Wondahful to seer ya," she said. "If yar wannar play, I'll ask the dawg to giver up his chah." She pointed at the Holmes lookalike, and collapsed back into her chair.

"You are all drunk," I exclaimed, in total surprise.

"Malkwa'z teaching us hvow to play this ancient dame," Ellie said.

Malka leaned over toward me, but forgot to lower the volume of her voice.

"Don't tell them the beah is auptional," Malka said, then winked. At least, I think she was trying to wink.

How long has Malka been stockpiling beer?

Malka had taught me to play Mah-Jongg when I was at UNE. Jewish rules. There had never been any beer involved. I laughed so hard that tears welled up in my eyes.

"Optional?" Ellie repeated. Her face was bright red. She put her arm around the plush corgi's shoulders.

"We tried to keep your dog away from the beer," Spencer said. Defeat was written all over his face.

I looked behind me. Sure enough, on one of Malka's expensive couches was a snoring Holmes. His head slumped off the couch, but his heavy rump ensured he would not end up with his nose against Malka's carpet. His face displayed a most contented grin.

"You're home early," Ellie said.

"Didn't the general schtups yah?" Malka asked.

"No," I said. "General Westmore only flirted with me."

"The ladies thought you'd succumb to the general's charms," Spencer said, "but I stopped them from placing wagers."

"No one would have bldamed you," Ellie began. "From what I hear, teh general's magnetism is intoxicating. He usually gets sa ady in his baed in under two hours."

"Really," I said. "Based on what evidence?"

"Priscilla's," Malka replied.

Had Priscilla confided in Malka about her sexual experiences before their rift? Or were Priscilla's sexual escapades the cause of their rift?

"Priscilla dumped Leonardo after only two months to start an affair with Jolly-Rollie," Ellie added, looking at Malka.

At least she is trying to sound sober.

"So, when was Priscilla seduced by Luke?" I asked.

"Oy vey, whatever happened to 'General Westmore?'" Malka asked, a sly smile creeping over her face. "Luke had Priscilla's panties at half-mast aun their first date."

"How did Leonardo take being dumped for Rolando?" I asked.

"We can ask him tomorrow," Ellie said.

"While I appreciate this information . . .," I began.

"You mean gossip," Malka corrected.

I ignored her comment. "How does this information add to my investigation?"

"Priscilla believed she could schtups ha way to tenure and grants," Malka said. "Sara might have been wooking unda orrdahs from Luke or Priscilla."

I have to agree. Malka's hypothesis makes Priscilla's sex life more than gossip.

"Does anyone have reason to believe Sara warmed Luke's bed?" I asked.

Malka and Ellie shook their heads. Spencer appeared to be falling asleep in his chair.

"I need to go to bed," I said, hoping everyone would follow my example. As much as I wanted to work on Sara's computer, I had no energy left.

"Malka, would you be so kind as to provide a car to take Ellie and me to the Cape Cod H-loop in the morning?"

"I'll have my limo take yar to the campus," Malka said.

I turned to Ellie and said, "Don't forget, we're having coffee with Leonardo at eight in the morning."

As I began walking up the staircase to the guest room, I heard Ellie yell at me. "Be sure to set an alarm; this isn't a smarthouse."

As I got to the top, I heard Malka say, "Pahdee-poopa."

Chapter 6
Wicked Wednesday

The next morning, the alarm on my wearable woke me. I decided to eat breakfast before getting ready for the day. The cottage was so quiet, I assumed the party animals were still asleep. Downstairs, I was dumb-founded by the sight of three people where white robes. Two women and one security guard were sitting at the dining room table, hands wrapped around mugs of hot coffee, heads bowed. They looked like members of a strange religious cult, quietly worshiping the dark brew as though it was a holy sacrament.

When Holmes saw me enter the room, he stopped begging for coffee. He knew I would never allow him to have any.

Who wants a caffeinated corgi?

"Good morning," I said, using a loud, cheerful, classroom-greeting voice. Malka glared at me. Ellie bowed her head lower. Spencer winced. Holmes whined, and jumped on the couch where it appeared Spencer had spent the night. On the coffee table sat a huge mug and a plate with crumbs. He had, at least, tried to stay awake. I was uncertain how successful he had been.

"We are meeting Leonardo at the university for coffee," I said. "Malka, would you like to join us?"

"With that schmuck?" Malka responded. "I have bedda things to do. Like aurganizing my lipsticks."

Ellie smiled at her with a knowing look.

"I got an ideer," Malka said, "You should leave Holmes with me so he can recovah from our pahdee last night. I'll be his body guahd. Besides, it's probably gonna shouwah all day."

Malka is probably right about the rain. Even though her moratorium on pets no longer includes Holmes, she will probably never stop grieving the deaths of her two poodles.

"Okay," I said. Holmes appeared to have his eyes half shut. "But no coffee and no beer. Promise?"

Malka chuckled, and let her hand drop to her side. Holmes walked over to her, wearing a goofy grin which earned him a chin scratching. Malka was full of surprises.

About an hour later, Ellie and I climbed into Malka's limo in the pouring rain. Spencer was going off-duty and Molly would meet us at the office.

On the drive, Ellie told me about a call from Yano. He had contacted her because Alisha was insisting on having her cybernetic limb removed.

"The call was rather chilling," Ellie said. "She talked about her implant as if it was an alien being with a mind of its own."

"At the same time, her request stands to reason if she is convinced that she cannot control her implant."

"Yano said he had found a murder case where the husband claimed his exoskeleton killed his wife," Ellie reported.

"Fascinating," I said. "Did he give you any details?"

"The incident took place almost two years ago in Montreal," Ellie said. "The husband pushed his wife off their fifth-story hotel balcony. He claimed he lost control of his entire exoskeleton."

"Had the man been in the military?" I asked.

"I thought the same thing," Ellie replied. "Military exoskeletons allow for remote access, but the man had never served."

"Was the murder recorded?"

"No, but there were over thirty witnesses," Ellie said. "The couple had been at a conference at the time of the murder."

"What kind of conference?" I asked.

"I don't know," Ellie said. "At the time I didn't think it was important enough to ask."

"Does Yano see a connection with Hernandez's murder?" I asked.

"Only that the husband claimed he wasn't in control of his body, and the couple worked at a college in Vermont," Ellie said.

Academics.

I felt a chill run down my back.

When we arrived at UNE, Leonardo and Molly were waiting. Molly was wearing her crisp Pinkerton's security uniform. Leonardo was wearing his ego.

After my iris scan opened the door, Ellie took over the operation of the self-driving food-cart which delivered her order. A thermos of coffee, a pitcher of iced tea, some berries, and assorted nuts filled the cart. Before MOM, the cart would have contained a continental breakfast with muffins, gooey pastries, and buttery croissants. Those sweet treats had been all but outlawed.

I doubt the French regulate their citizens as strictly.

"Thank you for the invitation, Cheryl," Leonardo said, and sat down on the large leather sofa.

"Good morning, Leonardo," Ellie said, taking her seat on the leather recliner.

I walked over to the cart and poured Leonardo a cup of coffee. I brought him the coffee on a tray with the MOM-approved morning snacks.

"Good morning, Ellie," Leonardo replied. He smiled at her as I set the tray down on the table in the middle of the sitting area. "We've missed having you on the research team."

"I miss *some* of the work, and all of the team," Ellie said. If she was lying, she was doing a fantastic job.

"Ellie, do you still drink your coffee black?" I asked. She nodded in affirmation.

"I don't think the DoD treated you fairly," Leonardo said, and placed his right hand on Ellie's wrist. He was wearing three heavy gold rings. Two of them had beautiful stones I failed to recognize.

"The DoD will never get over my Russian birth or that I was married to a Greek," Ellie said. I was impressed by the lack of heat in her voice.

Ellie looked like she was about to shudder, until Leonardo removed his hand. My first hypothesis was that he had previously made advances toward Ellie. My second hypothesis was that she had told him, in no uncertain terms, she was not interested. My third, and final, hypothesis was that Leonardo had been shocked by her rejection.

"I am still astounded how you were able to reduce the size of the micromotors on the exoskeletons, while increasing their power," Leonardo said.

I poured myself a glass of iced tea and took my seat on the recliner opposite Ellie.

"Leonardo, my congratulations on being made interim dean," I said.

Leonardo smiled, and bowed his head. I guessed his expression was an attempt to appear humble.

Leonardo wears humble like a bull wears udders.

"Ellie, what have you been up to these days?" Leonardo asked, in an awkward attempt to change the subject.

"I continue to work on exoskeleton research for medical, rather than military, applications," Ellie said, and smiled at me. "I'm taking a short leave of absence in order to assist my first mentor."

"Ah, yes . . ., he said. "You're assisting with the investigation into the researcher misconduct charges allegedly committed by the distinguished Dr. Sara Sheppard. I didn't think this was only a social invitation." He adjusted his Venezuelan scarf as if it were a medal.

"You were the department chair before Sara was elected," I said to Leonardo. "I suppose Sara relied on you to teach her about the duties of department chair."

He crossed his legs and showed off his expensive Italian leather shoes. If I were to guess, he paid the equivalent of most people's monthly mortgage for those loafers and had probably flown to Italy to buy them.

"Hardly. I think Sara ignored my advice because I rejected her sexual advances. Her numerous jealousies frequently cloud her judgment . . . about many things."

"You were seeing Priscilla at the time," I said.

"No, my affair with Priscilla had already ended. After all, I'm a married man." He twirled a gold band on his left hand. A self-righteous smile spreading across his face.

"Is your research still funded by the DoD?" Ellie asked. I appreciated her getting us both back on track.

"For the most part. Which is why I'm deeply concerned about what will happen to DoD funding if Sara is found guilty of misconduct."

"Who is your DoD contact?" I asked.

"General Westmore," Leonardo replied. His face was difficult to read. "Since you had dinner with the general last night, why do you need me to confirm what you already know?"

So much for polite conversation.

"Leonardo, I remember how you helped me apply for internal grants the first year I was at UNE," I said. "So, I am puzzled why you have not openly asked me for updates on my investigation. I would have preferred that over resorting to having Mycroft and Irene report my activities to you and having someone follow me and Ellie."

"I have no idea what you are talking about." Leonardo looked genuinely baffled, but not guilty.

"Mycroft, have you been reporting my activities to Dr. Leonardo Gonzales?"

"Yes, Dr. Locke," Mycroft responded.

"Mycroft," Leonardo said, "How are you sending the reports to me?"

"To your UNE email account, Dr. Gonzales," Mycroft answered.

"Mycroft, please report how long it has been since I last logged into that email account," Leonardo instructed. "Password "hillbillies.""

"Dr. Gonzales last logged into his email account 9 months, 16 days, 7 hours, 14 minutes, and 3 seconds ago," Mycroft reported.

So much for my trap.

"I stopped using my UNE email after the second time it was hacked last year," Leonardo explained. "The DoD set me up with an email account separate from the university's servers."

"I apologize for jumping to the wrong conclusion," I said. "I should have collected more information first."

My mind was racing.

How could I have made such a blunder?

"Cheryl, I don't want to presume to tell you how to conduct your investigation," Leonardo said, in a patronizing tone, "but you should consider that whoever programmed Mycroft to report your activities included my name as a red herring."

"Then how did you know about my dinner with the general last night?" I asked with the bluntness of a sledge hammer.

"When you are finished jumping to conclusions," Leonardo proclaimed. "The simple answer is that Sara told me, and I didn't ask how she knew."

I thought for a minute and said. "Mycroft, can you tell if the emails sent to Dr. Gonzales are being forwarded to another account?"

"Yes," Mycroft reported, "the messages are being forwarded to an email account outside the university."

"Sharp as ever, Cheryl," Leonardo's voice felt like a verbal pat on the head. "That is why I voted to hire you."

What chutzpah!

"Funny, I do not remember you being a member of the search committee who voted on my hire, Leonardo."

He shifted in his chair.

"Speaking of accomplishments," I continued, "I followed your research after leaving UNE. I was surprised you abandoned your agenda into sensory enhancements and switched to developing artificial muscle tissue. I noticed your proposal was incredibly similar to the one I had submitted to the IRB before I left."

"Dr. Kim asked me to review a copy of your IRB proposal," Leonardo said. "He thought I was the best researcher to evaluate its scientific merit. I agreed, since it was clear the DoD would fund the study."

"Curious," I said, "I left UNE before I had been informed that my grant would be funded."

"And now I know why you voted against Cheryl's tenure," Ellie said, heat rising in her voice. "You wanted to steal Cheryl's research on artificial muscles, as well as her research grant." The anger in her voice was even greater than the outrage I felt.

How did Ellie know he voted against me?

"I'm afraid I need to leave now," Leonardo announced. "I'm meeting with the Chancellor in five minutes."

As Leonardo left the room, I heard Ellie mutter, "Schmuck," under her breath.

I reflected on the conversation with Leonardo and realized I was being sucked into a cosmic black hole. Nothing would be gained by rehashing my tenure application. There was no point in determining who had followed me. Besides, I was happy with my WSF position.

"Let us go down to Sara's lab," I said to Ellie. "I am not wasting another second wondering who is spying on me."

I grabbed Sara's air-gapped computer and left the office with Ellie and Molly. Pinkerton agents are trained as detectives as well as security guards. The lab was the most likely place for a member of the research team to hide something.

In the lab, I began thinking out loud. "We should start with what we have learned so far. Sara is accused of falsifying her data. How was this discovered?"

"C. J. Hatfield reported to the IRB that her graphs did not match her data points," Ellie said. "He also claimed that the images of the cybernetic implant prototypes had been altered."

"Right, and Hatfield told me Sara would not let anyone see her analysis. So how did he know?"

"Maybe he was the one altering the graphs," Molly joined in.

Ellie looked from Molly to me and added, "Or he knew who was."

"We know she omitted data points which were outliers," I said. "A common practice. However, to ensure data integrity, she should have included them in one analysis and then removed them in the second analysis."

"Unless she was trying to hide that they were *ever* there," Ellie countered.

"So how did Sara end up with fewer data points on her graphs than she had in her data set?"

I had asked myself, but Molly answered. "Maybe she erased some."

I placed Sara's computer on one of the workstations. Since my iris scan would not allow me access, I put the computer into guest mode. A screen displayed a box for "User" and "Password." From the slip of paper in my pocket, I entered "Porkribs" as user and "Alpha 5 Delta 1 Echo 9" for the password.

The data tables were clearly labeled and included the outliers. I used some of the tricks my daughter had taught me to look for hidden files and remnants of deleted files. I would have the evidence I needed if there were duplicate tables without outliers. I could not find any. If Sara had used this computer to create bogus tables, she had destroyed all the evidence on the hard drive.

"Couldn't she have erased them, like with a pencil eraser?" Molly asked.

"Not a pencil eraser," I exclaimed, feeling my excitement growing. "Old-fashioned Liquid Paper, also called white-out."

Ellie shook her head and began outlining the steps. "First, she would need to print out the graphs. Then she would cover the points she wanted to omit, but she could not submit graphs with white-out to a journal publisher."

"She could scan them into a file, and no one would see the alteration," I said.

"Or she could make a photocopy." Ellie walked over to the far corner of the lab. She removed a dust cover from an old-fashioned photocopier that had been sitting there all along.

"Jackpot," Molly said.

"We will need to find someone who can tell if the copier's glass has been in contact with white-out," Ellie said.

"I also want to remove the copier's hard drive to see if Sara copied the graphs on that machine." I said.

"If you heat up the glass, any titanium dioxide in the white out would turn yellow," Molly told us.

"One more bright idea like that, and I will be asking the Worldwide Science Federation to put you on their payroll."

Molly appeared pleased with herself.

"There is probably a heat wand somewhere in the lab," Ellie said. "I remember using one to test a group of Skin-II samples."

"While we are looking for that heat wand," I said, "take out all the drawers you come across in case something fell behind them."

"Good idea," Molly said. "When you have thoroughly searched a cabinet, leave the door open. That way we won't duplicate our efforts."

"Look behind everything," I added.

After about 45 minutes, we were coming to the end of our search. I tried to open one of the lower cabinets, next to the one holding the small refrigerator. The door would not open with the lab's keycard. Ellie called down to the security office. A few minutes later, a campus security officer arrived with a master keycard. The cabinet still refused to open.

"What is in that cabinet?" I asked the security officer.

"I think it's where they store the battery packs, ma'am," he said. "But why would anyone need to double lock battery packs?"

Molly smiled at the officer and left the room. She came back a few minutes later with a small, square device which she held against the cabinet door. After a few seconds of flashing lights and whirling sounds, the door to the cabinet opened. Inside were two large battery packs. I tried to move them, only to discover they were either incredibly heavy or bolted to the floor.

The security officer tried to move them as well. They did not budge.

"I'll go back to the office and grab an extractor," he said, leaving the lab.

"I can probably move the battery pack," Ellie said. She rolled up her sleeve, revealing the control band for her exoskeleton. She touched it in a few places and smiled at us.

"I just needed to boost the power of the motors," Ellie said. "Nothing to be afraid of, Molly."

I glanced at Molly to see a horrified expression on her face. Apparently, Ellie had not told her about the exoskeleton.

Ellie came over to the battery packs and moved them out of the way as if they were feather pillows. Dust puffed out from the cabinet, leaving a layer of grime everywhere. On the cabinet floor was a stack of papers which had been hidden by the battery packs. On the pages were graphs, tables, and printouts from a statistics program.

"Jackpot!" Molly said again, but this time her voice was almost a whisper. "Don't touch them," she warned us in a louder voice.

Ellie touched her control band again.

"I don't want to drain the power out of my exo," Ellie said. "As it is, I will need to recharge it sooner than usual."

"Ellie, please call Dr. Fraser in the Criminology Department," I requested. "Tell her to send over someone who can do forensic tests on these papers."

While Ellie was calling Dr. Fraser, the campus security officer returned with a large machine.

"We don't need that," Molly said to the officer, "Ellie already moved the battery packs." She shot Ellie a big grin.

The guard looked at Eliana, with her slender fashion–model figure and exotically beautiful face. She gave him a most alluring smile. Speechless, he left the lab.

For years, that poor boy is going to wonder how Ellie moved those battery packs.

Chapter 7
Forensic Experts

I answered the knock on the lab door, expecting to see a forensic student. Instead Dr. Sophie Fraser stood outside the door. In her right hand was what appeared to be a forensic kit. In her left hand, she held a LEESH keeping a squirming beagle puppy by her side. She walked in and gave me a hug. Sophie was a few inches shorter than me, with shoulder-length, curly blonde hair and blue eyes.

"Like I'm gonna let a student have all the fun," Sophie said. "Cheryl, I took it for granted that you wouldn't mind if I brought Kirah with me."

She looked down at her beagle puppy, who appeared ready to chew the handles off the cabinets. "I know you're a dog mom too," she added and gave me a knowing look.

"Sophie and I were undergrads together," I said to Ellie and Molly.

"Roommates as well," Sophie explained. "At least, until *someone* got kicked out of the apartment for bringing in a dog."

I walked over to pet Kirah. As soon as I reached for her ears, the puppy plopped down and rolled over. Sophie was right, I was a dog mom, and Kirah knew how to get someone to rub her speckled belly. Obviously, the puppy had her own agenda.

"Nice to know we have the best forensic scientist in the region."

"Thank you," Sophie said.

"I was referring to Kirah," I corrected her, a cheeky grin on my face.

Sophie and I started laughing, as Ellie and Molly joined us.

"What do you need analyzed?" Sophie asked.

"We think someone tried to hide those papers," Ellie explained, indicating the pile on the floor of the cabinet. "We need to know who has touched them."

"I also want to know if this copier's glass has been in contact with titanium dioxide," I said.

"White-out?" Sophie asked.

"I think someone may have altered these graphs with white-out," I explained.

"I see you still have trust issues, you know," Sophie said, and smiled at me. "At the same time, I wish you had been less trusting of that psychopath you married."

"We are not going there," I said, exasperation in my voice. "We need to stay focused."

Sophie reached into her forensic kit and removed a large white envelope.

"Give me a hand, Cheryl," she said, as she opened the envelope.

I helped her spread the white film from the envelope over one of the work stations along the wall. Then she removed two more packets from her kit. One contained an instrument which resembled a large pair of tweezers with paddles on the ends. The other one contained a shallow silver tray with a raised lip and a clear lid. She picked up a page with the instrument and carefully placed it on the tray. She held the lid on top of the tray's lip as she walked over to the covered work station to lay down the tray. Carefully, she lifted the lid. If there were any skin cells on that paper, her movements were calculated to preserve them.

Sophie took out a small light wand and shined it on the page. Small purple spots showed up. She took an instrument that reminded me of a monstrous syringe and pointed it toward the purple spots. The spots were vacuumed into a vial. We were all mesmerized by her every move.

"Really, is this the best entertainment you can find?" Sophie asked. "This is going to take a couple of hours, you know."

I looked over at the pile of papers and began to think it could take days.

"Find something else to do, you know," Sophie ordered. "Something which doesn't involve watching over my shoulder."

Funny, I do not remember Sophie being this bossy as an undergrad.

"I would be happy to take Kirah on a walk," Ellie offered.

"Good idea," Sophie said, "Kirah has been known to chew up papers, you know, and anything else she can find."

"Would you like to come with me, Molly?" Ellie offered.

"I would love to," Molly said. "If you don't mind, Cheryl."

"Of course. Ellie may need protection from that ferocious animal."

"I guess I'll take an umbrella since we don't have your modified LEESH," Ellie said. She took Kirah's LEESH from Sophie, and the three ladies left the lab. Kirah's tail never stopped wagging.

I wish Kirah could tell me what they talk about on their walk.

"Do you have any suspects?" Sophie asked, returning my focus to the investigation.

"Yeah, all of the department faculty," I answered, "and most of the college."

Sophie laughed. "Sounds about right."

"I have a DNA database which includes all of the faculty, staff, and students at UNE, you know," Sophie said. "Please, don't tell anyone. I collected that material in public places, but I'm not sure about the legalities . . . .."

Sophie was always one to ask for forgiveness rather than permission.

"Do you want me to bring you any food?" I asked.

"Only if you're going to offer me some artery-clogging, off-MOM, snack," Sophie teased.

I blushed.

"How did you hear about that?"

"Are you kidding me?" Sophie asked. "There are more rumors around UNE than there are conspiracy theories on the Internet, you know."

"Look here." Sophie pointed to the top of a graph on the page. "What do you see?"

"White-out," I said. "The highest points on this graph have been concealed. Can you run a preliminary analysis and tell me who has been in contact with that page?"

"Not yet," Sophie said. "I will need more cells. Probably three pages should be enough for preliminary results."

In order to stay out of Sophie's way, I began examining the copier. I opened the paper tray. Considering the era of the photocopier, I expected to find old paper, yellowed with age. Instead, I found glossy white paper which was far too bright to be more than a few months old.

"Do you have a screwdriver in your bag of tricks?" I asked.

"A few," Sophie replied. "Help yourself. They're in the side pocket, you know."

After finding a sonic screwdriver, I opened up the front panel and removed some of the cams. Behind a roller, I located the hard drive. Removing the drive was simple enough. Now I needed to connect the drive to a computer to view what was on it.

"How much longer until you can tell me who has handled these pages?" I asked, trying to sound more patient than I felt.

"You're as patient as my pup, you know," Sophie said, and emptied the vial of cells into a small black box that she had set up on the adjacent work station. "The analysis is going to take at least an hour to run. The process of categorizing the cells into DNA groups is done cell by cell. Once the cells are grouped, they are identified in terms of source, skin, hair, nail, and so on. Finally, the device will estimate the amount of contact by taking into account how many cells and from where to determine who had the most contact with the page."

I am glad I do not sit in on her lectures.

A few minutes later, Ellie and Molly came back to the lab. They seemed to have allayed Molly's anxiety on the exoskeleton.

"Molly, do you have any concerns about continuing as our security guard?" I asked.

There was one more glass of iced tea from lunch. I poured it into a glass and took a long sip.

"Not at all," Molly said, and she smiled at Ellie.

"I've been meaning to ask," Sophie said to Molly. "Do you know my brother Spencer Fraser? He works for Pinkerton's too."

My iced tea nearly spewed out my nose.

Some investigator I am! I had not even considered the implications of two people with the same surnames, both working in the field of criminology.

Before Molly had a chance to answer, I said, "Sophie, he was our night guard last night."

Sophie laughed. "Small world, you know."

I debated telling Sophie about the drunken Mah Jong party and the unlocked door. Given my knowledge of siblings, I decided against it.

"While we are waiting for your results," I said to Sophie, "I should plug the hard drive from the copier into one of these computers. There should be a record of every page that has been copied."

I carried the drive to one of the work stations near the hub. On top of the black surface was a slot where I connected the copier's drive. All three women drifted over to the work station and stood behind me to look over my shoulder.

Sure enough, we saw the same graphs that were currently being analyzed by Sophie's apparatus.

"That machine must have copied tens of thousands of pages," I said. Just the thought of analyzing all the image files made my eyes hurt.

I cannot view every single one.

No sooner had those words come out of my mouth, than three black pages were displayed on the viewer.

"What's up with that?" Molly asked.

"I think someone forgot to close the copier's lid," I said.

Clearly, Molly did not have any photocopier experience.

"Oh, I could've sworn I saw a hand and a face," Molly said.

"Go back, Cheryl," Ellie leaned closer to the screen.

I went back to the first black page. Molly was right. There was a blurry image on the screen. The object must have been several inches away from the glass and moving.

"I see a hand," Molly said. Ellie and Sophie nodded in agreement.

The second black page came on the screen. "Is that a face?" Ellie asked.

"Shure looks like a face to me, you know," Sophie agreed.

"The image is too dark," I said, "Impossible to tell who it is without some tech-magic."

"Your tech-magic or mine?" Sophie asked, smirking.

Is that a challenge?

"Once DNA results are complete," I said, "we can try matching the owner of the DNA to the image on the screen."

As if on cue, Sophie's wearable emitted a noise. The loud buzz was followed by the blur of a beagle darting toward the only open cabinet for safety. The same cabinet where we had found the papers.

"Results are ready," Sophie said, as though announcing her cake had finished baking.

I sprinted over to Kirah before she could climb inside the cabinet and begin chewing up my evidence. As I scooped up the puppy, I noticed a two-inch hole on the side of the cabinet near the top, all the way in the back.

What is that hole doing there?

"The skin cells on these pages come primarily from three people," Sophie announced as though someone had won the lottery. "Hatfield, Nigel, and Sheppard. Trace amounts of skin cells can be attributed to janitorial staff and someone not in my database."

I looked at Sophie as though she had been speaking gibberish. "Trace amounts from someone *not* in your UNE database?"

"The number of cells is infinitesimal. Maybe the person had been inside the lab a few times and had no direct contact with those documents," Sophie explained.

I looked at the analysis on Sophie's computer. "What do you know?" I asked rhetorically. "The majority of the cells did not come from Sara."

"I'll need to test more of the papers," Sophie said. "An analysis of three pages is hardly definitive. There must be over fifty pages in that pile, you know."

Ellie came over and took charge of Kirah. Until those pages were safely moved to the work station, the energetic beagle needed to be contained with the LEESH while in the lab.

"We need to gather as much evidence as we can," I said. "Since we did not find a heat wand in the lab, maybe we should ask if the security department has one."

"Why do you need a heat wand?" Sophie asked.

I explained how we were trying to determine if the photocopier glass had been exposed to white-out.

"I have something which should work," Sophie said. She reached into her forensic kit and pulled out a device which looked a lot like an old-fashioned cheese slicer with a cord.

"Allow me," Ellie said.

Ellie took the heat wand from Sophie and began systematically waving it over the copier glass. Within seconds hundreds of yellow spots appeared on the glass. I took pictures of them with my wearable.

When the wand passed the lower left corner of the glass, a fingerprint became visible.

Thank heavens for careless criminals.

Ellie carefully heated the corner with the fingerprint. When it had stopped turning yellow, I took several pictures with my wearable. Sophie came over and transferred the fingerprint to a filament from her kit.

"Unless I get some help," Sophie stated, "analyzing these pages will take hours, you know."

I stepped into the hall and called Pinkerton's to request the services of Spencer Fraser. Then I called Provost Brown. When I enabled the video on my wearable, his holographic image was projected in front of me.

"How is your investigation progressing?" the provost asked. He sounded even more annoyed at my interruption than he looked.

"I have found some compelling evidence," I reported.

"Really?" the provost replied in a startled voice.

"Yes, which is why I am calling," I explained. "I need another security guard to protect us while the evidence is being collected and analyzed."

"I see," he said.

"One person can hardly provide security for two people and Holmes."

"I didn't realize Holmes was in any immediate danger," the provost said dryly.

I worked to keep my face and voice from betraying my thoughts.

If I ever see the provost again, I hope Holmes bites him!

"I'll see what I can do," the provost said, his voice devoid of confidence.

"Don't bother," I said, "I have taken the liberty of calling Pinkerton's and they are sending over another security guard. I just wanted to let you know about the expenditure."

Before Provost Brown had time to object, I ended the call.

Sophie joined me in the hall about halfway into my call. From the look on her face, I deduced she wanted to tell me something. When I disconnected from the provost, her expression changed. She looked at me as if I were a total stranger.

"I agree with your tactics, you know." Sophie's smile returned. "Spencer can help me collect forensic data, and no one else needs to be informed of this evidence."

"But?" I asked. "Your face says there is another question on your mind."

"When did you get so bossy?" Sophie asked rhetorically.

Should I consider that a compliment?

"I believe that hole you discovered," she said, "was used to stash the pages behind the battery packs."

I nodded in agreement. "Whoever doctored the graphs," I said, "probably thought they would return later and destroy them without being discovered."

"Less risky than throwing them away," Ellie added. "No way to know who might paw through the recycling bin."

Spencer arrived 30 minutes later. He showed no signs of the previous night's revelry. Sophie started barking orders, and he appeared practiced at helping his sister.

I turned my attention to the copier's hard drive.

"I wonder if there is a way see only the black pages?" I asked no one in particular.

"We can set a filter," Ellie responded.

She moved over to the work station and set her fingers moving on he controls. "Twelve more pages with similar images were found. I saved the pages to a file for easy retrieval."

"This copier can tell a story," I speculated. "I only hope to have the time to listen."

"What do you mean?" Molly asked.

"The copier has been used thousands of times, and each time the hard drive recorded what was copied," I explained.

"Some of those copies will have dates on them," Ellie added.

"Some will," I said, "but my fear is that analyzing all these pages could take months."

"Not for Mycroft," Molly said.

"Hmmm. I do not want Mycroft involved."

"Maybe General Westmore can help?" Ellie offered.

"I do not want him involved either."

"What about Watson?" Ellie suggested.

"Yes, I can trust Watson," I said. "However, I will need a secure data line to transmit the images to him. The lab has such a line . . .."

"But you'd need an access code," Sophie warned. "Access codes are one-time use only. Asking for one will alert people that you're transferring a large amount of data to your home."

"You could ask Yano for help," Ellie proposed. "I'm sure the police have secured data lines, and probably advanced encryption as well."

"Brilliant!"

In order to have privacy when I called the police station, I went outside into the rain. I stood under one of the catwalks to stay dry. I did not see anyone, but I activated my green-turtle communications scrambler as a precaution.

"May I speak to Detective Yano Johnson?" I asked the A.I.who answered my call.

"Johnson, here," Yano said after I was connected.

"Hello, Yano," I tried to sound like we were old friends. "This is Cheryl. I need to redeem the favor you mentioned at lunch."

Yano's sigh was filled with trepidation.

"Could transmit over a secure channel several terabytes of data to my iDom?"

"Is that all?" Yano asked, sounding relieved. "Given the depth of my debt, I was afraid you were going to ask me to break several federal and state laws." He chuckled.

"I will send Molly Fitzpatrick from Pinkerton's Security over to your office. She will have a hard drive with the file, the IP address, and passwords for my iDom. Could you hide the hard drive at the police station after the transfer?"

"Is it evidence?" Yano asked in an encouraging tone.

"Absolutely," I responded.

"Okay," Yano said. "I will put it in the Hernandez evidence locker."

I was immediately impressed with the subterfuge. No one looking for evidence regarding Sara's misconduct would look in the evidence locker for the Hernandez murder.

"Brilliant," I exclaimed. "There is just one more thing."

"Yes?"

"I need a fingerprint identified," I requested. "Would you be so kind as to run it through your database?"

"Doesn't UNE have records?" Yano asked.

"Are you kidding?" I replied. "The union stopped that practice decades ago. The faculty decided fingerprinting was too *demeaning*."

If the union catches wind of Sophie's DNA database, a violent uprising will ensue!

"Okay, but then *you'll* owe *me* a favor," Yano said with a chuckle.

"I am sure we can work something out," I agreed in a sultry voice.

I returned to the lab and nodded at Molly. She put the hard drive and the fingerprint filament into the pocket of her raincoat. The Pinkerton SDV would take her to the police station. Her activities were calculated to avoid arousing anyone's suspicions.

"Ellie, I believe Sophie's analysis will determine who falsified the charts," I said. "However, those were not the only charges of misconduct against Sara."

"Are you trying to clear her?" Ellie sounded incredulous.

"I only want to find the truth. I have no doubt that misconduct was committed. I am just not convinced that it was committed by Sara."

"What about the plagiarism?" Ellie asked.

"Sara was never sole author on any of the publications," I said. "In my experience with Sara, she is a terrible writer. Besides, plagiarism is no longer a misconduct issue, it has been promoted to a crime. If the IRB wants to pursue that charge, they need to file a police report."

Ellie looked at the IRB report on her display screen. "Next on the allegations list, 'conflicts of interest.' Hatfield accused Sara of failing to disclose her DoD agenda."

I shook my head. "Nothing there. General Westmore told me he directed Sara to keep certain aspects of her research hidden from the IRB. He also said this arrangement was due to DoD suspicions regarding Yong-Chun's continued ties to the Korean Empire. Sara's omissions would not be considered misconduct since she was protecting national security interests."

"We still need to address Hatfield's accusation that Sara received financial gains from her research."

"That charge is being investigated by the WSF accountants," I said. "Let me check and see if their report is back."

I was able to display the investigation notes from the WSF, but the accountant report was not yet complete. There appeared to be some issues with accessing the DoD ledgers.

At UNE, the Office of Research and Development audited Sara's account when Hatfield made his allegation. The details he provided led the auditors directly to the $250,000 missing from Sara's account.

"This only proves *someone* was moving money," Ellie said. "There is no trail which leads directly to Sara."

"I will call Frank and ask for his help with the money trail."

Once again, I stepped outside. At least the rain had stopped.

"Hello, Frank," I said.

"Hello, Cheryl."

The warmth in his voice is always so reassuring.

"I could use your help with my investigation," I said.

"I'd be happier than a clam at high tide to help you, Cher," Frank said.

"Frank, you were the principal investigator in several research projects with Sara," I said. "Would you please come to Sara's lab and help me review the auditor's report?"

"Why not just send me the report?" Frank asked.

Admittedly, Frank could have worked remotely, but I wanted him to join me in the lab. I needed to ask him about Hatfield's allegations regarding his father and the Egyptian Defense Department. Questions I could only ask in person.

"I want to show you what I have uncovered so far," I said. "I think I may have enough evidence to go to the Board of Regents."

"I'll be there in two shakes of a lamb's tail," Frank said.

Chapter 8
Traders and Traitors

Molly returned from the police station and reported that the files had been transferred to Watson, but Yano was had been called away before he could match the fingerprint.

"Yano said he'd run the print as soon as he returns to the station." Molly stated.

A few minutes later, I answered Frank's knock on the lab door. Kirah decided to defend the room against the intruder. Frank made cooing sounds and held out his hand to the puppy. Soon the beagle was soliciting belly rubs from a willing provider.

"I guess I've passed security and am allowed to enter," Frank announced, as he stood up. "Whatcha got?" he asked as he turned toward me.

I quickly summarized the discoveries we had made in the lab.

"I think we will know who falsified the data by the end of the day," I said. "Now I need to know who was skimming the research funds."

"How much do they say is missin'?" Frank asked.

"A quarter of a million dollars," I said.

"Those bean counters couldn't find water in a boot with the instructions written on the heel," Frank said. "Still, that isn't exactly pocket change."

"That is what I thought," I said. "I turned the grant management issues over to a WSF accountant. However, they do not have access to the DoD ledgers. Hatfield's last email contained detailed descriptions of the discrepancies. I cannot ignore them."

"Let's go back to your office," Frank suggested. "I'll need Mycroft's help for this."

Frank knows Mycroft is not secure. What is he up to?

"I am going to the office with Frank," I told the group in the lab. Molly started to follow me.

"I can protect Cheryl," Frank said to Molly.

"Cheryl," Molly began, "My job is to protect you. If anyone discovers you are looking at financial records, you may be in danger."

We both nodded for her to join us. When we got to the office door, Molly took a post outside.

Frank told Mycroft to scan his iris. I gave him an inquisitive look. "I have access to some files you don't," he explained.

"Entering stealth mode," Mycroft declared.

"You might have told me about stealth mode," I said.

"What?" Frank said with feigned shock in his voice. "You needed the exercise of walking down to Sara's lab several times a day. Your waistline will thank me."

Cheeky!

"You have a theory about what happened to the money," I said, somewhere between a statement and a question.

"Yes, I do," Frank agreed. "Now, let's compare the UNE records with the DoD's."

"Can Mycroft compare the UNE ledgers to the DoD ledgers and note any missing funds?" I asked.

Frank looked at me strangely. He repeated my instructions verbatim to Mycroft.

Seconds later Mycroft said, "There are no missing funds."

How can that be?

"Mycroft, display the report from Hatfield which identifies the discrepancies in accounts," I said.

The report displayed dates and amounts. I smiled in satisfaction that I was smarter than Mycroft.

"Mycroft, note any differences between the UNE and DoD accounting ledgers," Frank instructed. He looked at me with the smile of a father being patient with his know-it-all child.

If Frank pats me on the head, I will kick him in the shins.

"There are several differences in the accountings."

"Analysis," Frank requested.

"In June of last year, $150,000 was transferred from Dr. Sheppard's research account to Dr. Nigel's project," Mycroft began. "For the following ten months, Dr. Sheppard transferred $10,000 from her account into Dr. Nigel's on the first of the month."

You can only get answers to the question you ask.

"Mycroft, one-hour silent mode," Frank said. "Access code 'Queen to Queen's Level Three.'"

I heard a faint sound, like a computer going to sleep.

"There you go," Frank said to me. "Mycroft will not report anything from this room for an hour, including his current silent mode."

"I thought you did not program Mycroft," I said.

"Let's just say I *improved* on his programming," Frank corrected.

No wonder I have to be careful how I word my questions to Mycroft.

"Sara was moving her research funds to Bruce's project," Frank said. "The question is what was she trading them for?"

"Trading?" I asked, "Those transfers coincide with what Hatfield told the IRB. But Hatfield never said she was trading research dollars. Sara would need IRB permission to transfer money over to Bruce's project."

What was she getting in return?

"Did she make that request?" Frank asked. "Misconduct only occurred if she did not have authorization."

"Let me check the IRB records regarding amendments," I said. "The IRB would have had to approve it."

Frank laughed. "Do you know which IRB received the request?

Luke asked Sara to keep some of her research activities away from the IRB at UNE."

I felt like a rug had suddenly been pulled out from under me. Hell, the whole floor felt less solid.

"You know General Westmore?" I asked, when my mouth could finally form words again.

"Sure do," Frank said. "We went to the Citadel together. We've been friends for years."

"Why have you never told me?" I asked.

"You didn't need to know until now," Frank said. "I trust you'll keep that information to yourself. It's . . . complicated."

"Do I need to know *now* about your father's involvement with the Egyptian Department of Defense?" I asked.

"Ah, Hatfield took my bait." Rather than looking upset, Frank looked smug. "Who told you about that?"

"Bait," I repeated. "Bruce told me."

"Perfect," Frank said. "I was pretty sure after Hatfield hacked into my computer, he'd tell Bruce about my past."

"What is going on?" I asked.

"Cheryl, you've got a job to do for the WSF," Frank said. "You need to stay focused on your investigation. I'll explain everything once your work is done."

Ellie came running into the room. She looked shaken. Molly was close on her heels.

"Cheryl," Ellie said as she caught her breath. "Detective Johnson sent a campus security officer to the lab to tell you Dr. Kim Yong-Chun has been found dead."

"When?" Frank asked. The color drained from his face.

"How did he die?" My voice trembled so much I almost did not recognize my own words.

"All the security officer said was that Dr. Kim's body washed up this morning," Ellie replied.

"Frank, would it be safe to call the detective from this office?" I asked.

Molly remained silent.

"Sure," Frank said.

I called the police department and was quickly connected to Detective Yano Johnson. Both of us had video enabled.

"Yano, thanks for letting me know about Yong-Chun's death," I said. "Your involvement implies his death is suspicious."

"It's too early to determine if his death was a suicide or homicide." Yano hesitated. "I recognize Dr. Zelyonaya and Ms. Fitzpatrick in the background. Please introduce me to the other person with you."

Frank stepped forward.

"Hello Detective Johnson, my name is Frank Covington. Please access DoD file number U.S.F.C. one, seven, zero, one."

What happened to Frank's southern expressions?

Yano causally glanced at another display screen. Within seconds his glance became a stare. Then he began nodding his head.

"An honor to meet you, Dr. Covington," Yano said. The detective straightened up in his chair as if he were in the presence of a celebrity.

What in the hell did Yano see on that screen?

"Whadda ya know 'bout Dr. Kim's death?" Frank asked.

Can Frank turn his southern accent on and off?

"He drowned," Yano said. "His body was found in Boston Harbor between Castle Island and Spectacle Island. The preliminary coroner's report states he died sometime around four in the morning."

"Any signs of violence?" Molly asked, in a wary voice.

Before Yano had a chance to answer, Frank asked, "Was there a suicide note?"

"If there was a note, it wasn't found on the body," Yano said. "While there are no overt signs of violence, the word in cyberspace is that some people are happy he's no longer among the breathing."

Yano looked at me and added, "I'm already breaching protocol to tell you this much. Cheryl, but I thought if you're going to report your findings to Dr. Kim, you should know."

"I can report my findings to the Regents even without the approval of the IRB chair."

"I'll be in touch." Yano ended the call.

"I'm impressed," Frank congratulated me. "You've hitched your wagon to the biggest mucky-muck detective at the department."

Before I had a chance to ask him what he meant, Ellie stood in front of our small group and announced, "Sophie's report is ready, but she will only relay her findings once you're in the lab, Cheryl."

My professional demeanor and poor shoe choice kept me from running over to the cybernetics building like a child running to a toy store. Well, that and the fact I always look like an awkward penguin when I try to run.

"I take it everybody wants to know the identity of the *Copier Culprit*," Sophie said once the door to the lab was closed.

Copier culprit? Oh, no! Sophie is on center stage!

"Only if you are willing to skip the theatrics," I said dryly.

"Has anyone ever called you a 'party pooper'?" Sophie asked.

"Never," I lied.

Sophie tilted her head and looked at me with a less-than-convinced expression on her face. "Dr. Bruce Nigel was the primary person making copies of papers with white-out on them."

I reflected on my interview with Bruce. "I am not entirely surprised." Then I realized exactly what she had said. "Sophie, what do you mean by 'primary person'?"

Sophie looked at the readout from her computer. "In my professional opinion, C. J. Hatfield was at least present when some of the altered documents were copied."

"Where do we go from here?" Ellie asked.

"Normally, I would give my tentative report to the IRB chair."

I would have done that yesterday.

"I should call the Worldwide Science Federation. The WSF is responsible for officially informing the Board of Regents."

"Do you think the Board of Regents meeting will be cancelled?" Ellie asked.

"Maybe," I said. "At the same time, they are entitled to hear me explain my conclusions."

"Will ya be telling Sara 'bout your findings?" Frank's question reminded me that I remained in the dark about his involvement.

"Hopefully the WSF will allow me to tell Sara that my report will clear her of the most egregious misconduct charge. Not only am I convinced she did not falsify data, I believe Nigel and Hatfield fabricated the evidence against her. After all, Bruce may have altered the graphs, but the emails came from Hatfield."

"Shoot, I was hoping to have a big dinner with all the suspects sitting around a big table," Frank said as he stroked his mustache. "You'd start by talking about everyone's motives. In the end you'd unveil the villian."

"Right," Molly said, "and the murderer would confess because they had been cornered."

I laughed at the stereotypical scenario the two had described. "That sounds like an Agatha Christie novel. In the real world, I confine myself to determining if Sara falsified her data. The bean counters still need to establish if she was authorized to move funds. My suspicions about Hatfield and Nigel will need to be investigated separately, and by someone else."

I considered my next steps. "I need to make some calls."

"Do you need me to sing Mycroft another lullaby?" Frank asked.

I thought for a moment. I had not established if Bruce was getting reports from Mycroft. It was best not to let him know about my suspicions.

"That would be most helpful, but then I need to make the calls alone."

Frank nodded. "Understood."

Once again, Frank and I walked out of the lab and back to my office. He instructed Mycroft to assume the silent mode for another hour, and left.

I called the WSF on my wearable.

"Worldwide Science Federation, how may I direct your call?"

"Connect me to Dr. Louis Hawkins."

"Hello, Cheryl," Dr. Hawkins said. "How is the investigation going?"

My wearable projected a holograph of Dr. Louis Hawkins into the office. With his wizened face, he appeared to be over one hundred years old. His mind was sharper than most 20-somethings.

In the future, he will be considered one of the founding fathers of cybernetic ethics.

"I am nearly finished, and wanted to give you the preliminary results." I went on to describe the physical evidence, my interviews, and my information regarding the DoD's involvement and the secrecy.

"Well done," Dr. Hawkins said.

A scholar of few words, his "Well done" felt as if I had won a national award.

"May I have permission to tell Sara about my report?"

"Granted."

I looked around the office with thoughts of packing on my mind. There were a few things I would need to take with me. "Please let me know if I need to appear before the Board of Regents. Otherwise, I would like to go home."

"I should know within the hour."

As soon as I disconnected the call, I realized I had failed to tell him about the death of the IRB chair. Protocol dictated that Dr. Hawkins would call the IRB chair, the provost, and the president of the Board of Regents in a conference call. Well, he would know soon enough.

I turned my attention to calling Sara. I enabled video, and when she answered I could see her as well.

"Hello Cheryl," she said, "I understand Yong-Chun is missing."

News travels fast, and bad news travels faster.

I ignored Sara's comment. I did not want to discuss Yong-Chun's disappearance. I knew too many details which had not been released to the public.

"The reason I am calling is to tell you my part of the investigation is complete. My report to the Board of Regents will state you did not falsify your data." Sara remained silent.

"The WSF is still reviewing your research accounts," I added.

"Well, I wasn't stealing money from *those* accounts," Sara sounded offended.

Were you stealing money from some other accounts?

"Why were you putting money in Bruce's account?" I asked.

"I don't remember exactly," Sara said. "General Westmore wanted us to determine if the brain implants he developed would provide a more precise link to the cybernetic limbs."

I could feel the blood rush to my face. I took a deep breath to control my anger. "I see, and you decided to wait to tell me about this . . . because?"

"Because I thought General Westmore would back me up this time."

"I have already reported my findings to the WSF," I said. "Dr. Hawkins will be notifying UNE."

I saw a tear run down Sara's cheek.

"Thank you, Cheryl. Will you be speaking to the Board of Regents on Friday?"

"Dr. Hawkins will let me know if they still plan to meet. If I were a gambler, I would bet Friday's meeting will be cancelled. The board can simply read my report."

"When will you be going back to Seattle?"

"Tonight, if I can swing it," I said. "I can finish writing my report from home."

"Please wait until tomorrow. I want to take you out to dinner tonight. You and Ellie both. We can invite all the other faculty as well. Now that I've been cleared, we all have something to celebrate."

"That is generous of you, but it is a little premature."

"Nonsense," Sara said. "I'm confident I'll be cleared by the WSF accountants as well. I didn't do anything wrong. I want to celebrate with a small party. Who would you like me to invite?"

I was about to decline again when Sara added, "I don't want to celebrate alone." The tone of her voice spoke volumes about her pain.

"All right, but only if you limit the invitations to Ellie, Frank, and Malka."

"Done. I will make reservations at the Mistral. Will seven work?"

I looked at my wearable. It was a few minutes before four. "That works for me."

"Great, I will see you at seven."

I walked back to the lab and told Frank and Ellie about the dinner. Sophie had already started packing up her bag of tricks.

As if on cue, my wearable displayed a message from Dr. Hawkins.

The Board of Regents had cancelled their meeting for Friday, and requested my report be sent by the following Friday.

"Will you be needing security services tonight?" Spencer asked.

I was going to miss Molly and Spencer, but I no longer *needed* them.

"No. Thank you both for everything you have done. I will send a statement to your supervisor about your excellent service."

Molly walked over to Ellie and gave her a hug. By the time she hugged me, I could see tears in her eyes. She said her goodbyes to Sophie, Spencer, and Kirah.

"Say good-bye to Holmes for me," Molly requested.

I desperately wanted to cheer her up. "If I ever need security again, I will ask for you."

Molly walked out the door without looking back.

Sophie picked up the LEESH from a work station and walked Kirah to the door. "Keep in touch," Sophie said.

"It was great to see you again."

"When do we go back to Malka's?" Ellie asked.

Ellie's question reminded me that she needed to recharge her exoskeleton before dinner. "We can go now, if Frank will agree to have campus security seal the lab once we are all gone." I looked straight at Frank.

Frank nodded his head at me. "I'm at your beck 'n' call."

Since Malka's limo had returned home immediately after dropping us off that morning, Ellie and I took an air taxi to the H-loop.

Once on the Cape, Malka opened the front door. Holmes ran up to both Ellie and me. Ellie hurried by him to go to her bedroom, and I bent down to rub his belly.

"Your dawg's a petting sponge," Malka said as though she was bragging. She appeared to be freshening up for dinner party. Apparently, the Mistral was even more posh than the Oyster House.

"I can't imagine how Sara was able to get a table there fah tonight," Malka said. "That place is usually booked up months in advance."

I went upstairs to don the black dress I had worn Monday night. Malka had anticipated I would need it and put it in her cleaner. While fixing my makeup and hair, I saw my clutch purse on the vanity. I had been so busy with the misconduct investigation I had forgotten to have the wine analyzed. I called Sophie on my wearable. "Sophie, may I have one last favor of my favorite forensic scientist?"

"I will see if Kirah is available, you know," Sophie said.

I had that coming.

Sophie's face displayed well-deserved skepticism. "What do you need now?" Trepidation dripped from her every word.

I told her about the incident with the wine and asked if she could analyze the clutch purse. "I can send it to wherever you want, with a drone."

She was already home and needed the UNE lab to conduct the analysis. Rather than send the drone to UNE, we agreed there would be fewer questions if I sent it to her at home.

Sophie lived close to the campus and told me, "Cheryl, I will have your results before bedtime."

I called a drone service and within minutes my high-tech carrier pigeon arrived. Once I entered Sophie's location, I secured the clutch purse into the cargo compartment. The drone was on its way seconds later.

When Malka saw me outside, she joined me on the porch. She also wore a black dress, embellished with sparkling black crystals. Her simple diamond necklace with matching earrings made the overall effect one of sophistication and affluence.

"After all the times Sara tried to help Bruce with his research funding, he turned traitah on her. Why do you think he set ha up fah misconduct chahges?"

"I have no idea."

Why does someone become a traitor? Money? Power? Ideology?

Ellie opened the door to say she was ready. She wore a floor length black skirt topped with a brocade jacket that set off her ladybug necklace.

*   *   *

Frank met us at the front door to the restaurant. Sara had secured a table by the window.

"I wonder who she had to buy off to get this table?" Frank mused.

The menus were projected in front of us. Malka sat on my right and

Sara on my left. As I glanced over at Malka's menu, I noticed many entrees were dimmed.

"The MOM system is limiting my suppa choices based aun my health." Malka whispered in response to the question on my face. "I think the brewskies screwed up my medical profile."

We ordered meals through our wearables and a few minutes later the food was served by robots. The robo-servers placed a glass of champagne in front of everyone's table setting.

Sara stood up and tapped her knife on her glass as though everyone in the restaurant would want to hear her speech.

"I propose a toast to Cheryl, for all her hard work in clearing my name. I hope to repay her by becoming the next college dean."

Oh, the sacrifice!

"I believe that Cheryl is brilliant, although it didn't take a genius to see that the accusations against me were false. Cheryl's expertise in investigating researcher misconduct was wasted on these trumped-up charges. At the same time, I want to acknowledge Cheryl's fairness in seeing the obvious. A person of fewer scruples might have used this opportunity to seek revenge for having been passed up for tenure."

The customary "Here, here," was followed by the clinking of glasses.

If Sara does not shut up soon, no one will be able to eat their dinner.

I stood up and spoke next. "Thank you, Sara for your *charitable* words. A toast to Ellie, Frank, and Malka for their invaluable assistance during my investigation. Thank you."

"Well said," Sara interjected, derailing the custom of clinking glasses after my toast to the others.

Ellie stood up. "I propose a toast to Sara's vindication and Cheryl's tenacity for the truth."

Once Ellie sat down, we ate our dinners in the Land of Awww's.

Frank was the first to leave. I stood up for a good-bye hug.

"We need to say our good-byes now," Frank said. "I'm gonna skedaddle back to Georgia in about an hour."

I will not cry.

"Take care, Frank," I reminded him. "Call me tomorrow. I will be so happy to get home."

Frank whispered in my ear, "I'll be in touch."

Resuming my seat, I listened to Sara outlining how she would use the false allegations to become the next dean.

Leonardo is in for a big surprise.

As soon as Sara stopped to take a breath, I quickly announced it was time for us to leave. "Sara, thank you for the wonderful dinner. I wish I could stay longer, but the last three days have been exhausting. I need to get some rest before traveling home."

"Cheryl, I wish things had turned out differently with your tenure."

Ouch. She had to bring that up. Again!

"Actually, I am happy now with how things turned out," I confessed. "I admit to missing the research, but never the department politics."

"Thank you for suppa." Malka stood up and left without further conversation.

"Thank you for including me in this wonderful dinner," Ellie said.

As we walked out the door, I looked back at Sara, sitting all alone at the table. She appeared deep in thought. There was something odd about the expression on her face. Her countenance was not that of loneliness. She appeared neither happy nor sad. The image of her sitting there haunted me.

Malka, Ellie, and I took our seats in Malka's limo. A few minutes into our journey, I received a message on my wearable. Frank had booked me and Holmes on the 1 a. m. flight in first class.

Once we arrived at Malka's home, Ellie came into my room. As I packed my suitcase, Ellie sat on the bed and said, "I wish we would have had more time just for visiting."

"Me too," I said. "This has been the busiest three days in my life."

"Three days? Seems more like three weeks."

"Will you be going back to your research?" I asked. A tinge of sadness may have found its way into my voice. While I enjoyed my investigations, I missed being part of a research team which tried to make the world a better place.

"Probably," Ellie said. "At the same time, working with you has opened my eyes to other possibilities."

"You are always welcome to come stay with me in Seattle while you figure out what you want to do next."

"I can't stop thinking about Alisha," Ellie said. "I have a difficult time reconciling the video with my experiences. Alisha loved her husband. She was so devoted to him that when UNE offered her the position of dean, she told the search committee they were a package deal. UNE would hire both of them, or they could screw themselves. Well, not in those exact words."

I chuckled. Ellie was polite, but she could speak her mind when she wanted.

We lend toward each other for a hug. Ellie stood up and left my room. I had come to believe that if both people avoided the words "good-bye" we would see each other again.

Once the packing of my suitcase was finished, I began recording my report to the Regents. A couple of minutes later, Malka knocked on the door.

"Your flight leaves shortly. I thought we could visit a little before you left."

I smiled at the invitation. I had spent hardly any time with Malka and owed her a great debt for her support while I worked at UNE. "If you are willing to stay up with me, that would be wonderful."

We walked downstairs and sat on the back porch to stargaze. Malka handed me a large glass of wine, equal to her own.

As soon as I saw the wine glass, I said, "I almost forgot, Sophie owes me one last analysis."

I called Sophie on my wearable.

"I was wondering when you'd call, you know," Sophie said, instead of hello. She was dressed for bed.

"What can you tell me about the wine?"

"First of all, I'm glad you didn't drink it," Sophie began. "I found a drug, Roby-III, which is chemically similar to Rohypnol from the late 1990s. I have no idea where your general could have gotten the drug. Both have been illegal since the 2020s."

"I guess the general doesn't rely exclusively aun his charms," Malka said with a disgusted look on her face.

Sophie rolled her eyes.

I wonder if Frank knows about Luke's strategy for seducing women.

"Thank you, Sophie. I owe you another one," I said.

"Kirah and I will put it on your bill," Sophie agreed with a laugh.

"You are welcome to keep the clutch purse for your class."

"That makes it all worthwhile, you know."

Is she being sarcastic?

"Have a safe trip back to Seattle," Sophie said.

"I will try. Good night."

I took a sip of my wine and asked Malka, "What do you think about Sara's plan to become dean?"

"I wish she would try to become dean elsewhere," Malka said wryly.

"When are you going to retire? You could still work as professor emeritus, and then you would not have to deal with Sara."

"Now that no aune is telling me to retire," Malka said, "this might be a good time."

"Telling you to retire?" I asked. "What do you mean?"

"Early last yeah my memory was rapidly declining. Students were noticing, and they weren't exactly mum about the problem. Sara kept insisting I retire. She even got Alisha to crank up the heat."

"I have noticed no impairments," I said.

"Bruce helped me get a memory implant."

"One of his prototypes?"

"No, I was turned down by the Cybernetic Overseers because auf my age. Anyway, that is what they said. I think their decision had more to do with my politics."

Malka and I never discussed politics. We had silently agreed to disagree. Malka was a true dove. Because of my military service, she thought I was more of a hawk than my political views actually merited.

Malka took a sip of wine. "Bruce used a black-market connection in Korea to obtain the memory restoration implant. I had the surgery in China. Bruce is the aunly person at UNE who knows."

"That must be . . . uncomfortable," I said.

Malka nodded.

Had Malka known all along that Bruce was behind the fraud?

"When you first contacted me, you said that Sara had been unethical and got caught. Were you talking about the misconduct charges, or something else?"

Malka held my eye contact for longer than usual. Longer than was comfortable.

"Cheryl," Malka said. "I'm afraid."

She knew about Bruce from the beginning!

"I don't believe Sara is acting ethically with her research," Malka said. "She seems to be playing at another game. At the same time, she is far too clever to get caught altering documents."

Malka took a long sip of wine, and I followed suit.

"Bruce would gain the most from Sara's deparcha from the research project," Malka continued. "Forget about Leonardo's aspirations to be dean. If Sara was banned from conducting research, her funding would become Bruce's funding."

"Tell me why you are scared." I invited.

"When Bruce is charged with misconduct, he will likely air all of UNE's dirdee laundry in public."

I sensed the extent of her fears. Malka's implant was not only highly unethical, it was expressly against the cybernetics laws.

The pieces were adding up. "General Westmore probably approved the transfer of Sara's research funds to Bruce for some of his projects." I said. "They would have been risking everything if they did not get at least one IRB to approve the transfer. Frank thinks they were trading funds for something . . .."

Malka nodded in agreement. "Any idea what they were trading?" I asked.

"That's a mystery," Malka replied.

"I can aunly imagine what Sara would do with the information about my implant," Malka said. She took a longer sip from her wine glass while she fought back tears.

Chapter 9
Holmes and Homes

About an hour after midnight, I boarded the air bus with Holmes. There was no sleeper suite this time, but we were sitting in first class and Holmes had his own seat in which to snooze. We arrived Thursday, a little past 2 a.m. Seattle time. When I got home, Mori was pleased to see me, and thrilled to see Holmes.

I collapsed on my bed.

Mori woke me up at five in the morning, demanding food. Groggy from lack of sleep, I failed to realize her automatic bowl was still delivering her moist meals. Mori, however, was not satisfied with the chow in her bowl. She demanded companionship while she dined. Reluctantly, I took up my usual spot on the couch and Holmes joined me. We quickly fell back asleep. An hour later, Holmes announced his desire to go outside.

Pets should have snooze switches.

After walking Holmes and giving him breakfast, I crawled back to bed. I fell back asleep listening to the sound of Mori and Holmes playing. Politely, they took turns chasing each other. The clatter of their *zoomies* made me feel even more at home.

Two hours later, I rejoined the living and went to work. Although my notes were adequate, I wanted to verify some data for my report. As soon as I turned on Sara's computer, Holmes went berserk. His high-pitched bark was focused at the device.

I could barely hear Watson say, "Dr. Locke, I believe Holmes is reacting to a high-pitched whine coming from the equipment."

In order to save my eardrums, I took the computer outside, and placed it on a poolside table. I was half-tempted to throw it into the swimming pool.

I called my daughter.

"Hello Emily, are you busy right now?"

"Hey mom, what's going on? Did you find my missing earring?"

"Not yet. Holmes went nuts when I turned on Sara's air-gapped computer. Watson says he detected a loud, high-pitched tone coming from the device."

"What did you do?" Emily asked, subtle panic in her voice.

"I took it outside so Holmes would stop barking," I said, as if that should be obvious.

"Okay, Mom," Emily instructed. "Under no circumstance should you turn it off. Close the lid and send it to my office via drone."

"You sound worried."

"Mom, if Holmes is worried, so am I."

I contacted the drone service, and sent the laptop to Emily's home in Portland, Oregon. She had a fully-equipped computer lab in what could have been her garage. In addition to her telework for a hospital consortium, she was a highly sought-after consultant.

Holmes settled down as soon as the drone flew away.

I walked into my study and continued working on the report. A few minutes later, Watson announced the first match between the copier's image files and identification photos from the UNE security office. There were twelve copier images, and the first one had taken over twenty-four hours to match. Watson displayed the enhanced picture, which clearly showed the person to be Yong-Chun.

I was flabbergasted.

What was Yong-Chun doing in Sara's lab?

"Watson, connect me to Detective Yano Johnson."

A few moments later, Yano's face appeared on the viewscreen. "Hello, Yano," I said sweetly. "How are you doing?"

Yano smiled back at me. "When a lady talks with that much sugar in her voice, I get worried. Very worried."

"I have some news for you," I said, trying to recover my professional tone. "I am not sure what it means. Do you remember the image files you transferred to Watson?"

"Yes," Yano said. "They're from a copy machine. Right?"

"Right. The copier in Sara's lab which someone used to alter graphs and pictures."

"What did Watson discover in his analysis?" Yano asked.

"The first image Watson could identify is that of Dr. Kim Yong-Chun."

There was a charged silence, and then Yano asked, "Who else knows about this?"

"You are the first person I called."

"You haven't told Dr. Covington?" Yano asked, again.

"No, only you," I said, clenching my teeth because I sensed what he was going to say next.

"Cheryl, please don't tell anyone else. Not even Dr. Covington or Dr. Zelyonaya. The coroner reports that Dr. Kim was murdered."

"Frank and Ellie cannot be suspects," I contended, and then added, "Ellie was with Malka Tuesday night. Frank was probably at his hotel."

"They're not suspects," Yano said. "But they may act differently around our suspect, if they know."

"I will agree for now," I said. "There are eleven other images to match. However, I do not know how much longer the analysis will take."

"Speaking of the copier," Yano added, "I have the result of that fingerprint you sent to me. It belonged to the late Dr. Rolando Hernandez, the dean's husband."

"Noteworthy," was all I said, but Yano could probably see more on my face. I had not been expecting this result.

"Please keep me informed," Yano requested, "if for no other reason than to hear your sweet voice."

Is Yano flirting with me?

We said our good-byes.

"What was Rolando doing in Sara's lab? He was not part of her research team. How did he get white-out on his finger?"

"Insufficient information."

Watson's voice made me realize that I had asked those questions out loud, but he was right.

Next, I texted General Westmore and asked if Sara had requested approval to transfer money from her research account to Bruce's.

After lunch, I received a call from Frank.

"Hey Cher, have ya recovered from ya little jaunt out here?" Frank asked.

I told him about Holmes' reaction to Sara's computer.

"Where's the computer now?" Frank sounded worried.

"In my daughter's lab by now."

"Good," Frank said. "I reckon I was wrong about Holmes. He's a good guard dawg."

"Frank, I want to know more about your relationship with Luke."

"Another time," Frank said. Concern filled his voice. "Luke's in the hospital. His brain implant is malfunctioning."

"Oh dear. I texted Luke this morning to ask if the DoD's IRB had approved the transfer of funds. Is he going to be all right?"

The tone in Frank's voice revealed his concern. "Too soon to tell."

I decided this was *not* the time to tell Frank about the wine analysis.

"Do you know anyone at the DoD who could tell me if the funds transfer was approved by their IRB?" I asked, trying not to sound self-centered. "I could finish my report today if I had that piece of information."

"I'll see what I can do," Frank said. "I am trying to get clearance to see Luke in the hospital. I can be in Arlington in a few minutes if I take the H-loop."

"Arlington?" I asked.

"He's at a hospital operated by DARPA."

"DARPA?" I asked. "Home of the DoD's mad scientists?"

"Defense Advanced Research Projects Agency," Frank said. "They keep their super-secret projects there too."

"Keep me posted," I said. "If there is anything I can do, please let me know. You have always been there for your friends, especially me. I would love the opportunity to repay a small portion of your kindness."

"Stay safe, Cher," Frank said, and ended our call.

I continued dictating my report. As much as I enjoyed my home in Seattle, I was having a hard time transitioning back to being alone. My previous investigations had been rewarding, but they involved people I had never met before—and would likely never meet again. The UNE inquiry was different. I knew a lot of people there, so I had not been a lone koala.

Holmes seemed to sense my loneliness and dropped a tug-toy on my foot. He was obviously happy to be home. After a few minutes of tug, I called Ellie.

"Are you home in Maryland now?" I asked.

"Not yet," Ellie said. "I decided to stay with Malka a few days. I hardly had time to visit her while I was helping you."

I felt a twinge of jealousy. Again.

"When does your leave of absence expire?" I asked.

"In fifty-six days," Ellie said. "Malka thinks I should stay here and work with her husband."

Martin Goldberg was a world-renowned cybernetic transplant surgeon. I had to admit the position would be a good fit for Ellie.

"What would you be doing?" I was happy at her prospects and a part of me wished I could join her.

"He's developing nanites that re-write DNA in people with life threatening genetic abnormalities. If he is successful, so-called 'birth defects' will be a thing of the past. Genetics will be corrected at birth, or maybe in utero."

Her excitement at the possibility prevented me from engaging in a more philosophical discussion about genetic engineering and the ethics of genetic manipulation.

Maybe later.

"How is the report coming?" Ellie asked. "Anything I can help you with?"

"Kind of you to offer," I said, "but you should spend your time with Malka. The report is nearly finished. I had some trouble with Sara's computer, but I was only double checking what was already in my notes. I can finish my report without those files."

We said our good-byes, and she promised to call me once she made her decision about working with Martin.

A few minutes later, Watson announced, "Dr. Locke, I have identified more people from the copier images. There are two images of Dr. Bruce Nigel, four of Conrad Joe Hatfield, two of Dr. Leonardo Gonzales, and one of Dr. Rolando Hernandez. I cannot match faculty or students for the last two images, but I have determined they *are* of the same person."

"Expand your database to all images, even of people outside UNE." I directed. "Low priority." This was going to take days, if not weeks.

I took Holmes on a walk. I needed it more than he did. On our way back home, my wearable displayed an incoming call from a General Baker. Even with her short brown hair, she looked as though she had crossed the half-century mark a long time ago. She had one less star and fewer ribbons than Luke.

"Hello, is this Dr. Locke?" the general asked.

"Yes," I replied. "I should tell you. I am walking my dog and my location is not secure."

General Baker smiled. "That's fine. Our friend asked me to call you regarding an application you were inquiring about."

"I see."

"That application went through the proper channels and was approved."

"Thank you for letting me know," I said. I detected a strange tone in her voice. "Is there anything else I should know?"

"Our friend can fill you in on the rest. Please call him from a secure location."

"Understood. Thank you for calling."

As soon as the general said, "My pleasure, ma'am," she ended the call.

When Holmes and I returned home, we found Emily pacing in the living room. Her black jeans were covered with corgi fur from T'Paw and Spock. She was wearing a forest green t-shirt which showed off her red hair. T'Paw, Holmes' mother, was curled up on the couch, seeing no reason to pace with Emily. Holmes' brother, Spock walked with Emily looking as though this was one of his most favorite activities.

The furrowed brow on Emily's face, not the pacing, indicated she was worried.

"Mom, where the hell did this computer come from?"

"Hello, Emily, nice to see you too," I said, in a sarcastic tone to highlight her lack of greeting.

"Bother!" Emily rolled her eyes. "It is a good thing you sent this to me. If you had tried to access any files, the computer would have . . . for lack of a better expression, self-destructed."

"But it passed airport security," I protested.

"No explosives. Someone rigged the device to release acid onto one of two hidden hard drives if its security protocol is violated. Booting the computer outside the right geographic area was the first breach of that protocol. Accessing any file would have been enough for the self-destruct to commence."

I tried to keep up with what she was telling me. "If you had tried to open the welded case, the acid would have been released immediately. Quite an impressive defense system. I believe it was designed to pass most security checks."

"Two hard drives?" I asked. "I did not realize there was more than one."

"When I imaged the inside of the device, I found a second and third drive. When you turned it on, you activated a GPS tracing system tethered to the second drive."

What the hell did Sara have on that computer?

"Any idea what the third drive is for?" I asked.

"Not yet."

Emily's frustration was perceptible.

"Give me a break, Mom. I've only had the device for a few hours. And you say *I'm* impatient."

"I am surprised Sara did not ask for the computer back before I left," I said to myself, as much as to Emily.

I wonder if the DoD knows about the extra drives.

"I've never seen a computer with so many security modifications," Emily said.

"Considering your job, that is saying a lot. Do you think you can get past the security protocols and identify what is on those drives?"

"I'm pretty sure I can get past the security," Emily said, pride in her voice.

No stupid computer would get the best of my daughter!

"You need to take this computer back to UNE. A timer was tripped when you booted it. I hooked up my device which reads timers. The readout showed it was counting down from fifty-two hours when I left home."

A little more than two days.

We made airline reservations for Saturday morning. Emily agreed to come along. I was pretty sure I could reset the timer and GPS. However, if that did not work, Emily had more tricks and gadgets than I did.

Over dinner, I told Emily the amusing parts of my trip. The MOM-defying lunch with Yano and the dinner with General Westmore. Emily laughed in all the right places.

"I saw on Watson's newsfeed that some important person at UNE was murdered while you were there." Emily said.

"Yes. Dr. Kim Yong-Chun."

"Did you know him well?" Emily asked.

"I knew him, but not well," I replied. "When I was at UNE, I thought he was one of the more trustworthy people on the board. During my investigation, I discovered he had a less scrupulous side."

"Do you know why anyone would want to kill him?"

"I have been so busy with my investigation, I have not given it much thought."

I paused to consider the question. Emily waited for me to continue.

"My first guess would be that he had made a deal with someone, and they were not happy with the transaction," I finally responded.

"First a crazy dean who kills her husband during a golf game, and now an IRB chairman who gets sent to Davy Jones' locker," Emily said, with her usual flair for the dramatic. "I'm glad you're out of there."

I nodded in agreement.

After dinner, we moved to the observatory. Uncle Walter's home observatory was one of the reasons my dad had called his older brother eccentric—the euphemism for "black sheep." The room had a transparent ceiling for his astrophysics studies. On the wooden floor were rugs covered with depictions of various constellations. Stargazing was the most comfortable from the two chairs that were able to completely recline. The other seating options were basket-like swings that were equally comfortable. From the wear on the carpet, it did not take an investigator to know my uncle had spent a lot of time in this room.

I chose a recliner, and Emily made herself at home in one of the swings. She always liked to be moving. The swing also had the advantage of adjusting for her height. Although we were about the same height sitting down, she was at least two inches taller standing up.

She began telling me about her latest dating experience. Her social life was an endless source of amusement.

"Alister wanted to meet me at the retro bar called 'The Disco Ball,'" Emily began. "There is a Chinese restaurant on the first floor. The place is popular because of the fake bar food. You know what I mean, Mom. Onion rings, nachos, even hot dogs. They look real, but they don't quite taste like the real thing. Anyway, that's what the older folks say."

I gave her a *be careful* look.

Emily continued, "I met him at the door as planned. What we had not realized was that the place would be packed." She paused. "Finally, Alister spotted an open table near the back stairs. After we sat down at the table . . .," She paused. "I realized why it was vacant."

"Why?" I asked.

"Because the table was directly above the men's room in the restaurant below. A few minutes later, the stench from some dude taking a dump floated up. The smell was so bad, I got tears in my eyes and I felt as though my nose hairs were burning."

Emily wrinkled her nose in demonstration.

"What did you say?"

"I didn't know what to say." Emily confessed.

I could hear the smile in her voice.

"I was trying to pretend I didn't smell anything," Emily continued. "Alister apparently had drunk a few beers before I got there. He looked at me as if the horrendous odor was coming from me."

"What did you do?"

"Before I had time to do anything, he ditched me at the table. As he left the bar, I could hear him telling everyone on his way out that I had the worst nervous farts he had ever smelled."

We both laughed at the embarrassing story, but Emily laughed the hardest.

Just as Emily had finished sharing another adventure, Frank called. I told Watson to enable the video.

"Hello, Cher," he began, and as soon as he saw Emily, he added. "Hello, Squirrel."

"Howdy, Dr. Frankenstein," Emily retorted.

I always thought Frank treated Emily like the daughter he never had. He began calling her "Squirrel" during our first dinner together.

She had been so energetic, and changed topics so quickly, he said she reminded him of a squirrel running from tree to tree.

"What's the story 'bout that 'puter your mom brought back?"

Emily looked at him with delight. "I prevented the thing from self-destructing, but I won't know the entire story until I can access the second and third drives. We're flying back Saturday morning."

Emily went on to tell Frank all about the acid, GPS tether, and welded case. He appeared fascinated by everything she had to say. At the end of her description, she said good-night to Frankenstein, and left with her furkids.

"Do you have an update on General Westmore?" I asked.

"I had to pull a lot of strings, but I'm finally approved to see him. I'll be leaving in two shakes of a lamb's tail."

For Frank to pull more than one string was an indication of how difficult approval had been to obtain.

"Since you are going to be in the neighborhood," Frank said, "I could sure use your help."

"Anything you need. General Baker implied you had information about the transfer of DoD research funds from Sara to Bruce."

"That's a hornet's nest if there ever was one," Frank began. "The DoD approved Sara's transfer of funding to Bruce. However, the DoD auditors cannot figure out how the money disappeared from Bruce's account almost as soon as it arrived."

I could feel my brow constricting and my lips pursing as I tried to make sense of what he was saying. "Did you find out what Sara was trading for those research dollars?"

"Ya bet I did," Frank said. "Some brain implant technology a few prototypes."

Chapter 10
Logs and Logarithms

*F*riday morning, Mori woke me up in her usual way–by licking my eyelids. She always woke me fifteen minutes before Watson.

Does Mori consider this a competition?

With too little time to fall back asleep, I threw on my sweats and picked up Holmes' LEESH. I adjusted the settings to allow us to stay dry.

At first, Holmes refused to go out the front door because of the rain. This was becoming a rainy-morning ritual. I opened the back door to show him there was an equal amount of rain behind the house as well. He bowed his head and walked to the front door. For a dog with Welsh ancestry, his reluctance to walk in the rain was bewildering. He would only get his feet wet; the LEESH acted like an umbrella.

During breakfast, I asked Watson to review my agenda.

"Dr. Locke, your 6 a.m. conference call with Dr. Hawkins and the president of the Board of Regents is in twenty-five minutes. Ellie has sent a message asking you to call her before lunch. I finished proof-reading your report and corrected three grammatical errors. You have been invited to speak at the Cybernetics Ethics conference in Cairo this fall. The Samantha Heylighen Institute of Technology has requested your expertise in investigating a missing researcher. There are one-hundred-seventy-six unanswered emails in your inbox."

As I walked to my bedroom to get ready for the conference call, I gave Watson instructions. "Send a message to Ellie that I will call at seven-thirty. Send the conference planning committee the customary information regarding my speaker's fee. We will see how much they want me. Follow the usual protocol to analyze the emails and delete those which do not meet my current criteria. Also, send a big bunch of flowers to Malka with a "thank you" card."

"Very good, Dr. Locke," Watson replied. "What shall I tell the Institute?"

"Nothing," I replied. "And Watson, thank you for proofreading my report."

After I had showered and put on my professional façade, I went back to the observatory to wait for Dr. Hawkins' call. At precisely 6 a. m., Watson announced the conference call. Video was enabled.

"Good Morning, Dr. Locke," Dr. Hawkins said. "I am pleased to introduce you to Mr. Earl Cartwright, president of the UNE Board of Regents."

I was agog to be speaking to someone in New England who did not have a freaking doctorate degree. Probably a political appointment.

Mr. Cartwright wore a western shirt and a leather vest. His grey horseshoe mustache was the same color as his medium-long hair. I could see several pictures of horses, in addition to ribbons and trophies, behind his desk. If I had to guess, I would say he had already seen his sixtieth birthday. I considered it a safe bet that there was a cowboy hat in his office.

"Thank you, Dr. Hawkins. Nice to meet you, Mr. Cartwright."

"Let's not waste anyone's time," Mr. Cartwright began. "Did Dr. Sheppard falsify her data or not?"

"When I left New England, I was convinced she had not falsified any data. Forensic evidence links the altered charts and graphs to another researcher."

"Very good," Mr. Cartwright said emphatically.

His words may have said, 'very good,' but his tone said 'dismissed.' *I will not squirm.*

"However," I interjected, "I have another mystery on my hands in the form of her overly secure computer."

"This is new," Dr. Hawkins said.

"Yes," I said. "The air-gapped computer Dr. Sheppard had been using was confiscated by the DoD. General Westmore turned that computer over to me. I have discovered several irregularities about the device which warrant further investigation."

"Could this investigation reveal that Dr. Sheppard altered her graphs and images after all?" Mr. Cartwright asked. His blue eyes stared at me with the intensity of laser beams.

"No, I believe the forensic evidence clearly establishes that another party or parties are behind the alterations."

"Has the DoD established whether or not Dr. Sheppard had authorization to transfer research funds between her account and Dr. Nigel's?" Mr. Cartwright asked.

This man knows how to get to the bottom line.

"The DoD informed me that Dr. Sheppard went through the proper channels and had approval for the transfer. However–"

I could see Mr. Cartwright shift uncomfortably in his chair.

"However," I continued, "the DoD informed me that the money is missing from Dr. Nigel's account."

"That sounds to me like the WSF needs to investigate Dr. Nigel," Mr. Cartwright said, his gaze less intense.

"We need a formal request from the IRB to begin an investigation," Dr. Hawkins said to Mr. Cartwright. "As I am aware that the chairman is unavailable, I am willing to take a request from the Board of Regents."

I guess when someone is dead, they are the definition of "unavailable."

Dr. Hawkins shifted his focus to me. "Dr. Locke, you were previously of the opinion that the charges against Dr. Sheppard should be dropped. Do you have any new evidence which warrants a different outcome?"

"No, sir," I replied. "As we discussed, the charge of plagiarism is a legal matter and cannot be directly attributed to Dr. Sheppard. The accusation that she mistreated her GA cannot be supported by objective findings."

"What a bunch of horse shit!" Mr. Cartwright blasted. "Please forward your report based on the findings the evidence can support. I expect to receive it by Monday, if not sooner."

His request was quite clear. My report could not contain one iota of speculation.

"You can expect my report by the end of the day."

"Dr. Locke," Mr. Cartwright added in a much softer tone, "I think you did a sterling job with your investigation. I personally appreciate your thoroughness. And I'm sure ya got other fish to fry."

Dr. Hawkins told me I would be getting another assignment on Sunday. I told him that I would not be ready until Monday, at the soonest. We exchanged good-byes. The entire conference call took less than fifteen minutes.

"Dr. Locke, would you like a glass of scotch?" Watson inquired.

I smiled at the question.

It is 6:15 in the bloody morning and Watson thinks I need a drink!

"Watson, are you calling me an alcoholic?" I asked.

"No. I simply made a correlation between your current state of agitation and your usual method of relaxing."

Maybe I should talk to Emily about giving Watson a little less personality.

"Iced tea will be fine, Watson."

I finished my report in less than an hour and sent it to Dr. Hawkins and Mr. Cartwright. My usual sense of closure when wrapping up an investigation eluded me.

At 7:30 I called Ellie.

"Thank you for calling," Ellie began.

She looked uneasy.

"I saw Alisha yesterday afternoon," she continued. "I find her description of the murder . . . compelling."

"Please. Elaborate," I requested.

Ellie took a deep breath. "To begin with, she told me that when she moved her right hand over to the implant which was attacking her husband, she was trying to reach the kill switch."

Machines could malfunction for a variety of reasons. The Cybernetic Overseers required that all cybernetic implants, regardless of functions, to be equipped with at least one kill switch.

"Then why did she fail to engage the kill switch?" I asked.

"Alisha told me she reached the control, but it didn't work."

"So, you are convinced that a woman who was recorded killing her husband, is telling you the truth?" I hoped Ellie would see how ridiculous that sounded.

"Why would Alisha kill the man she loved?" Ellie countered.

"Because she knew about Rolando's multiple affairs?" I asked.

"Get real, Cheryl," Ellie chided, "most people in academia are shagging someone outside their marriage. Isn't that the point of professional conferences?"

I guess I had missed that point.

"As soon as you wrap up your WSF investigation, I would consider it a personal favor if you would analyze the logs from Alisha's implant," Ellie requested.

"I sent the WSF their report this morning. Send me the logs, and I will have Watson begin working on them. I will look at any anomalies on my flight tomorrow. Emily will be traveling with me."

I could hear Ellie say, "Malka, Cheryl is coming back with her daughter."

"Why are you coming back so soon?" Ellie asked. "We want to know if you've been flirting with Yano again."

Damn, they do not miss a thing!

I explained the issues with Sara's air-gapped computer, and that it would be another boomerang trip.

Malka insisted that Emily and I stay with her. I was happy to accept. Holmes would be thrilled to see his nanny again.

Shortly after our call ended, Watson announced the files had been received.

The logs Ellie sent only covered the day Rolando was murdered. I needed at least a month's worth of logs to determine if there had been a malfunction in the kill switch, so I sent a message to Ellie requesting more logs. She messaged back that she would visit Alisha and obtain them.

* * *

Halfway through my post-lunch walk with Holmes, the LEESH malfunctioned and both of us got soaked. Of course, Holmes wanted to snuggle up to me on the bed.

Whoever said the most affectionate animal in the world is a wet dog, was probably talking about Holmes.

I toweled him off and took a quick shower to warm myself up. I packed my suitcase for the Saturday flight. With no more appointments, I put on blue jeans and a Niners T-shirt. I renewed my make-up sparingly. Just as I was putting my hair in a ponytail, Watson announced Detective Yano Johnson was calling. He requested video.

Careful what you ask for.

"Hello, Yano," I said. "This should teach you to ask me to enable video on a Friday afternoon in my home." I tossed my long ponytail at his image.

Yano's face sprouted an enormous smirk. His mustache could not hide the twitching of his upper lip.

"I'll make a note to call you every Friday afternoon," Yano said smoothly.

He was wearing a grey suit jacket over a black turtleneck sweater. The pupils of his green eyes were dilated to the size of dinner plates.

He straightened up in his chair and added, "I hope I'm not disturbing you."

"Not at all," I said. "I sent my final report to the WSF before lunch. Ellie just sent me some cybernetic logs."

"The logs from Alisha's implant?"

Of course, he knows about the download. He probably approved it.

"Right," I said, not sure where the conversation was heading.

"I'd like to know the results of your analysis as well.'

"What is in it for me?" I asked, in a cheeky tone.

"We could work together for truth, justice, and the American way," Yano replied and smiled.

I love it when a man talks nerdy to me.

"It is our sacred duty to defend the world," I replied, barely resisting the urge to assume the Wonder Woman stance.

"There is a right and a wrong in the universe, and the distinction is not hard to make," Yano quoted.

That makes my spidey-senses tingle.

"I am the best there is at what I do," I said, channeling my inner Wolverine.

We both took deep breaths.

I attempted to sound professional again. "As long as you do not expect me to keep my analysis from Ellie."

Yano's smile widened. "I wouldn't think of it."

"Any leads on who killed Dr. Kim?"

"Nothing so far," Yano replied. "I've requested access satellite images from NASA and the National Weather Service. In case they recorded anything of value."

"I will let you know when my analysis of Alisha's logs is complete," I promised. "By the way, I am flying to Boston in the morning."

"Ah, you've succumbed to my animal magnetism." Yano's upper lip was twitching again.

"It is a long story," I said. "I was thinking that while we are there, my daughter and I might be able to help you with those satellite images. She is coming with me."

"Please call me when you land, and I will pick you up." Yano said, ending the call.

A few hours after Ellie received my message, I received three months' worth of cybernetic logs. I concluded the additional download must have been the reason for Yano's call.

I entered an algorithm for Watson and said, "Please use this set of rules to analyze the logs and report any anomalies which warrant my closer examination."

Mori informed me it was her dinner time, in no uncertain terms. Holmes sat by his food bowl, letting the feline do all the demanding. After feeding my furkids, I considered my own dinner. Tonight, I would dine alone for the first time in about a week.

After dinner, I sat in the observatory answering the few emails which warranted a personal reply. An incoming email caught my attention. The subject line was "Please call me when you're alone." There was no further information in the body of the email. The message was from Priscilla.

"Watson, please connect me to Dr. Priscilla Kennedy," I said, "match video."

If Priscilla enabled video, so would I.

"Thank you sooo very much for re, responding," Priscilla said.

She had enabled her video. Her blonde hair was styled in a 'messy' pony tail, and she was dressed in expensive club wear.

"What is going on?" I inquired, making a show of rubbing Holmes' belly. Priscilla considered pets a waste of time and money.

"I understand, someone said, you're chums with that detective officer fellow. The one looking into Yong-Chun's death." Priscilla flipped a strand of hair, that had fallen in her face, to one side. "Do ya know if he's searched Rollie's? Places. Ya know, office and home?"

"No, I do not," I said without elaboration.

"Uh huh. Could ya ask?"

The hair strand returned, and this time Priscilla tucked it behind her ear.

"What are you afraid he will find?" I asked.

"Never you mind." Priscilla whined, ending the call.

I was about to send a message to Frank, when Watson announced *he* was calling *me.*

"Good evening, Frank," I began. His face showed signs of fatigue, and his clothes were rumpled. He looked as though he had not left Luke's hospital room since he arrived yesterday. "I hope Luke is doing better than you look."

"I could use your help."

"Are you all right?" I asked. Frank rarely needed anyone's help.

"I'm fine," Frank began, "but Luke is not. Luke's bloody brain implant is malfunctioning."

I nodded to encourage him to continue.

"It's killing him."

"Where did the implant come from?"

"It's a DoD special order," Frank said. "Designed to regulate what someone remembers and what they don't." Frank drew his fingers through his white hair. "Luke's implant was designed to help him forget the atrocities of the Arab Wars. It blocks his memories of his capture and torture. For no known reason, early Thursday morning it started shutting down his autonomic nervous system."

"Frank, maybe you should talk to Bruce," I suggested. "He knows more about those implants than I do."

"I trust Bruce about as far as I could throw him," Frank responded. "Besides, this one didn't come from his lab. I designed the damn thing."

"*You* designed it?"

"Over ten years ago I developed five prototypes for the DoD. Luke's is the only one which actually worked."

"I'm afraid to ask," I said, "but what happened to the other four?"

"Two soldiers had their implants removed, due to unintended consequences."

"What unintended consequences?"

"The implants were supposed to block certain memories and retain others. The first malfunction occurred with an implanted solider attacking her comrades in their barracks. The glitch caused the solider to forget whose side she was on. Luckily, no one was seriously hurt. She was sedated by a dart. Her implant was deactivated and removed."

"Can someone deactivate Luke's implant?" I asked, and then realized Frank probably had already considered that action.

"I shielded Luke's implant after the DoD found evidence that the deactivation routine had been leaked to some underground terrorist cells."

"What happened to the other soldiers?" I asked.

"A sergeant on leave thought he was placing a blanket on another soldier, when in fact, he was suffocating his own daughter. No one had time to sedate him, so his wife shot him."

I felt goosebumps creep up my arms. "How terrible."

"Luckily the sergeant was married to a police officer. She shot him before the child suffered any permanent damage."

"You call that lucky?" I asked incredulously.

"She didn't kill him," Frank said, "just *incapacitated* him."

"That accounts for three implants," I said, "including Luke's."

"Right. The fourth soldier committed suicide. No one knows if the implant malfunctioned or his PTSD put him over the edge. The final implant is in a lab here at DARPA."

"If Luke's implant is malfunctioning, why not remove it?"

"The doctors are convinced he would not survive the removal because he's had the implant so long. The device has literally become part of his brain."

"How can this former cybernetic programmer help you, Frank?"

"I thought you could study the one in the lab and figure out a way to get around the shielding and reboot the primary functions. I may have designed the implant, but the man who programmed the device is dead."

Frank's words hit me like an ocean wave. "Rolando?" I whispered.

He nodded. "The late Dr. Rolando Hernandez."

Chapter 11
The Consulting Investigator

Mori and Holmes were sleeping on the foot of my bed when Watson woke me early Saturday morning. The sun would not rise for another hour.

I quickly showered and dressed. I could not waste any time before the flight.

"Have you finished the analysis of Dr. Patel's cybernetic logs?"

"Yes, Dr. Locke. There are several episodes which your algorithm identified as warranting further examination. Do you want to view them now?"

"No, Watson. I will do that during my flight."

I programmed my food printer for breakfast, grabbed the LEESH, and headed outside with Holmes. He walked out the front door, stood on the porch, and sniffed the air. The sun had started to shine, and the warmth felt good after all the rain. A goofy corgi-grin spread across his face until even his ears appeared to be smiling. He would be taking his sweet time on our walk, and I did not blame him.

After breakfast, I grabbed my suitcase and sent a message to my pet sitter to check on Mori while I was gone. As I was setting up Mori's automatic food dispenser, Emily arrived. She said her neighbor would be watching T'Paw and Spock. They were not used to traveling like Holmes.

On the way to the airport, I connected to Yano's wearable.

Yano appeared to be taking a walk when he answered. He was wearing an unusual head covering. The bowl-shaped cloth which covered his head, had something attached that looked like the top of a giant duck's bill–also covered in the cloth. I supposed it was to protect his bald head from the sun.

The head covering reminded me of pictures my dad had shown me of baseball players. With the abolition of college sports, due to safety concerns in 2040s, the demise of professional sports had not been a surprise.

"I wanted to tell you about a rather bizarre call from Priscilla Kennedy last night." I proceeded to tell him about our short conversation and then added, "It may have just been the booze talking, but I thought you would want to know."

"Interesting," Yano said. "We know she had an affair with Hernandez. Maybe I'll take another look at his home and office."

"Emily and I will be staying at Malka's house on the cape," I said.

"Nonsense," Yano said. "Cape Cod is pretty far from UNE. You can stay at my house in the Back Bay."

"That is kind of you, but I *am* traveling with my daughter and Holmes."

"Not a problem." Yano's smile widened. "I'll hire her too. Hell, I'll hire Holmes. The department can't pay as much as the WSF, but you can all stay with me."

Emily nodded.

"We accept," I said, and disconnected.

I looked over at Emily. She was biting her lower lip, a sure sign she was worried.

What is she worried about? Corgis? Air travel? Self-destructing computers? All of the above?

We placed our suitcases and Sara's computer in the wells under our seats. I gave Holmes the window seat. Emily and I sat in the aisle seats. No one was sitting next to her.

Frank messaged me after less than an hour on the plane. "Please, come to the hospital as soon as you can."

"I will," I replied.

Emily listened to her music.

I began examining the logs Watson had tagged as anomalous. I quickly determined gaps in the time indicators which meant I could not rely on the logs alone. I needed some of the video feed from Dr. Patel's home.

I messaged Yano that I would be ever so grateful if I could see the logs from Alisha's iDom.

He called me. "Cheryl, do you believe Dr. Patel lost control of her implant?"

"Too soon to tell," I said, "but it appears as though someone may have tampered with the logs."

"Are you sure?"

I shook my head. "I cannot be certain. The video feeds might help."

"I'll have to get my captain's approval to allow you access." Yano said. "You won't be able to bribe him with an extravagant meal. He's vegan."

Detective Johnson, you underestimate my arsenal of manipulation.

I called Ellie to let her and Malka know about my change in plans.

"Cheryl, I'm so glad you called," Ellie said. She had dark circles under her eyes. "When I went to see Alisha to get the record of her cybernetic events, we nearly couldn't complete the download. Since she couldn't convince anyone to remove her implant, she has refused to allow it to be recharged."

"What did you do?"

"I told her that if she didn't get the implant recharged, you would have no way to determine *how* she lost control of her arm."

I was flabbergasted.

No pressure there.

"I know I was overstepping, Cheryl. I didn't know what else to do."

"Did she allow the recharging?"

"Only partially. The implant will lose total power in three days." Ellie's eyes were wet, but she did not allow herself to cry.

I told her my suspicion about the time index. Ellie appeared to be cheered by the news.

"I have asked Yano to see the iDom's recording, but he says his captain will need to approve my access."

"What if Alisha tells the police to send it to you?" Ellie suggested.

"I doubt a request from their only murder suspect will carry much weight."

Since I could not do any more analysis on the logs, I listened to an old article on artificial tendons. The article was from the Journal of Cybernetic Technology by Dr. Les Gregson and Dr. Betsy Hopper.

* * *

When Yano picked us up, I was surprised to see he had a police car—on a Saturday.

"Yano, this is my daughter, Emily Locke. Emily, this is Detective Yano Johnson."

"Hi Yano. Sorry, Mom's a bit formal with introductions."

Did Emily just roll her eyes?

"Hi, Emily. I think parents believe it's their job to embarrass their children, at any age."

"We need to get to UNE right away," Emily said.

Did she expect him to put on the lights and siren?

Yano parked in the first spot on the UNE campus. Once the car stopped, Emily bolted out. She sat down on the curb and put the air-gapped computer on the ground. She placed a teacup-sized gizmo on the lid. When she read the information on the display, I heard her breathe a sigh of relief.

"The timer has stopped," Emily said. "The GPS tracker has been reset. I think the internal drives are safe. For now."

"Good," I said, "because I am starving. Breakfast was a long time ago."

Emily laughed.

"Why did you put the device on the ground?" Yano asked.

"Just in case the damn thing didn't reset. That acid could probably burn through the casing and anything else in its path–including my clothes and possibly my skin."

It was my turn to sigh with relief.

Yano took us to the closest restaurant. Holmes was less than pleased at waiting in the police car. Lucky for us, the place had some of the best Italian food in the neighborhood. After I drank a glass of wine with lunch, I felt the anxiety of the previous hours leave my shoulders.

"How can I help with your murder investigation?" Emily asked Yano.

"I need to take another look around Dr. Hernandez's office and home," Yano began. "The two of you can tag along and see if there is anything helpful on his computer."

"Emily, can you run a diagnostic routine and determine if anyone tampered with their iDom?" I asked. "And when you check the computer, let me know if you find any files that refer to General Westmore's brain implant."

"Sure, Mom," Emily replied. "Where are you going?"

"I promised Frank I would take a look at Luke's brain implant."

"The doctors were able to remove it?" Yano asked. "Will Frank be picking you up?"

"No, and no. I will take an air taxi to the H-loop. Frank is at DARPA, sitting vigil with Luke. In the lab there is an implant identical to Luke's."

We made plans to meet at the police department before dinner. Once onboard the air taxi, I called Frank for directions and security clearance. At the gate, I was issued a consultant security badge. The guard put one on Holmes as well.

Is Holmes strutting?

Frank met us at the door to the hospital. "Follow me," he said, not wasting any time.

We walked downstairs to the basement laboratory. I expected to see a glass case on a pedestal in the middle of the room with the implant being shrouded by an eerie light. The reality was disappointing. The lab looked more like the "Island of Lost Tech" than a place where cutting-edge science was performed. There was dust everywhere, and the floor was sticky. Frank opened a cabinet drawer and pulled out a cardboard box. The drawer appeared to be a repository of spare parts.

"Here is the fifth prototype," Frank said as he handed me the box.

I opened the box and took out a plastic bag containing a black speck.

"Can I see Luke?" I asked.

"If you want to help Luke, figure out how to reboot his implant."

I looked around the lab. Near a corner of the room, I found the equipment which would allow me to download this implant's programming. I could easily write a reboot code from the deactivation routine. The difficulty was getting the signal past the shielding.

After verifying no snacks had been left in the lab, Holmes found a pile of dust cloths where he curled up for a nap.

Frank spent another hour at Luke's side before returning to the lab. When he returned, I was no closer to saving Luke than when I left Seattle.

"How ya doing?" Frank asked, as if we had bumped into each other at a party.

"Stymied," I replied. "I have written reboot code, but I am no closer to sending the signal to Luke's implant than when I started. Are you sure these two implants are identical?"

"Yes, ma'am. The only difference is the shielding."

"Skynet, show me the shielding." The computer displayed the images and the chemical composite of Luke's shield.

"Skynet?" Frank echoed.

"No one bothered to name the computer assistant," I said. "So, I did."

"Interesting choice," Frank said. Apparently, he understood the reference.

"Frank, how was the shielding placed in Luke's brain?"

"The shielding is not in his brain. It was injected under the skin and covers the outside of his skull."

"Skynet, what chemicals would safely dissolve this shielding?"

"The chemicals required to dissolve the shielding would be lethal to the patient." Skynet replied.

Frank closed his eyes, and said, "The shield is fused with the bone. If the doctors tried to remove any part of the skull without anesthesia, the shock to Luke's system would kill him. Anesthesia would be equally fatal. We are stuck between the proverbial rock and a hard spot."

"Skynet, what would be the risk of drilling into the shield without penetrating the skull?"

"A five-micrometer hole drilled directly above the implant would allow a signal to evade the shield. The drill should be calibrated so as not to transverse the bone of his skull."

Frank grabbed a box which looked like an antique radio transmitter and ran out. By the time I found Luke's room, the general had been moved to a surgery suite. I sat down on the only chair in the room.

I hate waiting.

Less than an hour later, Frank came in. His eyes were wet. I feared the worst.

"You just saved Luke's life," Frank said, as a tear rolled onto his face.

I could sense his relief. "I'd like to see him," I said.

"I know. He won't be awake long. They've given him a sedative."

A few minutes later, Luke was transferred back to his hospital bed. He was barely awake and appeared exhausted. He looked at me, said, "Thank you," then closed his eyes and fell fast asleep.

Dr. Josephine Bell came into the room and told us that Luke's implant had rebooted and he was out of danger. The laser had cut the shield without penetrating the bone. Frank shook the doctor's hand and told her how grateful he was for her skills. She turned to Frank and asked, "Did you ever figure out how General Westmore came to have Roby-III in his bloodstream?"

Before Frank had a chance to answer, I said, "I think I know."

Chapter 12
Wines and Whines

I told Dr. Bell the story about how Luke had spilled my glass of wine at dinner, and Sophie's analysis that showed the wine had been laced with Roby-III. Frank listened closely and tapped on his wearable.

I hope Frank never learns that I suspected Luke used the drug to seduce women.

"That may explain several things," Dr. Bell said, once I finished my story. "I would guess that someone tried to gain access to Luke's implant."

"Apparently the person didn't have a clue about the shielding," Frank offered.

"Right," Dr. Bell agreed, "but the Roby-III may have, for lack of a better word, 'short-circuited' the implant, which caused the cascade failure."

"Now that we have opened the shield to his implant, it should be easy to download his implant logs," I said. "Since he also has a cybernetic optical lens, his logs may contain image files."

Dr. Bell nodded her head in agreement. "Keep in mind, some logs may have been corrupted by the reboot."

"Frank, who are you messaging?" I asked, once Dr. Bell had left the room.

"I asked Yano to send someone over to Luke's house to see if the wine bottle was still there," Frank said. "It's a shot in the dark, but knowing where Luke got the spiked wine could be helpful."

"Can you download the logs for Luke's brain implant and cyberlens while he is sleeping?" I asked.

Frank nodded.

He sent the logs to Watson, while I sent my iDom an algorithm to filter out irrelevant entries. As I looked at my wearable, I realized it was time to return to the police station and join Emily and Yano.

Holmes made huffing noises at me, a sure sign he was getting hungry. I left our passes at the gate and we proceeded to Yano's office.

"Mom, were you able to help the general?" Emily asked as I walked into the large ruby-glass and chrome office.

"Yes," I said. "General Westmore's life is no longer at risk."

This office is big enough for half a dozen police desks.

As if Yano could read my mind, he said "Since the proliferation of SDVs, the number of traffic patrol officers has dwindled. My office is a recycled break room."

"Impressive," I said. "The size, not the recycled part."

Why am I stumbling over my words like a school girl?

"What kind of food do you two ladies want tonight?"

Emily and I looked at each other and said together, "Seafood."

"Can we take Holmes to your house first?" I asked. "He is hungry too."

"Sure," Yano agreed, "my house is on the way to the best seafood in the Back Bay."

Yano's house was a three-bedroom unit on Beacon Street. I was amazed that a police officer could afford such a large home in an expensive neighborhood. From inside the house, we could see stunning views of the Charles River.

After Holmes ate, he laid down in front of a big window and quickly fell asleep as the last rays of sun shone on his belly. Yano took us to a fabulous seafood restaurant. I appreciated the casual atmosphere, since we had not changed into evening wear. Like many small restaurants, the quality of the food far exceeded the ambience. There was a sign on the door alerting diners that said their MOM system was 'down' this evening, and to excuse any inconvenience. From the look of the handwritten sign, the *inconvenience* had been going on for a long time.

After we finished our salads, I asked Yano, "Have you received your report about the satellite video pertaining to Dr. Kim's murder investigation?"

"Not yet," Yano said. "Tonight, let's celebrate the general's recovery, and the return of Dr. Cheryl Locke and company."

I tried to get into the celebration mood, but I kept wondering–

Is the murder of Dr. Rolando Hernandez related to the murder of Dr. Kim Yong-Chun? Who has been tampering with General Westmore's brain implant? Where did that wine come from? Why does Sara need an air-gapped computer with all that crazy security? What was Rolando doing in Sara's lab? How did his white-out fingerprint end up on the copier? Is Hatfield or Nigel behind Sara's frame-up? Or did they work together to get rid of her? Why did I order the swordfish, when I really prefer halibut?

No matter how I tried, there was one question I could not avoid.

What is Frank's role in this mess?

"If it's not confidential," Yano began, "how did your investigation turn out?"

"I found evidence which suggests either Hatfield or Nigel, or maybe both, altered the graphs," I said, "Sara has been cleared of the misconduct charges."

"Are you going to be investigating them now?" Yano asked.

"No," I said. "The WSF only allows an investigator to be assigned to one person per case. If that investigator finds evidence which points to others, new investigators are assigned to each person under suspicion."

Yano's eyes twinkled. "That makes sense. Having a fresh set of eyes on a case ensures the investigator is unbiased. Your work is a lot like mine. You find fraudsters, and I find criminals."

"I am not sure," I replied, "Our methods may be similar, but this is the first time someone *died* during one of my investigations."

Throughout dinner, each of us was interrupted by messages on our wearables. Ellie let me know she had found Alisha's wearable and downloaded the logs from the last 30 days. Emily received an update on her two corgis. Yano received multiple messages, but the only one he shared was that the enhancement of the satellite data had been completed.

As we arrived back at Yano's house, I read from my wearable, Watson has completed the preliminary analysis on Luke's optical implant.

"Do we start with Luke's cyberlens or the NASA satellite video?" Emily asked.

"Let's start with the satellite video," Yano said. "The murder of Dr. Kim *is* one of the reasons you two are here."

Holmes greeted me as soon as I walked in the door. Tailless, he wiggled his entire bum to show his excitement. Then he ran over to Emily and rolled over for a belly rub.

We all gathered in the living room, and Yano displayed the recording on a large screen.

"Keep your eyes on the yacht tied to the pier," Yano instructed. "The man walking up to the boat is Dr. Kim."

Even with the computer enhancements, I found it difficult to follow what was happening from this bird's-eye view. The satellite had been programmed to record the area, not a particular craft. Most of the image showed only the moonlight reflecting off the dark water. I could see both sides of the pier. Off to one side of the dock, I could see where the luxury yacht had been moored. Near the bottom of the screen, I could see something that looked like a small hut.

"What is that roof attached to?" I asked, pointing at a structure in the middle of the dock.

"It's a shed where the Coast Guard stows their gear," Yano replied.

Yong-Chun was greeted by a group of four men and two women. Two of the men and both women boarded the craft with the late chair of the IRB. The other two men left on the pier looked as though they were standing guard at the boarding ramp.

Emily jumped out of her chair. "Did you see the drone in the video?" she yelled, and started pacing around the screen.

"Yano, back up the video about ten seconds," I requested.

Sure enough, the unmistakable shadow of a tiny drone flying over the water could be seen near the ramp.

"Do you know what kind of drone that is?" Yano asked Emily.

"The drone appears to be a spybug. They can be a real challenge to security. They're so small, they often go undetected."

Yano tapped on his wearable while saying, "I'm asking the analysts to go back over all the footage and look for other drones. Thank you, Emily."

"Tell them to try to find an image of the actual drone," Emily said. "I might be able to identify the manufacturer at least."

Yano tapped on his wearable again. As we continued to watch, I could see the yacht depart from the pier. Near the stern, I noticed ripples of water behaving oddly.

"Can you zoom in on that spot?" I asked Yano, pointing to where I saw the disturbance in the water.

"What do you see?" Emily asked.

"I see it too," Yano said. "There is something attached to the bottom rung of the swimming ladder."

"Not something! Someone!" Emily shouted.

The person placed a second hand on the swimming ladder.

"Is that Luke?" I asked myself. I had not intended to ask the question out loud.

"The image is too grainy for a positive identification without further computer enhancement," Yano explained. "Why would General Westmore be following Dr. Kim?"

"Luke said he suspected Yong-Chun was selling research data to the Korean Empire," I replied. "Maybe the general followed him to get the evidence needed for his arrest."

"Conducting secret business transactions is easier to hide on a yacht than in the city," Yano agreed. "Especially when said vessel is flying the Korean Empire's flag. Anything which happens on board would be covered by diplomatic immunity."

"Luke's dark skin would make hiding at night considerably easier," I suggested.

"Yano, you said there were weather satellite images," Emily said, "They might show heat signatures."

"Wait," I said, "We should be able to see more if we view the record from Luke's cyberlens. The implant would have recorded everything he saw." Everyone turned and looked at me, even Holmes.

Yano's eyes looked tired as he asked, "How far back do the logs go?"

"Depending on his settings," I said, "the video may contain anywhere from twenty-four to ninety-six hours of his movements."

I glanced at my wearable. "It is after midnight, and I need to get some sleep. We can get a fresh start in the morning."

"You'll hear no objections from me," Yano said.

Emily and Holmes appeared to agree.

I took Holmes out to the backyard, where he quickly relieved himself and headed for the door. As we walked up the patio steps, I looked back at the lights over the Charles River. The view was quite beautiful.

Yano had thoughtfully placed a wide wooden plank at the foot of my bed for Holmes to use as a ramp. While I changed into a nightshirt, Holmes walked up the plank and plopped in the middle of the bed. It took quite a bit of effort to move him to one side so I could have a place to sleep.

How can a dog will himself to be twice as heavy than he actually is?

With the bedroom's east-facing windows, the Sunday sunshine poured into the room at dawn. Holmes continued to sleep while I showered and dressed. Only when I started downstairs, did he get off the bed and join me.

After Holmes and I returned from our stroll and finished breakfast, I heard Emily and Yano stirring upstairs.

"Let's grab coffee on the way," Yano said. "Cheryl, bring the logs from Luke's cyberlens. We can review them at the station."

"I have already had breakfast," I said, "what about you two?"

Do I sound like a mother or what?

"We can grab breakfast with the coffee," Yano said.

At the police station, the food and beverages were set down on a glass conference table in Yano's large office. Emily and Yano made ecstasy faces over the coffee while Holmes whined at their mugs.

I brought up the video log and displayed it on the table. Convinced there was no coffee in his future, Holmes curled up by my feet and went back to sleep.

The video showed what Luke saw beginning with Luke walking into his bathroom and starting the shower. I was pretty sure we did not *need* to see him take his shower.

Maybe another time.

I forwarded to one hour later and saw myself standing at Luke's front door with Sarge inspecting my hand. Jumping ahead another hour, we saw Luke entering a room where he picked up Sara's air-gapped computer. I skipped ahead another hour and we saw Luke looking at his wearable. The display read, Pier 6, midnight.

"Pier 6 is where the luxury yacht was tied," Yano said. "Can you back it up a little? I want to see who sent that message."

I backed up the video about two minutes. As Luke looked down on his wrist, his wearable displayed Incoming message from Priscilla Kennedy followed by the cryptic text.

"Yano, can you show the segment of the satellite video with the two women at the pier?" I asked. "I want to see if Priscilla was one of the women who joined Yong-Chun on the yacht."

Yano displayed the video segment I requested. The images were inconclusive regarding the women. The blonde may have been Priscilla, but the image was too grainy to be certain.

"Let's get back to watching Luke's cyberlens logs," Emily suggested.

We watched Luke carry a glass of wine left over from dinner into the great room. He sat at the piano and took a couple more sips of wine before he began playing. Without an audio track or sheet music, I had no idea he was playing.

After a while, he glanced at an antique clock on the wall. The time displayed a few minutes past eleven. Luke sipped more wine and carried the glass to the room where Sara's computer had been kept. He grabbed a duffle bag and drank the rest of the wine. After putting the bag into the trunk of his SDV, he got in the car, and turned off the autodrive.

"Mom, how did Luke turn off the autodrive?"

"Military vehicles have a switch," I explained, "so the SDV will have no record of where it was driven."

The video showed Luke driving to the harbor and parking. He got out of his vehicle and stood where he could see the yacht. Minutes later six people approached the vessel. Four men and two women. The men were wearing Korean-style suits, and the women were in club wear.

"They must not have seen Luke," Yano said. "Otherwise they would have *escorted* him off the pier."

Luke watched as Yong-Chun walked up to the yacht and talked to the others. Quickly Luke moved to a place that was dark and out of sight by anyone near the yacht.

"Where did he go?" I wondered out loud.

"I think he ducked behind the Coast Guard shed," Emily replied. Her eyes were tightly focused on the video.

Remember to blink, Emily!

"He's putting on wetsuit spray and scuba mini-gear," Yano observed.

Luke walked over to the side of the pier opposite the yacht and jumped into the water.

"Where are his fins?" Emily asked.

"He is probably using one of those directional propellers," I said. "They are quieter than fins."

The video showed what Luke saw as he swam under the pier and grabbed the yacht's ladder moments before the boat pulled away.

For over ten minutes, Luke stayed in that position. When the yacht slowed down, he climbed the ladder and hid behind a lifeboat. From where he stood, he could see the door to the main cabin.

A few minutes later, Yong-Chun exited the cabin. Luke followed him, darting behind the equipment on the boat for cover. A man taller than Yong-Chun walked up to him. His unusual height made the pant legs of his uniform look poorly tailored. They bowed to each other. Yong-Chun's bend was significantly lower than the taller man's bow. At first, they appeared to be having a casual conversation. After a couple of minutes, their body language changed dramatically. The discussion appeared to have turned into an argument.

Yong-Chun started to curl his fingers. His hands seemed to be about to become clenched fists. His entire body seemed stiff. Suddenly, the second man slapped him in the face. Yong-Chun's hands went flat, and his posture changed. He appeared to be pleading for something. The tall man turned his back on Yong-Chun and walked away.

Standing alone at the rail, Yong-Chun looked out to sea. Luke appeared to have run up to Yong-Chun and pushed him over the rail. The video from Luke's lens showed Yong-Chun's body splash into the ocean and sink.

I was dumbfounded.

"Did everyone see what I saw?" I said with a trembling voice.

"If you mean, did we all see General Westmore kill Dr. Kim Yong-Chun," Yano said, "then the answer is yes."

Chapter 13
Luke and Luck

"Not that," I said. "A few seconds before Luke charged at Yong-Chun there was a distortion in the video."

"I saw the glitch too," Emily said.

We both looked at Yano.

"Show me what you mean," Yano requested. "I must have missed it."

I backed up the recording to the moment before Yong-Chun was attacked. There was a second or two of static, followed by an abrupt change in the lighting.

"I see it now," Yano said. "What does it mean?"

Before I had a chance to answer, I got a message from Frank. Luke was awake and wanted to see me in person.

"Yano, I am at a loss for what that means," I replied. "I need to go. Frank says Luke wants to see me. I can ask him while I am there. Meanwhile, I will have Watson correlate this part of Luke's optical log with the log from his brain implant." I sent instructions to Watson from my wearable.

"I think I should go with you," Yano said.

"Luke may be reluctant to talk about Tuesday night if you are there. I should be back by lunch time."

As soon as I stood up, Holmes walked over to me.

"Mom, please leave Holmes with me," Emily requested. "He helps me not miss my Corgi companions . . . as much."

I left Emily and Yano watching the weather satellite feed. Holmes was eyeing their coffee cups again.

After I passed through the security gate, I met Frank at the door to the hospital.

"I thought I'd take you to his room myself," Frank said. "They've moved him out of ICU."

As I entered Luke's room, Frank turned and walked away.

Is Frank giving me privacy, or taking a break?

Luke looked pretty good for someone who had been knocking on death's door the day before.

"Thank you for coming so fast," Luke said.

"You look much better than the last time I saw you."

"Whatever happened, has had a weird effect on me," Luke began. His brows were knitted, and he was not smiling. "I can remember most of Tuesday night, but there is a span of memories that feel . . . well, foreign. Like they are someone else's memories."

"Tell me what you mean," I whispered.

"Frank said you had downloaded the logs to my optical and brain implants," Luke continued. "Can you help me make sense of this?"

"I will try," I said, "Start with what you did after I left."

"I remember playing the piano until late, and then going over to the pier to watch Dr. Kim. I had been notified that he was meeting with high-ranking members of the Korean military."

"Do you remember who alerted you that Dr. Kim was going to be at the pier?"

"Priscilla did. She has been to numerous parties on that yacht. I asked her to let me know if Kim was ever invited."

So that is where blondie gets her booze.

"The yacht is owned by Korean officers," Luke continued, "and I have long suspected Kim was providing them DoD research from UNE."

"What happened after Dr. Kim approached the yacht?"

"I released my drone and got ready to get on board."

"If you were using the drone to get evidence against Dr. Kim, why did you need to be on the yacht?" I asked.

"Those small drones are hard to control from a distance. I wanted to be sure that the drone recorded the evidence I needed."

That made perfect sense. I had assumed the duffle bag only contained Luke's scuba gear. Just like I had assumed Luke put the drug in the wine. The shadow we saw on the video must have belonged to Luke's drone.

As if I never heard about how to break down "assume."

"The record from your cyberlens showed you putting on scuba gear and jumping into the water," I said.

"Right," Luke said. "Shortly after I stowed aboard the boat, my memories go silent."

"What do you mean?"

"I have visual memories, but no voices to attach to them," Luke explained.

"I have only watched your cyberlens recordings up to the point where Dr. Kim was pushed overboard," I said. "Can you tell me what happened afterwards?"

"In these *foreign* memories I was subdued by two men," Luke's voice echoed his struggle to recall. He looked at the ceiling as if accessing the memories again. "You've got to believe me. I would never have killed Kim. I wanted him tried, convicted, and deported. I wanted to shame the Korean Empire!"

I believe you, Luke. Is your lens providing us with a deep fake?

I placed my hand on Luke's. "Try to stay calm."

"With my cybernetic arm, it would take more than two men to hold me," Luke added. There was no boasting in his voice. He was simply stating a fact.

"At what point do your memories have sound again?" I tried to make it seem like a routine question.

Luke looked at me and took a deep breath. "Later. About the time I was turned over to the police."

"What about Priscilla? You said she was on the yacht. Do you remember anything about her?"

"Not a thing," Luke said, as a curious expression spread across his face. "There is a fragment of a memory, I think it's one of mine, of another woman who looked familiar. I'm sorry, that is the best I can do."

He had formed a fist with his hand and looked as if he wanted to pound his bed. I worried that if he used his cybernetic arm, he could punch a hole in his mattress.

"Where did you get the dinner wine?" I asked, trying to sound casual.

"You mean the wine laced with Roby-III? The bottle arrived via drone with a 'thinking of you' note from Priscilla."

"I will keep you posted on what I learn from the correlation analysis," I said and squeezed Luke's hand in reassurance.

I left the room and proceeded down the hallway, where I saw Frank asleep in a chair. A half-eaten sandwich was on his lap. He looked so innocent. At the same time, I knew Frank was anything *but* innocent.

Back at the police station, I told Emily and Yano about Luke's *foreign* memories. When I finished, Emily asked, "Where is the drone now?"

"I forgot to ask," I said, embarrassed by my oversight.

"Let's get lunch," Yano suggested, and Holmes walked over to the door.

"Sorry, buddy," I apologized, "not all restaurants allow dogs."
Yes, Holmes you are a dog.

"He'll be fine here on my office couch," Yano sympathized.

On the way to the restaurant, I sent Luke a message inquiring about the present location of his drone. When he did not reply back, I assumed he was asleep.

If I do not hear back from him soon, I will message Frank.

Yano took us to a sushi bar. Emily had obviously let her food preferences be known. As we walked in the door, I whispered in Emily's ear, "East coast sushi is nothing like west coast sushi."

I ordered a salad. Yano ordered a rice bowl.

"What did the two of you learn from the weather satellites?"

"Only that the heat signatures on the pier match the recording from Luke's cyberlens–up to the point when he climbs out of the water and stows away on the yacht," Emily said. She was imitating my *teacher* tone.

Here we go again, milking the limelight.

I waited patiently. Yano smiled in a knowing fashion, but did not interrupt my daughter's report.

"Someone discovered Luke hiding, and another person led him to the sky lounge," Emily said. "That's all the satellite could show us of the yacht."

"In other words, Luke was captured." A shiver ran down my back.

Shortly after our food was delivered, I saw a message from Ellie asking about my analysis of Alisha's logs. My heart sank. I was being pulled in too many directions. I replied that I would visit Alisha in about an hour.

Emily's face told me all I needed to know about the sushi at this restaurant.

I took out a pen and started writing on a napkin. My daughter looked at me as if I had suddenly become a cavewoman.

"Starting from the beginning," Yano said. "Patel killed Rolando."

I wrote that on the napkin.

"Alisha says she was not in control of her implant," I added.

"She exhibited superhuman strength. Possibly an indication her implant was a military prototype," Emily added.

I added both to the napkin.

"Luke's logs show him killing Dr. Kim," Yano added.

I wrote, "Luke does not believe his memories of killing Dr. Kim Yong-Chun are real."

Yano nodded.

"We have two dead men," Yano said. "The only connection between Hernandez and Kim is that they both worked for UNE."

"Both had been Priscilla's lovers," I added.

"What else do we know?" Emily asked.

"There is the *other* murder," Yano added. "The one where the husband killed his wife using his exoskeleton while at the conference."

"Do they have a connection to UNE?" I asked.

"Not that I know of," Yano said. "But the M.O. is the same."

"What were their names?" I asked, pen poised above my napkin.

Yano looked at his wearable, and said, "Dr. Les Gregson and Dr. Betsy Hopper."

My ears rang, and I felt the blood drain from my face. Yano moved toward me as though he thought I was about to faint.

"I know those names," I said. "During my flight I read an article they authored about artificial tendons. Could that be the same Les Gregson who caused Sara to leave North Atlantic State University?"

Yano tucked my napkin into his pocket. "When we get back to the station, we need to consider if the connection between the victims has more to do with cybernetics than universities."

"You two go ahead," I said. "I promised Ellie I would visit Alisha."

Ellie met me at the door to Dr. Patel's hospital room. A police officer was seated in the hallway. The dean did not really know me. I had only met her a few times at gatherings where the food was more memorable than the people.

"Alisha, this is Dr. Cheryl Locke," Ellie said as we entered the room.

"Hello, Dr. Patel," I said, trying to give the woman back some of her dignity. Her days as dean and even professor may have been numbered, but she had earned her doctorate.

"Dr. Locke," Alisha said. As she spoke, she began to sob. "You've got to believe me. I did not kill my husband. I wasn't in control. My implant murdered him. I loved my Rollie."

"Please, call me Cheryl," I said. "Tell me the story of how you came to receive a military prototype implant."

Dr. Patel's eyes widened, and she regained some composure. "Military prototype? Are you sure?"

"Regular cybernetic limbs are not as strong as yours," I said. "It is the only possible explanation."

"When I came to UNE, I had a prosthesis. Priscilla said that since I was now Dean of the College of Cybernetics, I should have a cybernetic implant. I was thrilled to get rid of that prosthesis. I should have known it was going to cost me!" Alisha's anger was allowing her to speak more coherently.

"What do you mean?" I asked.

"When Abagail retired, Priscilla put pressure on me to approve the hiring of Sara Sheppard."

"Did Priscilla remind you that *she* had been the one to procure your implant?" I asked, even though I already knew the answer.

"Yes, and I'm embarrassed to admit it. At the time, the technology was so new it would have taken years to be approved for an implant. I felt like I had my own arm again. If I had known it had been designed for soldiers, I never would have accepted the implant."

Alisha's face reddened. "Cut the damn thing off me!" She was on the verge of hysterics.

"Dr. Patel, please calm down," I said. "I am here to help you."

The woman took three deep breaths and said softly, "Please, call me Alisha. I'm sorry for my outburst. Ellie said you are a cybernetic programming expert. Can you tell me what happened?"

"What I know is that your implant logs indicate anomalies which *suggest* someone hacked into your implant and took control of it."

Alisha started crying. "Who would want to do such a diabolical thing?"

"I do not know, but I intend to find out," I said. "In the meantime, you need to help me."

"You name it, I'll do it."

"You need to have your implant recharged and you need to start eating again. I do not want you to die while I am trying to find out who hacked into your implant and killed your husband."

What am I saying? I am an investigator, not a detective.

Ellie smiled at me. "Please, Alisha, will you do as Cheryl asks?"

"But what about the implant?" Alisha sounded on the verge of hysterics again. "I don't want it to kill anyone else."

I took Alisha's wearable from the drawer and downloaded a program from Watson.

"I am modifying your wearable to emit an ultra-high sonic wave. This wave will prevent anyone from accessing your implant. As soon as your implant has been recharged, put this wearable on your wrist."

Ellie smiled as she looked at the wearable, and said, "Brilliant."

"I got my inspiration from Holmes," I said and gave Ellie a hug.

"Thank you," Alisha sobbed, tears rolling down her face.

As I traveled back to the police station, I called Frank. "How is Luke doing?"

"He is resting. How are you doing?"

"I feel overwhelmed," I admitted, and told him of my visit with Alisha. "When Luke wakes up, ask him if he knows where the drone is now."

"Will do," Frank said.

At the police station, I walked in to find Yano giving Holmes a belly rub, while Emily sipped on her coffee.

How sweet.

I recounted my visit with Alisha for the second time. Yano created an eDoc which appeared before each of us like a translucent slate. He took out the napkin from lunch and said to his AI, "Two columns. Headings, Victims and Suspects."

The slate displayed two columns with the headings. "Add Hopper, Hernandez, and Kim under victims," Yano said. "Add Gregson, Patel, and Westmore under suspects."

The names appeared under the columns.

"Two of the three victims worked at UNE," Emily observed. The names Hernandez and Kim turned from black to blue.

"Right, but only one of the suspects worked there," I said. The name Patel turned blue.

"I have no protocol for this type of investigation," Yano said, "Normally, I would consider these murders as separate crimes. For each crime, we have a suspect."

"But every suspect denies they were in control of their assistive technology," I said. "Everyone but the general."

Yano instructed his AI, "Add second eDoc. First column heading: Motives."

"Patel was aware of Hernandez's affairs," Yano said.

I mustered enough composure to prevent me from rolling *my* eyes.

Before he had a chance to tell the eDoc to include that information, Emily said, with all the disgust of someone who had just turned thirty, "Adultery? For heaven's sake, they were watching golf. That's about as violent as watching mold grow. They weren't arguing."

Yano shook his head. "Happily married women do not attack their husbands."

"But," I interrupted, "if she was not in control of her implant, then someone else committed the murder using Patel's implant."

As instructed, the eDoc recorded "affairs" and "unknown" under Patel's motive.

"We have no idea why Gregson would want to kill his wife," Yano said.

The words: "affair," and "unknown" appeared under "Motives."

"In both the Hopper and Hernandez murders, the suspects blamed their actions on their technology," Yano said. The eDoc added the heading: Commonalities."

We all jumped as Yano's desk sergeant hurried into the office. The sergeant looked around the room and pointed to the first eDoc.

"You've got names to add to those docs," he said and handed Yano a small electronic tablet. After the sergeant left the room, two more names appeared on the lists: Gonzales and Bell.

Chapter 14
Rabbit Holes and Rapid Holes

"Who the hell is Bell?" Emily asked.

That cannot be the same Bell I was talking to yesterday.

"Dr. Josephine Bell. She was Luke's treating physician at DARPA," Yano stated.

A cold chill came over me. I felt my body flush. Luke's doctor was dead.

Yano put down the report he had been reading.

"Where is Leonardo?" I asked.

"No one seems to be able to find him," Yano said. "Hatfield has disappeared too."

"How was Dr. Bell murdered?" I asked.

"Gonzales was demonstrating a super-soldier exoskeleton at DARPA today," Yano's face screamed of disapproval. "The kind of exo which led to the creation of cybernetic ethical codes long before modern power enhancements were developed. Apparently, the designers of this exoskeleton got around the codes by classifying this invention as a 'massive robotic machine.'"

"How *massive* is massive?" Emily asked. Her dilated pupils and lip biting betrayed her anxiety.

"A little over 10 feet tall and weighing about 6,000 pounds," Yano answered. "The video shows Gonzales wearing the robotic machine which picked up Dr. Bell from the observation deck. Before anyone had time to react, she had been crushed by the robotic claw."

"When you find Leonardo," I offered, "I am willing to bet he will blame the machine and deny any desire to kill Dr. Bell."

"I know better than to bet against my mother," Emily said smiling at Yano.

Yano nodded in agreement.

As well they should!

"Where was Hatfield during the demonstration?" I asked.

Yano looked at the slate containing the report. "He was standing next to Sheppard and Kennedy, two rows behind Bell." Yano said.

Gonzales' name appeared under "Suspects" and Bell's name under "Victims."

"What could Leonardo's motive be?" I asked. "Bell is DARPA, not UNE."

Yano consulted the slate again. "Apparently Bell and Gonzales were married while undergrads," Yano said, "and divorced as graduate students. Does anyone want to guess her reason?"

"Oh, she probably got tired of his conference trips," Emily replied.

I will never be able to think about conferences in the same way again.

Yano looked at a notification on his wearable and said. "Frank Covington is here with Luke's drone. Any objections to asking him to join us?"

I smiled at Emily, and we both said, "Send him in."

Frank entered carrying a small object in his right hand, and a large metal box in his left. The heavy box was about the size of Mori's transport crate. The drone was about the size of a large dragonfly. He placed both objects on Yano's table.

"Have you reviewed the logs?" I asked Frank.

"Nothing to review," Frank said. "Someone musta beat us to the drone. I had Luke activate the homin' signal as soon as he woke up. The drone's data has been wiped clean as a whistle."

Emily stood up and walked over to the heavy box. "Has anyone checked the records of this control box?" She asked. When no one responded, an impish grin crept over her face.

Frank shook his head. "I didn't know the box had separate storage."

The grin on Emily's face widened. "Most people don't know about the backup recordings. These spybugs are so small, they're easy to lose or destroy. That's why they're equipped with a transmitter to send their data back to the control box as a safeguard against lost information."

"Why didn't Luke know about the backup logs?" Yano asked.

Frank tapped on his wearable and said, "I'm askin' him."

Seconds later, Frank read the reply, "He says he borrowed the drone from Bruce."

"Kim's murder doesn't fit the M.O. in two ways," Yano said. "First, he was not killed by a physically augmented person. Second, his relationship with those on the boat was professional, not personal."

"He had a personal relationship with Priscilla," I suggested.

"But she wasn't hurt," Yano retorted.

"At the same time, the murders seem connected," Frank said. "After all, the Koreans attempted to use Luke's augmentations to cover up Kim's murder."

"I agree," Yano said. "We need to stop looking at the murders as individual events and start looking for the connections."

"May I join y'all in your jaunt down that rabbit hole?" Frank asked.

Yano nodded. My gut told me that Frank could not be entirely trusted; maybe I would learn his secrets by working with him.

"I can't wait to find out what the drone recorded," Emily interjected. "Looks like I have two mysteries to solve."

Frank looked at Emily and ran his hand through his white hair. "Two mysteries? What mystery do you need to solve besides the drone?"

"The mystery of the air-gapped computer," Emily said, in one of her more dramatic voices.

I was so relieved when Emily had stopped the timer on Sara's air-gapped computer, I had completely pushed the device out of my mind. Frank and Yano looked at each other with the same surprised expression I was wearing.

"Divide and conquer," I suggested. "I can retrieve the image files."

"Yeah," Emily said, "my skills are more suited to figuring out a way around the weird-ass security on Sara's computer."

Holmes walked over to me and huffed. "Someone is hungry," I said.

"We all are," Emily said and glanced at her wearable. "It's nearly seven o'clock."

"Frank, you're welcome to join us for dinner at my house," Yano offered. "Given the late hour, we will probably have something light."

"Thank you for your generous offer," Frank replied. "But I agreed to stay at Luke's house and keep Sarge company at night."

Frank agreed to meet us at Yano's office in the morning.

I fed Holmes while Yano put together a platter of cucumber chips, hummus, pita bread, and chicken salad for dinner. The meal was light yet satisfying. After our meal, Emily walked Holmes. I went to bed early, leaving Emily and Yano discussing how difficult it would be to control another person's implant. Less than 10 minutes later, Holmes and I were sound asleep.

*　　*　　*

Early the next morning, Emily popped into my room. "Dr. Frankenstein set me up with a computer lab at DARPA. He says the lab is state-of-the-art."

Must. Not. Roll. Eyes.

"Air taxi?" I asked.

"Well, I'm not riding Holmes," Emily said with a giggle.

At the mention of his name, Holmes sat up and yawned. Our Monday had begun. I had an hour to eat breakfast, walk Holmes, shower, dress, and meet Frank at the police station. I sent a message to Dr. Hawkins that I was still tied up.

Where did the weekend go?

The lists we had created the day before greeted us as we entered Yano's office. Holmes made himself at home on the couch.

"When I investigate misconduct," I said quietly. "I usually start by following the money."

"Yes," Frank said, "one of the five common motives for murder."

"Loot, love, loathing, lust, and lunacy," Yano recited.

"The DoD has funded billions in cybernetic research," I concurred.

"And some of that money has gone missin' at the DoD," Frank added.

"Means, motive, and opportunity," I recalled from Sherlock Holmes. "Do you solve them in a particular order?"

"This is like a complicated multiple regression, Cher," Frank replied. "We solve for all three factors at the same time."

"How do you know so much about murder investigations?" I asked Frank.

"Another time," Frank replied.

"No way, bucko!" I barked. I stood up, putting my hands on my hips. "If you expect me to trust you, explanations are due. Now!"

Frank looked genuinely hurt. Yano stared through his coffee to the bottom of his mug.

"Fair enough," Frank drawled. "I suppose it is about time."

He walked over to me and encouraged me to sit down.

"I've been working with Luke to uncover who is selling UNE research data to other countries."

"Countries? As in more than just the Korean Empire?"

"China and Venezuela as well," Frank answered. "I took Egypt out of the market."

Holmes came over and laid across my foot. He could sense my emotional turmoil, and his warmth was comforting.

"Luke and I are 'Gerald,'" Frank went on. "The author of those negotiation emails you read. Luke was the one who encrypted and passworded the file so you wouldn't miss it. I told him that wasn't necessary."

Damn, I have been played!

"And who decided to infect the file with a virus?" I asked.

"That must have come from Sara," Frank replied.

"What were you and Luke buying?"

"Backdoors," Frank said. "The DoD instructed Sara to equip all the military exoskeletons and implants with remote control abilities. Either Sara or Priscilla decided to create backdoors to those remote controls. Anyone with the passkey could then activate the remote-control and turn the person into a puppet. Malka told me she suspected Sara was selling the backdoor access to other countries. I needed the passkeys to protect the soldiers who have this technology."

"That probably explains the air-gapped computer," Yano offered. I startled at his comment, having forgotten he was still in the room.

"Malka?" I said with more surprise than question in my voice. "How is she involved?"

"Her husband noticed an abnormality in a cybernetic arm he implanted," Frank said. "Once he finished the surgery, he ran the routine diagnostics on the implant. As they were transporting the patient to the recovery room, he saw the fingers move."

I was stunned. "Had the firewire already been disconnected?" I asked.

Frank nodded his head.

Movement from the cybernetic limb should have been impossible if the person was under anesthesia. Maintenance, charging, and diagnostics were all performed with firewires attached to tiny, hidden ports. Remote kill switches should only shut down a device.

"What did he do?" I asked.

"Nothing at the time," Frank said. "Martin told his wife he thought there had been a mix up and the man was given a military implant."

That made sense. Martin had been one of the surgeons DARPA recruited to implant soldiers with their cybernetics.

"Let me get this straight," I said. "Either Priscilla or Sara equipped their implant prototypes with a means for the limb to be manipulated by remote control."

"That means it is possible that Alisha was not in control when her arm killed her husband." Yano said. His eyes were as wide as a superhighway.

"Is Priscilla or Sara 'Felicity?'" I asked.

"I don't know," Frank said, rubbing his hand across his face.

"Last night," Yano began, "Emily told me that in order for a person to control Patel's arm with a purpose in mind, that person would need to be able to see what she was doing."

"Of course." I tried to sound like his statement was a given, even though this was the first time I considered the logistics. "I had come to the same conclusion."

Yano must not get the impression that my daughter is smarter than me.

"Alisha would have to be close enough to Rolando for the killer to use her arm to grab his throat." I added.

Frank smiled with approval.

"Was their iDom been breached?" Frank asked.

Yano shook his head. "No way to know. The forensic team didn't consider the possibility, and the iDom performed a self-reset."

"You are not done, Frank," I said. "What was in the file Yano accessed when we learned about Yong-Chun's death?"

Frank looked at Yano. "I didn't tell her," Yano said, and returned to studying the bottom of his mug.

"The file in my Pentagon record contains several awards and citations. I was recruited to be an operative while attending graduate school at Duke. I was an undercover agent while earning my doctorate at ETH Zürich in Switzerland."

"And you never told me?" I fought back tears.

"Spies stay alive by keeping secrets," Yano offered.

The word rang in my ears. *Frank is a spy!*

"Frank is a hero," Yano explained. "He has put his own life at risk to protect our country several times. He was almost killed helping General Westmore escape during the Arab Wars."

No wonder Frank knows so much about Luke's PTSD.

"Were you undercover when we worked together at UNE?" I asked, unsure I wanted the answer.

Frank nodded. "Cher, that doesn't diminish our friendship in any way."

"So, you asked me to investigate Sara, because you needed to know about the backdoors," I said, plugging the holes in my understanding.

Frank nodded his head again.

"Are we still friends?" Frank asked, with pain in his voice.

"I guess," I said and brushed the tears away from my eyes before they could fall.

Yano changed the heading on the display from "Suspects" to "Weapons." Frank and I nodded in approval.

Yano added an eDoc to the display. At the top were four columns: Victims, Weapons, Motives, and Opportunity.

"Was Leonardo a weapon?" I asked.

"I'm not sure," Yano explained. "Unlike the other *weapons*, he went into hiding after Bell was killed."

"Right," I said. "We should not jump to any conclusions."

Says the gold medal winner of the Olympic conclusion-jumping event.

"We also need to consider there may be more than one air-gapped device," Frank added.

"Now all we need to do is figure out *how and why* one of those people would want to kill Gregson, Hernandez, and Bell," Yano said.

Easy-peasy.

"I cannot shake this feeling that somehow Yong-Chun's murder is connected," I said. "I hope we can figure out how."

"Let's view the video from the control box," Yano replied.

"Roll 'em," Frank said. His southern accent had returned.

Apparently, Luke had programmed the spybug to attach itself onto the bottom of one of the windows around the sky lounge, an enclosed flybridge with windows on three sides and a sunroof. The interior space held a full bar, and comfortable couches and chairs grouped for conversation. We observed the Koreans talking while they watched a monitor. They all stood when Yong-Chun entered the lounge.

Where are the women?

Outside the sky lounge, the drone had recorded the sounds of the waves hitting the yacht. I was about to tell Yano to kill the audio, when I heard a raised voice among the splashes.

"Yano, can you filter out the water noises, and enable a translator?" I asked.

"I would need to have one of the folks in the lab do that. I'm just a detective."

"I guess that is not part of the training at the police academy," I joked.

I took the playback controls out of his hands. Since the police A.I. did not know me, I used my wearable to link the audio to Watson and told my iDom to filter out the water noises. The voices become conversations.

"Enable translator," I instructed Watson. Korean utterances were transformed into understandable words. We watched as Dr. Kim Yong-Chun entered the sky lounge. As they exchanged greetings, I felt my wearable buzz. The message read, Tell Frankenstein I've slain the monster.

"Pause playback," I shouted.

Chapter 15
Computers and Commuters

"Emily, what did you find?" I enabled a video connection.

Before she had a chance to answer, Yano made a cut-throat gesture with his hand to me and shouted to Emily, "Don't say anything."

"Police stations are always under attack from hackers," Yano explained. "We have more officers monitoring our communications firewall than in patrol cars, thanks to cyberspace and SDVs. Our security prevents eavesdroppers within the building, but for conversations over a wearable, you need to go to the communications closet."

"Hold on, Emily," I said, "We need to move to another room. One with communications shields."

"Hurry!" Emily's eyes were wide with either fear or excitement. At which point, I was ready to run.

As Yano escorted me to the communications closet, I received a message from Luke on my wearable. Sara is asking for her computer back. The timing was not lost on me.

The closet lived up to its name. About the size of a janitor's storage room, the black metal walls hosted a bank of electronics that created a low-pitched hum. There was only room for two chairs, but at least they were comfortable. Yano synched my wearable to the shielded transceiver. I imagined DARPA had similar protection.

"What did you find?" I asked, trying to sound calm.

"First of all, I have downloaded all the drives to Watson. They are encrypted in layers. It will take a while to crack the code."

"Anything else?" Yano asked, not knowing about my daughter's flair for the dramatic.

Emily slowly brushed a stray strand of red hair out of her face and adjusted her lab coat.

Now is not the time to be milking the limelight, little girl.

"This computer is equipped with an RF transceiver," Emily reported, "As well as a microwave transmitter."

"In other words, the air-gapped gizmo, that is not connected to any networks, is capable of sending and receiving messages from a host of other sources." I said.

"Right." Emily looked a little deflated.

"I just got a message from Luke. Sara wants her computer back. Could that thing have sent her a message that you are trying to look under her skirt?"

"A message could have been sent at any time before I got to the lab," Emily considered, "but . . . not since. On the other hand, maybe the shield from the lab was the alert. Up to that point, the damn thing may have been sending her a signal through one of the transmitters."

"And once inside the lab," Yano said, "the signal was cut off by DARPA's shielding, and Sheppard probably assumed the computer was back in Luke's custody."

"Now what?" I asked.

"I'm going home," Emily said. "I miss my pups. Watson can help me decode the data from the drives at your place."

Speaking of pups, I forgot about Holmes!

"Fair enough," Yano said. "I will make your flight reservations. Let's meet for lunch after you pack."

"Do you need the device for anything else?" I asked.

"No, I've seen all the way up her skirt," Emily said, smirking.

"Then leave the computer in the lab," I instructed Emily.

We returned to Yano's office, where Frank was providing Holmes with a belly rub while they waited for us. Yano engaged a sound isolator and made the glass walls opaque. Conversations in an office were easier to secure than wireless communications.

After I recounted Emily's discoveries, Frank said, "Luke says Sara wants her contraption back. I told him to stall."

"She must think I have given it back to Luke," I said.

Frank stared at me.

"If the computer has been sending signals to Sara all this time, then this is the second time the signal has been interrupted." I explained.

"The second time?" Yano repeated.

"I was given the computer at Luke's home in Brookline," I said. "Sara was not all that happy that Luke had confiscated it."

"And his home is shielded," Frank added, following my logic.

"So, when Luke gave it to me, I took it outside the shield. Sara probably knew Luke would give the device to me. The blasted thing was probably sending signals to Sara up until Emily took it to DARPA today, where it was shielded again."

"Isn't Sheppard's lab also shielded?" Yano asked.

"With all those different transmitters," I said, "Sara could easily have programmed her shield to allow for the transmissions."

"Where is the computer now?" Frank asked.

"I told Emily to leave it in the lab," I said. "I hoped Sara would think it was at Luke's house again."

"Quick thinking," Frank complimented.

"At the time, it made sense." I smiled.

Yano looked at me and asked, "If your daughter is finished with it, why not just give it back to Sheppard?"

"Unintended consequences," Frank answered.

I looked at him and nodded. Yano looked puzzled.

Frank took a deep breath, and explained, "If Luke gives Sara back her equipment, will she think the DoD has given up trying to hack into it? Or will she assume the DoD has already done that?"

"Sara's thoughts are not my concern," I said. "She has already been cleared of misconduct. We need to focus on who is controlling other people's cybernetics to commit murder."

"Fair enough," Frank said.

"There is still more video to watch," I reminded them.

A buzz on my wearable let me know Emily requested a change in plans.

"Yano, can you book Emily's flight to Seattle instead of Portland?" I asked.

"Sure."

He tapped his wearable and the new flight information was sent to Emily.

"Resume playback," Yano requested the A.I.

Once again, we watched Yong-Chun enter the sky lounge.

"Good evening, General," Yong-Chun said. While bowing deeply, he kept his legs straight and both arms by his side. The elderly man held out his right hand. As Yong-Chun shook his hand, he supported his right forearm with his left hand to show his inferior position. After the handshake, Yong-Chun took a small box out of his jacket pocket and offered it to the general with both hands. The general took the small, beautifully wrapped gift, and set it on the table next to a chair.

"Are you well?" the general asked. "Your family asks about you frequently."

"I am well," Yong-Chun responded.

Yong-Chun turned to the tallest man and said, "Good evening, Colonel." He bowed deeply again, but not as deep as he had when greeting the general. The colonel was slow to offer his hand, keeping Yong-Chun bowing as if the man wanted Yong-Chun to break with tradition. Next, Yong-Chun greeted *Professor*, and then *Doctor*. His bows to them were not as deep as the one he had given the colonel. Titles only, no names. The five men sat down in the lounge chairs.

"Mr. Kim, I have heard that a researcher at your school was charged with misconduct," the general said. "How did you let this happen?"

Wow, the general has no respect for Dr. Kim's title.

The colonel's carefully shaped, straight eyebrows rose.

"The researcher has been cleared of all charges," Yong-Chun said.

"You must not let this kind of thing happen again," the colonel said. "You can't afford any scrutiny."

Yong-Chun stood up, walked over to the bar, and poured a glass of scotch.

"I understand," he said, offering the drink to the colonel. The colonel took the drink and nodded his head in approval at the gesture.

"Before we get started," Yong-Chun said, "I want to go outside and look at the stars. I rarely get to see them with all the bright lights in the city."

Yong-Chun bowed to each man and left the lounge.

The drone was still recording the activities in the lounge. The professor and doctor were holding a private conversation at the far end, too far away to be recorded. The colonel left the lounge.

Yong-Chun's voice came over the audio. As he was heard pleading for his life, the video showed the general walking briskly to the door. The colonel shouted something about honor. We heard scuffling, and then a splash. The other two men in the lounge ran outside.

The general yelled at the colonel, "What happened?"

Before the colonel could answer, we heard a woman scream. The professor appeared to run in the direction of the sound. He returned holding a gun to Luke's head. The professor was nearly carrying the groggy soldier.

"You don't need the gun," the doctor said. "He'll be as obedient as a new recruit."

The professor walked Luke into the lounge. He did not appear convinced that his gun was unnecessary. Luke's face was expressionless. The doctor looked Luke over and tapped on his wearable. He smiled at the display and walked over to the colonel.

"Welcome aboard, General Westmore," the general said. "We've been expecting you."

The colonel nodded, and the doctor took a small bag from behind the bar. The doctor gave Luke an injection. A few moments later, the professor put his gun back in the holster. Luke was unconscious.

The professor took out a small device and began tapping on the controls. Within a few minutes, he ejected a small chip.

"Our intelligence says that the general's brain implant is shielded," the doctor said.

"That is why I am going to implant a video into his cyberlens," the professor said, with pride in his voice. "When the general regains consciousness, and attempts to remember what happened here tonight, he will see images of himself killing Kim."

"Are the images strong enough to overcome the implant?" the colonel asked.

"That is where the Roby-III comes in," the doctor said. "Not only did we manipulate the delay in the drug's effects, the general will have no memories other than the ones given to him through his cyberlens."

The Korean faces were expressionless. I could hear the faint sound of a woman laughing in the background.

Even though implanting the chip into Luke's cyberlens was bloodless, I felt sick to my stomach.

"Pause playback," I croaked, my throat dry.

"They knew about the shielding," Frank said, more to himself than to Yano or me.

"Given that those men have the ability to implant memories in the form of images, I think we need to consider that this recording could also have been tampered with," I said.

Frank looked at me, eyebrows approaching his hairline. "Good point."

Yano added, "I like your suspicious nature, Cheryl. You take nothing at face value."

You have my ex-husband to thank for that.

I walked over to the control box and stared at it. This device was not all that complicated. It could easily have been hacked—if the hacker knew the drone was transmitting the surveillance video.

"I'll send the control box down to forensics," Yano said. "They'll be able to determine if the recording is real."

"Do you have the autopsy report on Dr. Kim?" Frank asked.

"Yes." Yano brought up the report on a viewscreen near the far end of the office. I did not follow Frank over to look. I knew the report would contain images of the autopsy as it was performed.

"What are you looking for, Frank?" I asked.

"I may be barkin' up the wrong tree, Cher," Frank replied. "I'm checkin' to see if Kim had any implants."

Yano walked over to the screen and began reviewing the report alongside Frank. "The coroner told me the cause of death was drowning," Yano said. "I admit I haven't had time to read the entire report."

"Dr. Kim was not a healthy man," Frank said. "He had an artificial heart."

Yano pointed to the report. "And he had a brain implant . . . no, make that two brain implants."

"Do you see that scar?" Frank asked while he pointed at one of the images from the report.

He has to be talking to Yano, because there is no way I am going to look at a scar on a corpse.

Yano nodded at Frank. "Dr. Kim had been tortured at least once."

A reminder on my wearable alerted me it was time to meet Emily at the café down the street.

The outdoor seating allowed Holmes to join us. As the four of us walked down the street, I enjoyed the brightness of the sunshine after such a dark morning.

Emily was already seated, and I took the chair next to hers. Even though I never wanted to be a drone mom, always trying to keep tabs on what she was doing, I had enjoyed working with her.

"Emily, who is meeting you at the airport?" I asked.

"Jasper is picking me up with my pack. The four of us are going to stay at your house."

So glad you asked permission from the homeowner.

Emily and Jasper met in middle school, and they had been friends ever since. My suspicion that they would date when they got older never materialized. I never quite understood why Emily was so close to him, but I appreciated how he supported her.

Before Emily could tell us what she thought all the encryption was hiding, our waiter approached the table carrying a water bowl for Holmes.

Moments after the waiter took our food order, I received a message from Dr. Hawkins telling me about my next investigation. I sent a message back that I was unavailable for the next several days. I was fine and would explain later.

Dr. Hawkins worries like a mother duck.

"I really can't tell what is on that computer," Emily said. "The encryption is unevenly layered. First, I will need to develop an algorithm to separate the layers. Good thing Watson has so much computing power."

"Well, Uncle Walter *was* an astrophysicist."

Lunch was over too soon. Emily hugged both Frank and Yano good-bye.

"Maybe between the four of us, we'll be able to find where Mori hid my other earring," Emily whispered in my ear as she gave me a hug. I doubted the efforts of Spock and T'Paw in solving the mystery, but Jasper was bright in his own way.

"I love you, baby girl," I said. "Stay safe." Emily boarded the air taxi.

Yano put his hand on my shoulder. "That's quite a daughter you've raised."

The four of us walked back to Yano's office. As soon as we entered the reception area, Holmes started his eardrum-piercing bark as Dr. Bruce Nigel stood up. He had dark circles under his eyes and his clothes were disheveled. Bruce scanned the room constantly.

In a voice barely louder than a whisper, he said, "I think I know where Gonzales is hiding."

"Shure ya do." Frank's voice was devoid of any conviction.

"Come with me to my office," Yano said.

"Can we go somewhere else?" Bruce asked. "I don't want to be seen in a police station."

"Too late," Frank interjected.

"I told the desk sergeant I was looking for my lost cat," Bruce said to Frank. As he looked at Frank, his face betrayed dislike.

How did those boys ever work together?

"There is a coffee shop across the street," Yano offered.

"Do you mind if Cheryl and Frank join us?" Bruce asked. "It will look more casual that way."

"I cannot take Holmes into a coffee shop," I objected.

"Officer Evans," Yano called.

"Yes, Detective Johnson?" the pimply-faced officer answered.

"This corgi needs protective custody for the next hour or so. Can I be assured that you will let no harm come to Dr. Locke's pooch?"

"I will guard him myself," Officer Evans boasted.

"His name is Holmes," I said, "and do *not* let my dog convince you to give him any coffee."

A puzzled look spread across the face of Officer Evans as he took the LEESH from me. Holmes gave me the stink-eye.

Once everyone had their drinks, we sat down at a table away from the windows. I positioned myself under a cooling duct, hoping the breeze would blow the coffee smells away from me.

"Where do you think Dr. Gonzales is hiding?" Yano inquired.

"Cuba," Bruce said, without hesitation.

"What evidence do you have?"

"Where else would he go?" Bruce asked rhetorically. "His father is in exile there, and there hasn't been an extradition agreement with Cuba for more than a hundred years. It's the best place for him to hide."

"In other words," Yano continued, "this is only speculation on your part."

"Not entirely," Bruce said. "C. J. received a message on his wearable just before he went underground. Leonardo's signal was off the coast of Florida."

"Where is Mr. Hatfield?" Yano asked.

"Off the coast of Florida as well." Bruce looked a tad embarrassed. "I pinged his wearable when he didn't respond to my text."

I was flabbergasted. Pinging another person's wearable required synchronization between the two parties or uploading a mirror program to the other person's wearable. Other than those two methods, eavesdropping another person's wearable was supposed to be impervious to hacking.

"I'm convinced C.J. has been in contact with Sara," Bruce went on. "You should subpoena her emails."

Whoa there, professor! You should never try to tell a lawman what to do.

"I will take that under advisement," Yano mumbled. "Is there anything else?"

"Yes," Bruce said, "I need protection. I'm being followed."

"Who would be following *you*?" Yano looked directly into Bruce's eyes.

Bruce squirmed in his chair and said, "If I knew that, I would simply give you the name so you could arrest him." He attempted to return Yano's gaze.

"Let's start with *why* anyone would be following you?"

"Because Rolando gave me a computer the day before he was murdered," Bruce said. "He told me he wanted it out of his house in case the owner came back for it."

"Did he tell you the name of the owner?" Yano inquired.

"No," Bruce said, "and I didn't ask."

"When did you and Rolando become such close friends?" Frank probed, without taking his eyes off his coffee cup.

"We were not friends," Bruce blurted out. "I considered him an academic mercenary, but he *was* the dean's husband. I had my own future to protect."

"Mercenary?" Frank repeated, not quite under his breath.

"Rolando had no qualms about doing research off the record," Bruce explained, "if the price was right."

"Why didn't you tell the police about this computer after Hernandez was murdered?" Yano asked. There was no twitching in his lip, or twinkle in his eyes. He was in full Detective Johnson mode.

"I – I – I didn't want anyone to-to know I had it," Bruce could barely get his words out. "Especially after Rolando was murdered."

"Yet, the person who killed Hernandez was in police custody," Yano said. "Unless you believe that someone used Patel to kill her husband."

Yano let the idea land on Bruce, before stating his next conclusion. Bruce refrained from taking the bait.

"Well, if you think someone is following you because of the computer," Yano said, "then you must have told *someone* you had it."

"I didn't tell anyone," Bruce said emphatically. "I think C.J. may have seen it when I was cleaning out Sara's lab."

"Why did you take it to the lab?" I asked.

"Shielding," Bruce replied.

"If Gonzales and Hatfield are in Cuba, neither one could be following you," Yano sounded as if he was talking about the blueness of the sky.

"Maybe *one of them* told someone," Bruce said. The fear in his voice seemed authentic.

"Tell me more about your relationship with Hernandez and Hatfield," Yano requested.

"C.J. was one of Rolando's lab rats," Bruce explained. "Rolando was experimenting with programmed brain implants. I supplied him with implants for his research, before I knew how he was using them."

"I'm not a scientist," Yano said. "In layman's terms—what is a programmed implant?"

"C.J. wanted to be a highly skilled computer programmer," Bruce began, "but he didn't want to spend years studying coding. Rolando offered C.J. a brain implant which contained all the programming skills of a decade of study, in a neat, twenty-micron chip."

"How much did he owe Hernandez?" Frank asked.

You are skipping over the down payment, Frank.

"I have no idea," Bruce said, he looked up at the ceiling. "Given his expected earnings, the balance could easily have been six, maybe seven, figures."

"How did Hatfield become Sara's assistant?" I asked.

"I don't really know. She claims he was blackmailing her, but she refuses to say how. I think they were working together."

Working together?

"The evidence he provided regarding her misconduct," Bruce continued, "was hardly ironclad."

"I agree," I said. "In fact, I found evidence which suggests that *you* set her up."

"Why would I do that?" Bruce asked.

"That is a good question," I said. "Maybe you wanted to become a program director. Maybe you had other motives."

"I'm no fan of the *distinguished* Dr. Sara Sheppard," Bruce admitted. "But I had nothing to gain if Sara lost her DoD research money. After all, she was transferring some of those funds to me."

"Speakin' of those bucks, would you care to enlighten us as to how those funds disappeared after they were transferred?" Frank asked.

Bruce's face drained of color.

"I have no idea," Bruce whispered.

Chapter 16
Lost and Found

*Y*ano arranged for Officer Bean to take Bruce home in a police car.

"Bruce, make sure the entire neighborhood sees you giving the computer to my man," Yano said.

Just before Bruce left, I referred him to Pinkertons, and recommended Molly Fitzpatrick and Spencer Fraser. The police would not provide protection without evidence that Bruce was in danger from anything other than his imagination.

Once Bruce was out of the room, Yano looked at Frank and me, "Do either of you think Hatfield and Gonzales are in Cuba?"

Frank shook his head saying, "The only believable thing Bruce said, was that Hatfield's wearable was off the coast of Florida."

I looked at Frank, and said, "Did you forget about the computer given to him by Rolando the day before the murder?"

"That computer's probably got more clues than a corgi has tickle spots," Frank said.

"All the airports, hyperloops, air taxis, and toll-booths have been put on alert for Hatfield and Gonzales," Yano said. "Only a matter of time before we catch them."

"That covers the land and air," Frank said. "What about sea?"

"The A.I. has checked all passenger lists on ferries, chartered boats, freight barges, hydrofoils," Yano replied. "Certain private vessels and those flying a foreign flag are more *difficult* to monitor."

"Routine roadblocks," Frank scoffed. "If you catch them with any of those, they want to be caught."

"Right," Yano agreed. "We can't even be sure they are traveling together."

"If you two will 'scuse me," Frank said casually, "the time has come for me to use my well-developed snooping skills."

I stood up and Frank walked over for a hug good-bye. Yano walked him to the front door. When the detective returned to his office, I felt a bit odd as I suddenly realized we were alone.

I am a mature woman. I do not need a chaperone.

Yano's green eyes were twinkling. He sat down at the conference table and motioned me to sit next to him. I was tempted but decided to sit across from him instead. I wanted to be able to see those green eyes. Yano leaned over the desk and said softly, "I've been meaning to ask you, what does Sherlock Holmes mean when he says 'the game is afoot?'"

I slipped off my right shoe and ran my foot along the inside of his ankle. I smiled as Yano seemed to lose his ability to form words.

"Excellent." Yano's upper lip quivered.

"Elementary," I purred and smiled. If the desk sergeant were to come in the office now, I doubted Yano would stand up. But it was not the desk sergeant who interrupted us.

"Dr. Locke, I have identified the final person whose image was caught on the copier." Watson's voice was unexpected. Yano gulped in a noisy breath.

"Please tell me the name," I said.

"Thae Song-thaek," Watson replied. "He is the Korean colonel the drone recorded on the yacht."

I had forgotten that when I asked Watson to translate the drone recording, he had gained access to the surveillance video. Watson had been following my instructions to expand his image search beyond UNE personnel. As soon as Yano heard the name, his finger began flying across his wearable.

"The image is blurred due to the distance between the colonel and the copier," Watson explained. "From my analysis, the colonel was not using the copier. He was simply in the vicinity when someone else used the machine."

Yano looked up from his wearable and said, "According to social media posts, Colonel Thae Song-thaek has a rather nasty reputation as a *truth extractor*." Yano's eyes no longer twinkled.

"In other words, he is good at torture," I said.

I walked over to Yano and put my hands on the back of his neck. "There is nothing more deceptive than an obvious fact." I said, quoting Sherlock Holmes again.

I felt a notification and looked at my wearable. Frank had sent me a message saying he believed Hatfield had fled to the West Coast.

So much for Florida.

"Dr. Locke, are you expecting a visit from Conrad Joe Hatfield?" Watson asked.

"No, why?"

"Because he just tried to enter your house," Watson explained.

"Show me," I instructed.

Within seconds, Watson displayed an image of Hatfield trying to turn the doorknob to the backdoor while holding what appeared to be a high-tech lock pick. Behind him, I could see a duffle bag and some food on the table near the pool.

"Obviously, I'm not the only man trying to get your attention to-day," Yano remarked. The twinkle in his green eyes had returned.

"Watson, broadcast my voice."

Since Hatfield's wearable was on a cruise in the Atlantic, it was logical I could not talk to him over his wearable. Unless he had a relay with some squid.

"Mr. Hatfield, you have three seconds to convince me that I should not call the police–starting now!"

"Hello, Cheryl," Hatfield responded. "Your house has an impressive security system. I was only slightly disappointed when I couldn't break in."

"Two seconds."

"Touchy, touchy," Hatfield said, in a taunting voice. "I've got the evidence you need to end the selling of UNE research."

"What *kind* of evidence?" I asked, squeezing as much skepticism into my voice as I could.

Hatfield looked around. In a smugly conversational tone, he said, "If you're not going to call the police, then would you be so kind as to allow me entry into the house? Our chat can be overheard, and I'm an easy target out here."

"I will let you in the pool house," I said.

Hatfield changed direction and walked over to the table by the pool. As he picked up his technological doodad, he said, "I could have done *that*, myself."

He pulled out a duffle bag from behind a chair and carried both to the pool house.

The security on the pool house was not as sophisticated as my home system. At the same time, it was not as simple as a padlock.

"Why did you run after Dr. Bell was killed?" I asked.

"Are you kidding me?" Hatfield quickly responded. "I'm probably next on the hit list."

Suddenly Hatfield shouted, "Drone!"

Watson opened the door to the pool house and Hatfield practically threw himself inside.

"Watson, did you detect any drone activity in the vicinity?" I asked.

"Yes, Dr. Locke, that is why I opened the door. The drone had been sending a signal to my surveillance system that made it appear to be a crow. Once Mr. Hatfield shouted, I enhanced the video and determined that the *bird* was actually a drone."

"Where is the drone now?" I asked.

"It got away," Watson said, "but not before I fried the circuitry. The drone will appear to have been struck by lightning."

Did Watson sound proud of himself?

"Cheryl, I had no idea you collected antiques," Hatfield said into the microphone of my citizen band radio.

"I do not like you, *Mister* Hatfield," I said. "I might be able to get past that, if you start addressing me as Dr. Locke."

"As you wish, *Doctor* Locke." His tone of voice spoke volumes to his contempt for having to address me with my title.

"The pool house is secure. That radio is the only transmission which can get past the shield and it only connects to my wearable. The signal is encrypted and cannot be intercepted. To ensure your safety, I have asked Watson to lock the doors and windows."

"You mean I'm a prisoner?" He sounded like Mori when her dinner was late.

"Prisoner? More like a trespasser, blackmailer, and traitor. You can thank me later for saving your life. I will contact you again in one hour."

The time was 2:15 p.m. I disconnected the transmission before Hatfield had a chance to respond.

"Bravo!" Yano said, clapping his hands. "Note to self. What others have said about the temper of a red-head is a gross understatement."

If I had not been so worried, I would have bowed at his compliment. Instead I started pacing. Yano gave me an inquisitive look.

"My daughter and Jasper will be arriving at the house in a few hours. I need a plan to keep them safe. Any suggestions?"

Yano put his index finger across his gray mustache and leaned into his hand. "I can contact the local police and tell them to pick Hatfield up." He stroked his mustache and added, "That is what I would *normally* do."

"No. As much as I enjoy the image of Hatfield crying in the darkest and most barbaric of jail cells, I do believe his life *is* in danger."

Yano shut his eyes momentarily. "What if we treat your pool house as a safe house . . .? I could have a couple of FBI agents stay with him. Protective custody and all."

"Better," I said. "How long will that take to set up?"

"Less than an hour," Yano promised.

"I will let Emily know," I said, as we started tapping our messages. "Do you have any objections to me letting Frank know that we have found Hatfield?"

"No. But you're not exactly *required* to tell him everything. You know. Like how we *caught* Hatfield." Yano's face turned slightly pink.

The competition of male egos is always a source of amusement.

"Of course not," I said, with as much innocence as I could muster.

Emily responded quickly. She estimated that she and Jasper would arrive at my house in about two hours. Plenty of time for the FBI to take Hatfield into "protective custody" at the pool house.

I quickly sent a message to Frank. "Hatfield is in custody. You were right. He is on the West Coast now."

Yano stopped tapping on his wearable and said, "All set. The FBI is sending over two agents to babysit Hatfield. They'll be there in less than an hour."

The time was now 2:35 p.m. A few minutes later, Officer Bean entered Yano's office with a computer in his hands. "Dr. Nigel gave me this computer," he reported.

I was surprised by how much it looked like Sara's air-gapped computer.

"If you want my hypothesis," I offered, "that computer is what Priscilla was worried the police would find at Rolando's home or office."

"You think the computer belongs to Priscilla?" Yano asked.

"Not entirely sure," I said. "However, I would *not* be surprised if it has a security system equal to that of Sara's."

"I think I need to interview Dr. Priscilla Kennedy again," Yano said. "This time I have better questions to ask. Starting with whether or not she is missing a computer."

"While you are interrogating Priscilla," I said, "I will contact Emily and ask her to talk me through disabling the protection. Given her experience with Sara's computer, I doubt she will have any trouble. I want to send this one to her for further analysis."

Officer Evans entered Yano's office with Holmes.

"I take it that you can resume custody of this *pooch*," Officer Evans said. There was no humor in his voice.

"Of course," I said.

Officer Evans left and Holmes plopped down under the conference table. His customary goofy grin had been replaced with a look of exasperation.

Officer Evans is obviously not a dog person.

"If you need any tools, ask the desk sergeant," Yano said.

Yano left the office at 2:45. I called Emily a couple of minutes later. She was still on the plane back to Seattle.

"What's up, Mom?" she asked.

"Do you remember Conrad Joe Hatfield?" I said softly, so as not to be heard by the other passengers.

"He's that smarmy guy?" she whispered, following my lead.

"Well, he is in my pool house. Yano is having the FBI send agents over to place him in protective custody. So, don't go over to the pool house."

"Okay," Emily said, hesitation filling her voice.

"Sitting on Yano's desk is another air-gapped computer which looks remarkably like Sara's," I said.

"Don't touch it!" Emily shouted.

Do not scare the other passengers, Emily.

Emily reduced her volume as she noticed a few heads had turned in her direction.

"How can I help?" she asked.

"Could you talk me through disabling the security protocols, so I can send it to you?"

"Sure," Emily said. "Now that I understand the system, it should only take about twenty minutes."

True to her word, Emily led me through deactivating the computer's protections in less than twenty minutes. There was one important difference. This computer was not sending a signal echo like Sara's device.

"Now, the question is, how can I safely send this to you?"

"The distance is too far for a regular drone," Emily said.

"I will work it out," I stated. "It is time for me to talk to Hatfield again."

"Be careful, Mom," Emily said.

As I was thinking about what I was going to say to Hatfield, I looked outside the window. Parked on the street was a black limo with Korean Empire flags and diplomatic plates.

Wow! Those Koreans know all about stealth.

I quickly sent Frank a message.

At exactly 3:15 I connected my wearable to the radio in my pool house. "Mr. Hatfield, this is Dr. Locke. In a short time, a couple of FBI agents will be joining you in the pool house. Rather than have you arrested, Detective Johnson has agreed to put you in protective custody until you can be safely transferred back here."

"Protective custody?" Indignation filled Hatfield's voice.

"Would you rather wait in a jail cell?" I asked.

"No, I'm sure this hut is more comfortable."

After I said good-bye to Hatfield, I looked around Yano's office for a book of a certain size and shape. Once I found the right one, 'The 150th Anniversary of Superhero Comics,' I took off the color-jacket and wrapped it around the computer. I returned the wrapped computer was to the bookshelf. I put the book into my carrycase and left the office.

"Sergeant," I said, approaching his desk, "what is the safest means of sending something *this* size to my house in Seattle?" I held up my carrycase so he could see the size I needed.

"That's too far for a drone," Sergeant Obvious said. "You'll need a special carrier service."

"Could you be so kind as to find me one?" I asked, trying my best to sound like a damsel in distress.

"When do you need it?"

"Well, I am going to take Holmes on a short walk down the street to the café," I said. "So, in about thirty minutes." I tried to make my body language indicate it was no big deal.

"I'll do my best, ma'am."

As I walked out the door, I noticed a man studying the portrait of the police chief on the wall outside the police station. Even though his back was toward me, I recognized the cut of his suit. He was from the Korean Empire. My heart started beating faster.

Using a make-up mirror, I verified the Korean art critic was following me. I needed to get to the café before he got to me. I could feel perspiration dripping on my forehead.

Two blocks from the café, I began to wonder if bringing Holmes with me had been a good idea. My willingness to take risks did not justify putting my furbaby in danger. Holmes' nose twitched as he sniffed the air. I took a deep breath. The smell made me realize that what I had previously mistaken for cheap aftershave, while walking with Ellie, was likely Korean cologne.

The Korean art critic increased his speed. At this rate he would catch up to me before the end of the block. There was no way I could outrun him. If I tried to return to the police station, I would run right into him. I suddenly realized the best-case scenario was he would seize the carrycase without hurting me or Holmes.

Why had I been so impulsive?

There was no need to prove this man was after the computer. Even more important, I did not have a plan for preventing him from grabbing the carrycase or what would happen when he realized the computer was not inside.

I stopped walking and using a store window's reflection looked behind me. The Korean art critic was the general who had been on board the yacht. Suddenly I felt a burning sensation in my left shoulder.

I see the SNAFU fairy has visited me again!

Another Korean, who I had failed to notice, was right beside me. He held a hand dart. When the general caught up, he tore the carrycase from my shoulder. Holmes barked as loud as a German Shepherd. The world began to spin and I felt myself pour onto the sidewalk like melting ice cream. I knew I was about to lose consciousness, and worried what would happen to Holmes when I collapsed.

Suddenly, I felt strong hands lift me into a vehicle.

Was I being kidnapped?

I could no longer keep my eyes open. The last thing I know was Holmes jumping in and sitting next to me. Somehow knowing Holmes was safe, made everything all right.

Chapter 17
"The Plot Thickens"

*E*ven before I opened my eyes, I had an impression of the room. My sense of smell told me I had been here before. The memory evoked a feeling of safety. I could feel the sofa I was laying on and the blanket on top of me. The room was quiet.

I opened my eyes and, to my surprise, saw General Luke Westmore sitting in the chair next to me. He smiled at me, but it was a forced smile.

"How long have I been out?" I asked, trying to sit up.

Luke reached over and gently pushed me back on the sofa.

"A few hours," he said. "Don't try to sit up. That poison has a vile reputation for agonizing headaches before death. The drug I gave you should neutralize it. Temporarily. You still need the antidote."

"What happened to Holmes?" I trembled. My mind was fuzzy.

Did Luke just say I am about to die?

Luke stood up, walked over to the door and opened it.

He yelled down the hallway, "She's awake."

Holmes raced into the room. Frank followed a few moments later. My corgi jumped up on the sofa and began licking my face with abandon. His bum wiggled in delight.

The two men exchanged worried looks. "The antidote is on the way," Frank said.

Holmes finally settled down next to me. I put my arm around him and he rested his head in the crook of my elbow.

"Luke was able to grab you before they carried you off," Frank said, his voice full of apology. "But I'm afraid the computer is now in the hands of the Korean Empire."

I started laughing so hard I could barely breathe. My laughter seemed to cause the two men even more concern.

"Actually," I said, as soon as I could talk again, "the Korean Empire has 'The 150th Anniversary of Superhero Comics' in their hands. I *borrowed* it from Yano's office."

Frank and Luke exchanged looks and put on forced smiles.

I began to sway, and their worried expressions intensified.

"But the message said you had Priscilla's computer," Frank said, "and that a limo from the Korean Empire embassy was parked outside Yano's office."

"Where is the computer now?" Luke asked.

"Sitting on the bookshelf in Yano's office wearing the book's color-jacket." I grinned, convinced I was the cleverest woman alive.

I felt another wave of dizziness wash over me and realized I might not be alive much longer without the antidote. I stroked Holmes' head, not certain who was being reassured.

Luke responded to his wearable and left the room. A few minutes later, he returned with a worried-looking Yano and a medical case. Luke took out a hypo-spray, placed it against my neck, and released the antidote.

"You'll feel right as rain in a few minutes," Frank said.

"What happened?" Yano asked.

I recounted the events the best I could. I told them about how Emily had talked me through disabling the computer's security system, and about the limo. When I got to the part about contacting Frank, he added to my story.

"When Cher messaged me 'bout the computer and the limo," Frank began, "I knew she didn't appreciate the danger of her situation. I figured Luke could get to her faster, so I told him what Cher had told me."

Luke took over. "Fortunately, I was on my way to DoD headquarters," he explained, "which is only a block from Yano's office."

"Tell Yano what you did with his superhero comic book," Frank said.

I explained how I used his book as a decoy and left the office with the Korean art critic in tow. I could see Yano clench his teeth and narrow his lips. He looked away from me.

Why is Yano so angry about the book?

"As I approached your office," Luke said to Yano, "I saw Cheryl walking along with two men closing in on her. She seemed to be aware of the fellow behind her, but not the man across the street walking on her flank."

I nodded my head and explained how I had used the storefront to see who was following me.

"I wish I had been faster," Luke said. "The man on her flank crossed the street and ran up to Cheryl. He injected her with the neurotoxin before I was able to secure her. I recognized the man behind her, even without his uniform. His name is General Kim Jong-eun."

Even I knew *that* name. General Kim Jong-eun came from a long line of corrupt and ruthless leaders. Each one more merciless than his father before him.

"I guess I am lucky to be alive," I realized.

"Holmes bit the man who attacked you, before jumping up into the SDV," Luke said with what sounded like admiration in his voice.

Or is Luke jealous?

"I had no idea a corgi could jump that high." Luke smiled at Holmes.

With a running start Holmes could jump fences. Providing he could run long enough and the fence was not too high.

"Yano, tell me about your interview with Priscilla," I requested.

"You were right," Yano began, "the computer we got from Nigel was Priscilla's. She had left it–"

Holmes started making odd noises and looked around the room frantically. Yano stopped talking abruptly. My head started spinning.

"Wow, I am feeling dizzy again . . .." I said, closing my eyes.

I heard a commotion. Voices were all around me, but I could not make out what they were saying. I felt Holmes press against me, and then everything turned black.

Waking up the next time was a dramatically different experience. I had no sense of the place before I opened my eyes. I was in a hospital bed among wires, tubes, and monitors. Malka was sitting vigil this time. My head was throbbing.

"I need to let Ellie know you are awake," she said.

Fingers moved across her wearable as though she was using a keyboard.

A few seconds later, Ellie came into my room.

"How are you feeling?" Ellie asked.

"Like a zombie."

Ellie laughed nervously.

Was I about to become a member of the walking dead?

"Was there something wrong with the antidote?" I asked.

"Martin thinks the poison was spliced with virus DNA," Ellie explained. "This would cause the toxin to be antigenically different every time the virus replicates. As a result, it's grown resistant to the antidote developed by Dr. Bell."

Ellie's face betrayed her emotional pain. I could only imagine how I would feel in her place. I fought back the urge to cry. I knew that Emily would take care of Holmes and Moriarty, but they would miss me.

"Thank you for telling me the truth," I said. "Can he cure me? I need to know if I am going to die."

"My husband is working haud to make sure that doesn't happen," Malka said.

"Dr. Goldberg is programming nanites to remove the virus DNA from the toxin," Ellie said. "If that is successful, then the antidote will work."

"I see," I said. "Where are Frank, Yano, and Luke?"

Malka and Ellie exchanged looks.

"Trying to find Holmes," Malka said hesitantly.

"Holmes ran off while you were being put in the air ambulance," Ellie explained.

"Please hand me my wearable," I said.

Malka looked puzzled, but handed me the wearable anyway. I placed my finger on the underside, and activated a locating signal on Holmes' collar. He would come directly to my location.

"Who wants to wait in the lobby and bring Holmes to me?" I asked, and smiled at the two women standing by my bed.

"I will," Malka said, and left the room.

The effort had increased the pain in my head. I wanted to howl.

"Ellie, please tell 'The Three Stooges' I have summoned Holmes and they can stop looking for him." I tried my best to smile, but my head felt like it was about to detonate.

She smiled and walked over to me. Ellie sent the message from my wearable so it would appear to be coming from me.

I need to remember that.

In a little over twenty minutes, Malka came into my room with a dirty, wet, and exhausted Holmes.

Ellie lifted Holmes onto my hospital bed. I scratched his head and felt like the tears would fall again. My furbaby presented me with his belly. Malka put water in a small bowl she had taken off the bedside table and Holmes sat up to take a long drink. His face reflected his gratitude.

A blue synthetic nursing-unit came into my room and announced everyone had to leave because Dr. Goldberg had ordered a procedure. Malka smiled at me.

"You're going to be all right, Cheryl. We'll wait auutside your doah."

"Sedative dispensing," the SNU announced softly.

201

I felt Ellie take Holmes off my bed as a strange sensation of warmth crept over my body.

The next time I opened my eyes, the dawn light was streaming through my window. Holmes had been cleaned up, dried off, and placed in my bed. He was snoring contentedly. My headache was gone, and so were my friends.

I spotted my clothes on a chair and got up to get dressed. I did not make it very far.

A white blur speeded to my side. "Stay there," the SNU said harshly, and lifted me back onto the bed.

The SNU was only about four feet tall and looked like an upside-down white compost bin with a round top. I could see six armatures of various lengths, attached at different heights around the cylinder-shaped body. On top of the unit were input keys, lights, a camera, and speakers.

"Thank you," I said. "Do you have a name?"

"Your name is Dr. Cheryl Locke," the SNU answered.

"Not my name. What is your name? What do I call you?"

"Nurse," the SNU responded.

So much for bedside manner.

"Do you require further assistance?" Nurse asked.

"I need help getting dressed," I said.

"If you will stay on the bed, I will help you with getting dressed," Nurse said.

Holmes yawned and Nurse moved away from the bed.

"I need to alert security about this intruder," Nurse said. Three of the SNU's six arms pointed at my corgi.

"Nurse, this is my dog, Holmes," I explained. "There is no need to alert security."

Nurse brought me my clothes and helped me dress without saying another word. Apparently, my reassurances were not completely acceptable because Nurse assisted me from the side of my bed away from Holmes.

"Thank you," I said. "One last thing. Will you help me to that chair?"

"Why do you thank me?" Nurse asked.

"Because you helped me," I replied.

"An unnecessary exertion of your limited energy," Nurse retorted.

Oh, how I miss Watson.

Nurse left the room once I was in the chair. My wearable was on the table next to me. I picked it up and saw it was 5:34 a.m. on Thursday. Somehow, I had lost two entire days. I was about to send messages to my friends when Yano walked in.

"How did you know I was awake?" I asked. I could not tell whether I was happier or more surprised by his arrival.

Yano came over to me, smiled, and kissed the top of my head. "I didn't," he said, "I have been so worried about you. We have much to talk about. After I walk Holmes."

He took the LEESH out of a drawer by my bed stand. Holmes appeared to be familiar with this routine.

Was he the one taking care of Holmes during my recovery?

While the two guys went for a walk, I looked at the messages from Emily.

The first one said, Mori has been tormenting Jasper. The first morning here, Mori hid in the bottom bathroom cabinet. When Jasper got out of the shower, she jumped up and bapped his butt cheeks. Mori scared the bejabbers out of him.

Later that morning she said, Last night, Mori woke up Jasper every few hours by jumping on him from the dresser across the room. She seems to think Jasper's stomach is a trampoline.

Around lunch time, she wrote, Frank told me what those Koreans did to you. He told me to stay here because I couldn't be of any help there. He said my analysis of Priscilla's computer was the best way I could help you. You better survive, Mom. No one is going to love Mori the way you do.

The next day she texted, Your cat keeps trying to convince us that she's starving, even though we feed her twice a day. In fact, I think she has gained a few pounds.

Only my daughter would update me on my cat while someone was in protective custody in my pool house.

I decided to contact her. She was likely worried.

"Hello, Emily," I said into my wearable.

"Hi, Mom," she responded quickly. "Please enable your video."

"I probably look like hell," I said, but enabled the video as my daughter requested.

"You kinda do look like hell, Mom," she said laughing. It was the sound of her relief.

I reached for the brush from my bag, but realized I was still too weak to brush my own hair.

"What is going on?" I asked. "I have a few days to catch up on. Have you heard anything from Hatfield?"

"Yeah," Emily said. "One of the agents came over to the house to tell me Hatfreak was worried because he couldn't raise you on the radio."

"What did you tell the agent?" I asked.

"To tell Hatfreak that when you wanted to talk to him, you'd be in touch," Emily said. "Hey, I'm almost finished downloading the data from the computer you sent me."

How did Emily get Priscilla's computer?

"The neighbors are still buzzing about what was in the small box delivered by military escort," Jasper said.

"Hi, Jasper," I made my voice loud enough for him to hear me. "Be sure to keep my daughter safe."

"The sight of that military heliodart landing in the yard drove my corgis crazy." Emily giggled, and added, "I understand Hatfreak hid in a closet until he understood they were *not* assassins. What a wimp!"

One of these days your eyes are going to roll right out of your head.

Yano returned with Holmes, fed him breakfast, and refreshed his water bowl.

"I'm glad you're okay," Emily said. "Let me finish up with the computer, and I'll contact you when I'm done. In about two hours."

Once the call ended, Yano took the hairbrush off the table and started brushing my long, red hair. It felt wonderful.

"The SNU said they can release you if you have someone to care for you," Yano said. "The poison is still working its way out of your system. You're going to be a little unsteady on your feet for a few more days. Ellie is on her way."

"Awesome," I said. Getting out of the hospital would be a relief.

A few minutes later, Nurse brought me a breakfast tray. At least that was what she called it. The word bland would be an understatement. The food did not taste bad; it was tasteless.

After I finished eating, Yano explained, "Everyone's fighting over where you are going to stay during your recovery. Malka lost because she is not currently staying in her smarthome. I think Frank and Luke are duking it out now over who's got the better security."

Did anyone think to ask me where I want to go?

"I want to go home," I said.

Yano's face fell.

"You can't travel yet," Ellie objected as she walked through my door.

Malka was right behind her and walked over to me. She put her arm around my shoulder and gave me a very un-Malka-like hug.

Is she going to get all motherly on me?

Frank followed her in, but there was no more room by my chair. He settled for scratching Holmes' head.

"Where is Luke?" I asked, as my room filled with people. Frank went out to the hall and found more chairs.

"He is making arrangements for a soldier to be your bodyguard at his house," Frank said. "Lieutenant LeClerc will also help you with whatever you need while you recover."

That gives new meaning to the expression 'bodyguard!'

Ellie's face fell, and she looked slighted. Luke walked in the door.

"I am sure Ellie can take good care of me," I argued noticing the expression on her face.

"I know she can," Luke agreed. "However, Lieutenant LeClerc can also protect you. She has black belts in several martial arts."

Ellie laughed and said, "I can't top that."

I looked around the hospital room at my group of friends. The sight brought tears to my eyes. Even though I was thankful for my job with the Worldwide Science Federation, the last few weeks had reminded me how enjoyable it was to work among people I knew and liked.

"We all know how academia hides dirty politics under a veil of scientific inquiry," I said to everyone. "If we are going to stop these murders, we all need to help Yano by telling him everything we know."

"While I appreciate your advocacy," Yano said, "this place is not secure."

"My house is secure," Luke said. "I want everyone to come to my place so we can start to connect the dots."

Yano frowned at the suggestion.

"No offense, Detective, but I'm sure Cheryl will be more comfortable at my house than in your office."

Malka did not appear to be listening. Perhaps she thought she was not included in the invitation.

"Malka," I said, "can you come over to Luke's place with us?"

Malka looked at me for a few awkward moments and asked, "Why?"

"You have known these people a long time," I said. "Your experience and insights are critical." I squeezed her hand in friendship.

"Everyone should come to my place to debrief," Luke said.

Frank shot Luke a look, and the general walked over to Ellie.

"That includes you," Luke invited her with a smile.

Ellie's face welcomed his overture.

Frank helped me walk out to the military transport. I was still wobbly on my feet. Ellie helped Holmes onto the seat next to me, and she sat on his other side.

"I'll be there shortly," Malka said, as her limo arrived.

Yano came over to the transport and stuck his head inside. "I have an errand to run," he explained, "but I'll come over as soon as I can."

While on board the transport, I saw that Emily had sent me a picture. The image was captioned, Look what Mori just brought me.

In the picture, Mori stood on my desk with the stolen earring in her mouth. Emily had placed her other earring by cat's paw for the picture. In the background I could see Priscilla's air-gapped computer.

I stared at the picture. There was something about the image that spurred my mind to connect the pieces in a whole new way. I quickly texted Emily with a suggestion for dealing with the encrypted data from the air-gapped computers.

Thank you, Professor Moriarty.

Chapter 18
"Once You Eliminate the Impossible"

A little while later, we were gathered in Luke's study. Yano was the last to arrive. He presented me with a new carrycase. It was painted with superheroes.

"Have you figured out how you're going to get my book back?" Yano asked. He still looked surprisingly perturbed.

The prophets of technology had underestimated the human need to connect with our reading. The enjoyment of reading a printed page. The music created by turning the pages. The smell of the ink. The artistry of the interior design. The feel of the books in our hands. We still loved our books. Sadly, they were less common than they had been a hundred years ago.

Finding *that* book would be a challenge. I doubted it was still available. If the general did not destroy it, perhaps it would find its way to a used book store. A dangerous place for a bibliophile like me.

My daughter signaled me, and I announced, "Emily has important news that will interest everyone."

A holographic image of my daughter appeared in the center of the room.

"Mom, you were right," she said. "I told Watson to match up the uneven layers of the data set from Priscilla's computer with the one from Sara's. Together they provided a list of people, places, technology, and codes."

Frank sprang to his feet. "You found the backdoors, Squirrel!" he exclaimed.

Emily smiled. "You're welcome, Dr. Frankenstein."

"Mom, they said," Emily pointed at Frank, Yano, and Luke, "that the best way to help you was to crack this computer."

"Now that I've done that, can I join you?"

"No, Emily," I said. "At least there are agents around Hatfield. I don't want you in harm's way with those Koreans out here. No need to worry. I have a bodyguard here. I will be home soon."

I blew Emily a kiss as her image flickered out.

"Backdoors?" Ellie asked.

"The DoD had intelligence suggesting that Sheppard and Kennedy were selling the codes used to shut down or remotely-control cybernetic technology," Luke explained, "including limbs, exoskeletons, and brain implants."

Ellie shivered as though someone had walked on her grave.

Is Ellie's name on that list?

"Cheryl, I know you're a cybernetic programmer," Luke said, "but *how* did you figure out the data set had been divided between two computers?"

"Mori stole one of Emily's earrings," I explained. "When my cat returned the earring, Emily sent me a picture of the pair. I realized that having one earring stolen was as bad as having both stolen. Earrings are worn in pairs and women rarely wear one without the other. Then the thought occurred to me that the computers did not just look alike, they were also a pair."

"Where is Priscilla now?" Malka asked.

"She wasn't taken into custody," Yano replied. "After she admitted that the computer was hers, she refused to answer any more questions until she could lawyer-up. Her lawyer was quick to point out that withholding information about her computer was not enough to keep her."

Malka was listening so intently, if she had been a puppy her ears would have been standing straight up.

"Why divide the data set?" Yano asked.

"If you'll remember," Frank said, "Luke and I thought Priscilla and Sara were selling the backdoors either together or separately."

"They probably didn't trust each autha," Malka added. "By dividing the files they were selling, neitha could double-cross the autha."

Had Priscilla double-crossed Malka?

"I'm relieved Emily has Priscilla's computer," Luke added. "This should prevent either of them from selling any backdoors for now. We have Sara's computer. Felicity is out of business."

"Who is Felicity?" Malka asked.

"Felicity is Sara and Priscilla," Frank answered. "Together they were sellin' the remote access codes."

I wonder what Malka would say if she knew about Frank's secret life.

"I brought the eDocs with me," Yano announced.

As Yano walked over to hand a small device to Luke, I noticed that Holmes had snuggled up with Sarge and they were snoring a duet. Luke activated the device, and the pages of notes we had made were displayed before us.

"In order to arrest Priscilla for murder, I need a solid case to present to the district attorney," Yano said.

"Priscilla obviously knew Rolando and Yong-Chun," I recounted, "because they worked at UNE. Any ideas about her connection to Josephine Bell?"

"We need to find a compelling reason why Kennedy would want to kill Bell," Yano said.

Ellie started to pace around the room, much like she used to do when we were brainstorming.

"Can you dig into their histories and discover if they shared anything in the past?" I suggested. "These murders feel personal."

"I'll send word to my A.I. to retrieve both women's history," Yano said.

"What about Hopper?" I asked. "Is the murder of Betsy Hopper connected to the other three murders?"

"Who is Betsy Hopper?" Frank enquired.

"She was at a cybernetics conference," Yano explained. "when her husband tossed her over the fourteenth-floor hotel balcony."

"Let me guess," Luke said, "he blamed his implant."

"Actually," Yano said, "he blamed his exoskeleton."

Ellie's face turned unnaturally white. Tears filled her eyes, making them look glassy. Her mouth moved, but no sound came out. Her hands shook by her side.

I tried to rush to Ellie, but nearly passed out in the process. Luckily, Malka was faster than me and guided Ellie to a chair. Luke ran into the room with a cold compress for Ellie's head. I had not even seen him leave.

"I will be fine," Ellie said to everyone. Gradually color returned to her face, and she thanked us for our concern. She turned to me and added, "Cheryl, you should not try to do anything quickly for the next several days."

A few minutes later, Lieutenant Jeanne LeClerc entered the study. Her athletic physique was obvious under her Army uniform of light-green with its buttoned-down V-neck shirt over dark-green slacks. Her shirt was decorated with two rows of ribbons which were placed below her three weapons medals. On her sleeve, a Special Forces patch identified her unit. Her blonde hair was pulled up in a knot. She looked at everyone in the room and announced, "If you will all move to the dining room, lunch is ready."

If Frank had not looked up so quickly at the sound of Jeanne's voice, I would have missed the moment of recognition on both their faces.

I need to ask Frank how he knows a member of the Army Special Forces.

The table was set with octagonal ceramic plates and tall glasses. A mixed salad and a terrine of onion soup sat on the sideboard. Three large trays had been placed on the small table at the side. Sliced croissants sitting next to a goose liver paté were on the first tray. On the second one, smoked salmon and thinly sliced strips of beef brisket were beautifully arranged. The circular third tray held several types of cheese surrounding a baked Brie, with slices of baguettes tucked around the edges. A small jar of fruit preserves held a knife. On the table, the pitchers of ice water and iced tea were sweating from the cold. My stomach rumbled at the sight.

I guess MOM has not joined the Army.

At the head of the table, coffee cups surrounded an ornate coffee urn. Ellie poured herself a cup. "Hmmm, that's a good French roast," she said, after taking her first sip.

Jeanne sat next to me, which gave me the opportunity to learn a little about her. She was born in France, and her parents had been in the diplomatic corps. Until the age of 14, she attended French schools. After her parents were killed in a bombing at the embassy, she lived with her aunt and uncle.

"How sad for you to lose your parents like that," I said. "Did you miss France?"

"Not really," Jeanne answered. "I moved to New Orleans and lived with my aunt and uncle until I finished high school. My family is why I joined the Army after college."

"What kinds of martial arts have you studied?" I asked.

"I first studied Angam pora in Sri Lanka."

"I thought that practice had been banned over three centuries ago," I said.

"The techniques survived within a few families. I met a soldier who had relatives in Sri Lanka. He helped me find a master."

"Luke bragged about all the black belts you have earned."

Jeanne laughed, and glanced at Luke. "I've studied martial arts in the U.S. and other countries. My black belts are in Judo, Shodokan Karate, and Brazilian Jiujitsu. However, there are no 'belts' in Angam pora. Last year I attended Helankada Mangalya. It's somewhat like a graduation."

"How is Angam pora different?" I asked, and hoped Jeanne understood I was truly interested, not just making conversation.

"Although fighting with weapons is taught within Angam, I was primarily interested in the unarmed combat techniques of Gataputttu, Pora Harammba, and especially Maru Kala which uses nerve point attacks."

"I guess being a soldier means being able to kill your enemy."

"To kill someone with a weapon means you don't have to look them in the eye," Jeanne said, locking eyes with me. "To kill someone with your bare hands is . . .well . . . different."

I think I will skip asking her how she knows.

After lunch, we returned to Luke's study. A short time later, Jeanne joined us.

"I have the history report," Yano announced as he displayed it. "There was no evidence that Kennedy knew either Bell or Hopper."

"I believe these murders were committed by the same person," I said.

Where is the connection?

"As long as aurr theory of the crimes requires the murdera to be connected to the victims," Malka said, "it's impossible Priscilla is the killa. She didn't know Bell aur Hopper, so what possible motive could she have?"

Every professor in the department has a motive to want at least one other professor dead.

Finished with his nap, Holmes came over to me for a belly rub.

My mind raced, and I said, "I think I know *how* to figure out who is killing all these people." My voice was soft. I was speaking more to myself than those in the room.

"How?" Ellie asked.

"By properly identifying who the *victims* are," I said.

"But, Cher, the victims are in the morgue," Frank said.

Yano nodded. "You were the one to convince me they were all killed by hijacked technology," Yano said in a somewhat dismissive tone. "We've been down that road."

"No," I said emphatically. "We went down the wrong road because we identified the wrong people as victims."

I continued to rub Holmes' belly.

"When I was being kidnapped," I said, "the one thing on my mind was that I would never forgive myself if anything bad happened to Holmes."

"You never should have taken that risk," Frank said.

"Agreed," I said, trying not to sound like a scolded child. "I promise I will never put Holmes or myself at risk like that again."

"I see where you're going, Cheryl," Ellie said. "We *have* been looking at this all wrong."

"There are no connections among the people who were murdered," I said, "because they are *not* the victims. The victims are the people who are now forced to live with the memory of having killed someone close to them."

"How ghastly!" Jeanne said, and put her hand in front of her mouth.

I was surprised by her reaction. A few minutes ago, she had been telling me about learning to kill a person with her bare hands by attacking their nerve points.

At Yano's instructions, the eDoc headings changed. 'Weapons' was replaced with 'Victims.'

"Oy vey!" Malka said, and rose to her feet. "I didn't realize that Betsy Hoppa was married to Les Gregson. He was the chair auf the department where Sara worked before she came to UNE. If anyone would want Gregson to suffa, it would be Sara."

"Alisha Patel was interim dean at the college where Sara was denied tenure," Frank reminded us.

"How does Kim's murder fit this pattern?" Yano asked.

"We don't actually know who killed Kim," Luke said. "We've been working under the assumption it was the Korean colonel, but anyone on the yacht could have killed him."

"If Sara was behind his murder," I said, "then Luke was the intended victim. What better way to make the general suffer than to discredit him? After all, Sara believed she would become dean after Alisha's conviction. Besides, Luke could have protected her from the humiliation of a misconduct investigation by informing the IRB that she had DoD clearance for what she was doing."

"What about the drugged wine Priscilla sent me?" Luke asked.

"We've been working under the assumption that she sent the wine because her name was on the gift card," Yano said.

"Who let you chaps know that Holmes had been found?" I asked.

"You did," Luke responded.

Frank and Yano nodded in agreement.

"No, Ellie did," I said. "She used my wearable to let you know he had been found. The message would have appeared to be sent by me. Sara could have simply signed Priscilla's name to the card."

"Sending the message on Cheryl's wearable was basic multitasking," Ellie explained. "I didn't have to tell you Cheryl was awake because the message appeared to come from her."

"That brings us to the Bell murder," Frank said.

"Let us consider that Sara's victim was Leonardo," I said. "The question remains how she would know that Josephine meant more to him than his current wife?"

"Pillow talk?" Ellie offered. "Leonardo could have told Priscilla, and she could have told Sara."

"Sounds plausible," Yano observed. "But we will need more convincing evidence to persuade the D.A. that Dr. Sara Sheppard killed four people in order to make four *other* people suffer."

"We have most of the why's," I said. "Now we need to uncover the how's."

"I'll mosey on up to Montreal and visit the hotel where Betsy was killed," Frank said. "See what people remember. Talking to someone over a wearable is not as effective as talking to them in person."

"Ellie, why don't you ask Alisha to suppa?" Malka asked. "In aurda fah Sara to have used Alisha as a murdering marionette, we'll need a theory about how Sara accessed their iDom."

Ellie nodded in agreement. She was still staying with Malka, and the two ladies left while quietly talking about their plans.

"That's enough for one day," Yano said. "Be careful you don't overexert yourself, Cheryl."

"You're welcome to stay for dinner," Luke invited.

"Please," I added. "Do stay."

"Thank you, I will," Yano said. "In the last few days, I have found dining alone to be increasingly disagreeable."

"Perhaps you should get a dog or cat," Luke suggested.

Did I just grow a tail and whiskers? Why is Yano looking at me like that?

Luke divided the cooking among the others. I was left out of the collaborative culinary adventure and *ordered* to sit outside while Jeanne grilled the watermelon and avocados. Yano was instructed in how to make cauliflower fried-rice, while Luke assembled Thai chicken lettuce cups and sautéed the shrimp. The only thing more impressive than the delicious food was Luke's skill at cooking and teaching others.

We were all trying not to talk about the case, and we all failed at one time or another.

"With the evidence on Priscilla's computer," Yano said, "She could be arrested for treason. Selling those backdoors would certainly qualify."

"She's under surveillance," Luke reported, "and I would like a little more time to discover who she contacts and who she avoids."

Yano nodded in agreement. "Has she communicated with Sara?" he asked.

"Not as far as we know. I will pull up the logs again in the morning."

"When are you going to question Hatfield?" I asked Yano.

Yano looked at Luke, and then at me.

"In the morning," Yano replied. "How did you know?"

"Considering Hatfield was blackmailing Sara," I explained, "that seems a logical next step. Have you let Emily know?"

"No," Yano said. "The fewer people who know, the less danger there is in the transport."

"Please tell me you are *not* sending in another heliodart," I pleaded with Luke. "Emily said the neighbors are still buzzing about that special delivery."

"Not much gets by you," Luke declared with a grin. "We're staging a chemical spill and evacuating the area. In the confusion that invariably follows with an exodus of that size, we'll get Hatfield to a transport and bring him back here."

"Not bad," Jeanne said. "Who will be handling his interrogation?"

Luke smiled at her. "Yano will. Hatfield is not a military matter."

"I read about Hatfield in the briefing for this assignment," Jeanne objected. "He is suspected of having information regarding the sale of DoD research to other countries. Doesn't that make him a military concern?"

There was no argument or disrespect in her voice. She sounded as though she could have been talking about what we would be having for breakfast.

"This is a civilian crime, not a military one," Yano explained. "Hatfield has never been in the military."

"That is too bad," Jeanne mused. "He'd probably be less of a *stupide* if he had joined the military. The Navy *probably* would take him."

After dinner, Yano said good-night to everyone and went home. Jeanne helped me change into my nightgown.

"Luke will let Holmes out with Sarge this evening," Jeanne said. "The backyard is fenced and the two canines have bonded."

"Be sure to let him into my room, even if I have fallen asleep. Holmes is used to sleeping with me."

"In that case, he will need a lift," Jeanne said, and left the room.

A few minutes later, she returned with an automatic dog-lift and set it next to my bed. Given Sarge's age, I was not surprised that Luke had such a device in his house or that Sarge shared Luke's bed.

The next morning, I woke up hugging the edge of the bed. Taking up most of the bed were Holmes and Sarge, performing an encore of their snoring duet. I did not even have enough time to use the bathroom when Jeanne rushed into my room. Wearing civvies, I barely recognized her.

"I put a stabilizing bar in the shower," she said. "I will wait here in case you need me."

After I showered, Jeanne helped me get dressed although I felt I could have done that on my own. The dizziness seemed to have passed.

I entered the dining room with my bed-buddies in tow. While I fed Holmes, Luke fed Sarge. After they ate, Luke let them out to the backyard.

"I can't believe how those two have bonded," Luke said.

"Holmes seems to think Sarge is a long-legged corgi," I said.

"And Sarge seems to think Holmes is a short-legged German Shepherd," Jeanne offered.

"I was told you like eggs," Luke said, as he pointed to the frittatas and cheese soufflé on the table. There was a tray of beautiful pastries, but I only wanted the egg dishes.

I wonder how many young people join the Army to get away from MOM.

"Have you heard anything about Hatfield?" I asked.

"He's in a waiting room at the police station right now," Luke replied. "Yano wanted him to relax before the interview."

Frank sent a message that he would meet me at Yano's office. He wanted to share what he had learned about Betsy Hopper and Les Gregson.

Just as I ate my last bite of frittata, I received a message from Yano requesting me to join him for Hatfield's interview.

"Luke," I said, "could you summon an air taxi for me? I need to meet Frank at Yano's office."

"Jeanne will be happy to take you," Luke said.

The reason Jeanne was wearing jeans and a t-shirt quickly made sense. She wanted to blend in with the herd of humanity in the city.

The lieutenant smiled saying, "You still need protection, Cheryl."

"Can you leave Holmes here for the day?" Luke asked. "I haven't seen Sarge so playful in years. I didn't realize he missed the company of other dogs."

I looked over at Holmes. He was giving Sarge a corgi-style play bow. Sarge had a huge grin on his face. Even though he was slow getting up, Sarge started running after Holmes in a merry game of chase.

How could I break up such a friendly game?

"Sure," I said. "Holmes can use some paw-pal time himself."

When we arrived at the police station, Yano was seated behind his desk and Frank sat in the visitor chair across from him. I took a seat on the couch. After all, Holmes would not be using it.

Everyone assumed that since Luke had sent Jeanne with me, she must have all the necessary clearances. She moved a chair near the door. My bodyguard positioned herself to be able to see people before they entered the door, and provide me with protection. Her focus seemed to be on the people outside the office, rather than the conversation in it.

"Oh, good," Yano said, "you're here. Now we can get started."

"Who has Sara contacted?" I asked.

"As far as Luke's surveillance is concerned," Yano replied, "only her manicurist."

"Is her manicurist Korean?"

"I will check on that." Yano tapped on his wearable.

"So, we knew that Gregson and Hopper were attending a conference," Frank said. "When I asked the hotel staff to check their records from the event, I learned that Priscilla and Sara were also at the conference and hotel."

Yano tapped on his controls and the two-year-old conference agenda appeared before us. On Saturday, Priscilla and Sara had presented their research regarding remote controls of cybernetic implants as safety precautions.

"Frank," I said cautiously, "what are you holding back?"

"I suppose I must look like the 'cat that ate the canary,'" Frank mused. "Sara's hotel room was next door to Gregson and Hopper's. Priscilla's was directly above them."

"How could *that* be a coincidence?" I asked.

"Oh, it wasn't," Frank said. "The hotel records showed that Sara called several times about whether Gregson had reserved a room. Once they confirmed he had, she requested the room next door. Sara claimed she wanted to surprise them for their wedding anniversary.

"After the murder, the police interviewed all the staff. Everyone they interviewed mention that Sara's behavior was rather odd."

"How so?" Yano asked.

Frank turned toward Yano and said, "When Les and Betsy were checking in, the desk clerk casually mentioned that many people were celebrating their anniversaries at the hotel that weekend. Betsy told the clerk that they would keep that in mind when they had their anniversary in a little over three months."

"What about Kennedy?" Yano asked.

"Priscilla requested the room on the other side of Gregson's room, but someone had already reserved it. So, she was offered the one directly above."

"And who was on the other side?" I asked before Yano had the chance.

"Conrad Joe Hatfield," Frank said with a smug smile.

Frank has probably memorized all the occupants of the rooms on at least three floors.

There was a chime on Yano's wearable and he announced, "Time to talk with Mr. Hatfield."

Chapter 19
"Whatever Remains"

"Why don't you simply hook him up to a LieGauge?" Jeanne asked. "That's what we do in the Army if someone is suspected of violating the Uniform Code of Military Justice."

"Many years ago," Frank explained patiently, "the U.S. Supreme Court ruled that biological means of lie detection was inadmissible in court because that would violate the sixth amendment regarding the right of the accused to cross-examine the witnesses against them. A person cannot cross-examine a machine."

"I cannot lie during my interview either," Yano added. "The court ruled that lying to a suspect is considered entrapment."

"Nowadays," Frank continued, "police interviews focus more on getting information than getting a confession."

Yano commanded, "Review instructions," as he left the room. Moments later, we heard the AI's voice.

"Once inside the interviewing room, the interview will be broadcast into this office. If any of you see or hear something the detective should be aware of, say it out loud. I will get the message to the detective. Keep in mind that because you have been asked for assistance with the interview, conversations in this room will be recorded along with those in the interview room."

We watched on the viewscreen as Yano entered the room. Tall windows gave the large room an airy appearance. Next to each over-stuffed chair sat end tables holding pitchers of ice water and a couple of glasses. Hatfield had moved one of the ottomans over to his chair and was resting his feet on it. There appeared to be the remains of food on the table next to him.

"Do you need anything?" Yano asked, as he moved an ottoman over to his chair.

"Am I under arrest?"

Yano paused to rest his feet on the ottoman, mirroring Hatfield's position.

"No," Yano said casually, "after that near drone attack, I decided you might really need protection. I went to great lengths to ensure your safe return."

"What do you want?" Hatfield asked, suspicion dripping from every word. "No one goes to that much trouble if they don't want something."

"I want to keep you safe until you're given the opportunity to tell me what you know about the selling of UNE research," Yano said.

"I see," Hatfield said, nervously shifting in his chair. "Yong-Chun was selling research proposals and closing summaries to the Korean Empire."

Knowing the A.I. would send everything to Yano, I said, "Closing summaries are what researchers submit to the IRB chair when their research project is completed. Those reports must be approved by the chair before the study can be published."

Frank nodded at me and added, "The summaries outline the results before anyone else knows them. Only Dr. Kim would have had access to them."

"Please *help* me, C.J." Yano's voice sounded as though he was requesting a personal favor, "I don't understand why the Korean Empire would have killed the person selling them secrets."

I doubt I could force my voice to sound as though I was asking Hatfreak for help.

"I'm pretty sure they found out that Yong-Chun was selling to others, outside the Korean Empire," Hatfield said in a smug voice.

Yano poured himself a glass of water and sipped it. He appeared to be in a relaxed conversation, asking a friend for advice.

Yuck!

"Yong-Chun sold to the highest bidder," Hatfield explained. "I know he sold Cheryl's proposal to Leonardo after she was denied tenure. Rumors have it that Leonardo voted against her in order to get his hands on her proposal."

"How do you know so much about Dr. Kim's sales of UNE research?"

"Bruce told me," Hatfield replied. "He claimed to have evidence that Leonardo was making copies of Sara's research papers in the lab. He never told me what that evidence was, and I could never figure out how Leonardo got into the lab."

"What kind of researcher does that?" Yano sounded offended.

"Leonardo is devoid of ideas," Hatfield rambled on, superiority filling his voice. "In order to keep his position, he was always looking for a research agenda he could steal from someone else. I think that is why he had an affair with Priscilla."

"I'm sorry, C.J.," Yano said. "I don't see the connection."

"As department chair, Priscilla would know who was working on what research. I'm sure their pillow talk was purely *academic*." Hatfield laughed at his own joke.

"Any idea who sent the drone after you?" Yano asked.

"That could have come from any of a number of sources," Hatfield's smile momentarily disappeared. "Most likely Sara sent it, but it could have been from Leonardo or even Bruce."

"Why would Dr. Nigel want to send a drone after you?"

Hatfield looked out the window for a few moments. Then he stared at a wall hanging. Finally, he got up and began to pace.

"Have I said something to trouble you?" Yano asked, as though the two men were close friends.

"Well," Hatfield said slowly, "Cheryl already figured out that Bruce was behind Sara's frame-up. He was so jealous of Sara, it was ridiculous." Hatfield paused for a minute and added, "I think Bruce mistrusted Sara so much his suspicions were spilling over to me."

"Speaking of Sara," Yano began, "she wasn't very nice to you, was she?"

I think I am going to puke.

"I knew what I was getting into," Hatfield said smugly.

"There's a *rumor* that you had some leverage over her."

What a euphemism! Leverage.

"It's true," Hatfield said. "Everyone tries to find an advantage. The competition for research assistantships is pretty cut-throat."

I quickly did the math in my head. According to the IRB complaints, Hatfield had been her assistant for about two years. That matched the date of the conference where Hopper's murder took place.

What is the connection?

"Ask him if he applied to be her assistant before or after the conference in Montreal," I said.

"Did you apply for your assistantship before or after you attended the cybernetics conference in Montreal?" Yano asked.

Hatfield's face betrayed his surprise at the question, but he quickly recovered.

"Before," Hatfield blurted out, and then quickly added, "but she didn't interview me until afterward."

"Conference hotel rooms can be so unpredictable," Yano said. He sounded as though they were only discussing hotel rooms and not murder. "Every year there is a police conference in Quebec. The first time I went, my room was exceptionally nice. The next year the room they gave me was a disaster."

"You should have reserved the same room as the year before," Hatfield offered.

"Do you reserve certain rooms?"

"Usually, if I've been to the hotel before."

"Had you ever been to the Montreal hotel before the conference?" Yano asked.

"No, that was my first time in Montreal," Hatfield said.

Yano sat quietly for about an entire minute. To me those sixty seconds felt like hours. Hatfield started tapping his fingers on the armrest to break the uncomfortable silence.

"Is that all?"

Yano shook his head. "Tell me about Dr. Hernandez's research."

"Look," Hatfield's voice had a note of agitation, "Bruce had a side business selling brain implants. Rolando was one of his customers. Rolando programmed one and sold it to me. Unethical, maybe. Illegal, I don't think so. After all, I was his research subject."

"What did Nigel expect to gain from framing Sara?"

"I told you," Hatfield said, "Bruce was jealous of Sara being made program director."

"But she was transferring research funds into his research account." Yano said, "You can see why I'm puzzled. If Sara was convicted of the misconduct, Nigel would lose that DoD money."

"Maybe he was more jealous than greedy," Hatfield offered.

"Or maybe more than one person was involved in framing Sara," Yano speculated. "Someone who was afraid that eventually auditors would find that funds targeted to Nigel's research weren't being transferred. Someone who owed another person a large sum of money."

Hatfield appeared stunned. He paced around the room again. Yano sat still, watching the information sink in.

"What are the chances that the money missing from Nigel's research account will match deposits Hernandez made?" Yano asked.

"I know nothing about that," Hatfield said—a little too quickly.

Liar.

"Is there anything else I should know about the *leverage* you have on Sheppard?" Yano asked.

"Nothing relevant," Hatfield said, closing his eyes briefly as if to make Yano go away.

"Very well," Yano said, "thank you for your time and assistance. The police sergeant will show you out."

Yano stood up to leave. Hatfield grabbed the arms of his chair in an apparent attempt to stop his hands from shaking. His face turned pale.

"What about ensuring my safety?" Hatfield asked. Panic filled his voice.

"I'm sorry, C. J.," Yano said sympathetically. "I jumped to the wrong conclusion about the risks. Your evidence about the sale of UNE research is solely based on hearsay. You're probably safe. You probably weren't the drone's target."

"What if I tell you how Sara has been selling codes to access the remote control of the military grade exoskeletons?" Hatfield asked. His eyes were half-open and his lips quivered.

Yano turned to Hatfield. The detective's countenance was one of the best poker-faces I had seen in a long time. "I'm only interested in this *story* if you have any first-hand evidence of your allegations," Yano said.

"I had enough evidence to convince Sara to hire me," Hatfield boasted.

Yano returned to his chair and sat down. After placing his feet back on the ottoman, he softly said, "I'm listening."

Hatfield blinked away the drop of sweat that had fallen from his brow onto his eyelashes. "I asked the hotel to put me in a room close to Sara's," Hatfield began. "I wanted to see who she knew. Who she liked. Who could put in a good word for me."

"Go on," Yano said.

"Friday night, Les was on the balcony with his wife," Hatfield recalled, "Sara was on her balcony too. With her computer." Hatfield wiped more sweat from his forehead with his sleeve.

"I take it you were on your balcony as well," Yano added.

"Right. The weather was so pleasant, I arranged with room service that I would eat dinner out there. I think Les and Betsy had made the same arrangement, even though their meal was served a few minutes *after* mine."

Does the man really think he is that important?

"And Sara?" Yano probed.

"Sara didn't come outside until I had finished dinner. She was acting peculiar."

"How so?"

"As she walked around on her balcony, she stayed in the shadows as if she was hiding. Unless someone was looking directly at her, they wouldn't have seen her."

"Were you looking directly at her balcony?"

Hatfield stood up and resumed his pacing. Yano waited patiently for him to answer. Finally, after almost a minute, Yano said, "You must have been looking at her balcony to see her *peculiar* actions, C. J."

A look of near panic appeared on Hatfield's face.

"Maybe you wanted to know if she had a lover in her room. Or maybe you only wanted to know what kind of music she listened to."

If Yano does not stop kissing the man's arse, I am going wash his lips after the interview.

Hatfield resumed his seat. "I think there was another person with her," Hatfield said. His eyes looked up toward the ceiling for a few seconds, and then he shut them tightly. "A man. He looked Asian, probably Korean."

"Why Korean?" Yano asked.

"Because Yong-Chun was Korean," Hatfield responded.

"Was the man Dr. Kim?"

"I'm not sure," Hatfield said, as a few more drops of sweat left his brow. "He seemed taller than Yong-Chun."

"What did you do next?"

"When Betsy started screaming," Hatfield said, gripping the armrests again, "I looked to see what was happening."

"Why was she screaming?" Yano asked.

"Because her husband had picked her up and was walking toward the rail," Hatfield's voice was devoid of emotion. "I will never forget the look on his face as he held her over the rail. He looked . . . bewildered. People at the outdoor café below started screaming. Then she rolled off his arms into the air."

Hatfield mimed the gesture.

"Did you look back at Sheppard's balcony?"

"As soon as Les tossed Betsy from the balcony," Hatfield said, "I wanted to see Sara's reaction. She had been looking at them just before the incident."

"What did you see?" Yano asked.

"I saw the man bow to Sara."

I have seen better expressions of horror on masks in a Halloween store.

"Then I saw Sara take a device that looked like a high-tech frisbee off the balcony table as she and the Korean walked back into her room."

"Then what?" Yano asked.

"The hotel security entered Les' room and stayed with him on the balcony until the police arrived."

"Go on."

"Later, during my assistantship interview with Sara, I asked her about what happened," Hatfield continued. "I asked her why she was with a Korean on her balcony, and why neither of them tried to stop Les from killing his wife. Instead of answering my questions, she hired me."

Of course, Hatfield, it is all about you.

"I see," Yano said. "Anything else?"

"The morning before Yong-Chun was killed, I overheard a *conversation* between Sara and Priscilla," Hatfield said. "Does this count as hearsay?"

Hatfield was back to being smug.

"Please, tell me about the conversation."

Yano could not sound any friendlier if he was hosting a children's show.

"Well," Hatfield began, "it was more like an argument. Apparently, Sara had removed some codes they were supposed to be selling together, and Priscilla was so hot she started yelling. Sara said she had taken the codes because their customers wanted demonstrations of what the codes could do with the right equipment. Priscilla asked if Yong-Chun knew, and Sara said if she told him, the general would kill her."

"Which general? Which *she*?" I was on the edge of my chair.

"Yano, is Hatfield referring to the Korean general or General Westmore?" Frank asked.

"What's the name of the general?" Yano asked.

"Sara didn't say," Hatfield replied. He sat further back in his chair and relaxed his shoulders.

"Was Sara saying that if *she* told Dr. Kim, or did she mean if Priscilla told Dr. Kim?" Yano asked.

"I have no idea," Hatfield said.

"Anything else about the conversation?" Yano asked, "Even a trivial comment may be important." Subtly, the detective continued to mirror Hatfield's body language.

"I heard Sara say that she was going on the yacht with Priscilla."

So much for trust among colleagues.

"Look," Hatfield said, "you have to understand that several people would like me to feed the fishes. Sara, Priscilla, the Koreans, maybe even Luke Westmore."

"Why would General Westmore want *you* dead?" Yano sounded as though he was stifling a chuckle.

"Maybe he found out I tried to hack his brain implant," Hatfield said. Yano raised an eyebrow.

Jeanne looked as though she wanted to run to the interview room and kill Hatfield with her bare hands. Frank walked over to her and put his hand on her shoulder.

"Why did you try to hack into the general's implant?" Yano asked, carefully keeping his tone neutral.

"Sara asked me to," Hatfield replied, sounding like a child. "She said someone had given her a code and she wanted to see if it was the general's backdoor."

Frank whispered something into Jeanne's ear, and she relaxed.

"But I couldn't get through," Hatfield said, as if that made the attempt innocent. "Either she was wrong about the code, or his implant was shielded."

"Mr. Hatfield, you no longer need to worry about someone trying to kill you," Yano said.

Hatfield smiled.

"You are under arrest for blackmail, buying an underground brain implant, and stealing money from the DoD. For starters."

Hatfield's face no longer held a smile when an officer came in and put black metal bands around his wrists and ankles. Their small size belied their ability to control the wearer.

"After processing, place Mr. Hatfield in a high security cell," Yano instructed.

"I want a lawyer!" Hatfield yelled. "And not some washed-up public defender."

"Get one," the officer said, escorting Hatfield out the door.

As Yano left the interview room, the A.I. announced, "Recording complete."

"Good job," Frank said, as Yano walked into the office and walked over to shake the detective's hand.

"Remind me never to play poker with you," I said, by way of congratulations.

Is Yano blushing?

Yano looked at the door, his mind still in the interview room. I interrupted his deliberations. "May I offer a few hypotheses?"

"Please do." Yano's green eyes twinkled at me.

Chapter 20
"However Improbable"

"First, when Betsy was murdered," I postulated, "Sara was most likely demonstrating her control over Les' exoskeleton to the Korean."

Frank added, "Sara must have chosen Les because she was angry at him for thwarting her chances of becoming department chair."

"She had a database of hundreds of backdoors," I said, "and chose to demonstrate the codes while getting revenge on Les."

I wonder what Priscilla saw from her balcony that night.

"Do all researchers have such homicidal tendencies?" Jeanne asked.

"Many do," Frank said. His face did not betray whether he was joking or serious.

What a great place to work!

"Sheppard waited a long time before conducting her next demonstration," Yano said.

I nodded in agreement, and added, "I suspect that Sara was successful with her first sale to the Korean government."

"In the two years between the murders of Betsy and Rolando," Frank said, "Sara switched her research from exoskeletons to cybernetic implants."

"Although Sara had demonstrated control of Les' exoskeleton," I said, "she needed to prove to the Korean Empire that she possessed backdoors to cybernetic implants as well."

"Wasn't that the point of the Hernandez murder?" Yano asked.

"Unlikely," I said, "there were no Korean witnesses to the Hernandez murder."

"So, what was the point?" Jeanne asked.

"I believe Sara needed to practice controlling a cybernetic implant, before conducting another demonstration," I hypothesized. "She used the opportunity to exact revenge on Alisha. She had never gotten over being denied tenure. I think Sara assumed the provost would appoint her interim dean. She had not planned on the misconduct charge."

"Logical," Frank said, and I bowed to him.

"How does Dr. Kim's murder fit in with your revenge theory?" Yano asked.

"Sara still needed to demonstrate her control of cybernetic implants to the Koreans," I said. "But I do not think Yong-Chun was Sara's intended target."

I thought for a minute, reflecting on what was planned rather than what happened. "I believe Sara intended to demonstrate her control of Luke's cybernetic implants by having him kill Priscilla that night."

"A double-cross?" Jeanne asked.

"Yes," Frank said. "Priscilla might not have been the love of his life, but they had an affair. A rather passionate one, I've been told."

Frank needs a reality check with Luke.

"Since Hatfield failed to hack into Luke's brain implant," I said, "Sara must have tried to control his cybernetics by other means. She failed to realize that his cybernetic limbs were similarly shielded. Am I right, Frank?"

He nodded in agreement.

"When Colonel Thae Song-thaek killed Yong-Chun," I continued, "Sara suggested moving on to Plan B."

"Implanting the fabricated video of Luke killing Kim into Luke's cyberlens," Yano finished. "The Roby-III makes that scenario even more plausible."

"Why would the colonel kill Dr. Kim when he was providing them with UNE research?" Jeanne asked.

"He probably found out that Yong-Chun was selling to customers outside the Korean Empire," I said. "If Hatfield knew the IRB chair was auctioning research to the highest bidder, it follows that the colonel would as well."

"The colonel was shortsighted," Jeanne said. "He shut off the sales of technology to others while ending it for the Koreans as well."

Heads around the room nodded in agreement.

"May I make a suggestion?" I asked.

"Like I could stop you," Yano said, his lip twitching.

"You need to prevent Bruce and Priscilla from leaving the area," I said.

Yano used his wearable to order their detainment. "Good call."

"Are you going to bring Dr. Sheppard in for questioning?" Jeanne asked.

"Jeanne," I said, turning to my bodyguard, "it is unlikely Sara will confess to the murders. The means and motives are exceptional."

"Cher is right," Frank said. "Yano will collect more evidence by interviewing those who would betray her."

"And who would that be?" Jeanne asked.

"The first person who tries to leave town is a good place to start," I suggested.

Hours passed. We decided to leave get some lunch and walked back to the café where Holmes had been treated like royalty.

"There is one thing that bothers me," Frank said to the group. "Who used Sara's keycard after the misconduct investigation was underway?"

"I would guess Yong-Chun. He had already left the room when I asked the provost to secure the lab."

"Do you have any ideas about who put the hole in the cabinet?" Frank asked.

"That must have been Bruce," I said. "He knew the documents with white-out would reveal the charges were fabricated. He needed a place to stash them until he had a way of getting them out of the lab."

"Is there anything left to figure out, Cheryl?" Jeanne asked. As with most of her questions, I heard no agenda in her inquiry.

"I still do not know who followed me and Ellie when we went for our walk," I said. "My mind keeps going back to the similar smells I associated with both the stalker and General Kim."

Frank tapped once on his wearable and said, "Compare the gait of the person who followed Dr. Locke in the 600 block of Springfield Street with the gait of the people at the dock on the night Dr. Kim was killed."

I had *never* seen Frank ask for any A.I. assistance.

"Who are you asking?"

"Isis," Frank responded, "my iDom."

"The gait of Dr. Kim Yong-Chun is a match," Isis responded.

Was Frank's iDom named after the Egyptian goddess, or someone else?

"Kim must have worried you'd uncover his involvement during the misconduct investigation," Yano said.

We strolled back to Yano's office after lunch. On the way, his wearable made a peculiar noise. "Dr. Kennedy has just tried to board a ship to Asia," Yano announced.

"I was hoping she would be the one," I said. "How soon will she get here?"

"Not long," Yano replied, "but I would guess she won't talk without her lawyer present."

Yano's prediction was correct. Priscilla was brought into the police station and refused to talk to *anyone* until her attorney arrived. I was stunned to see Mr. Earl Cartwright, president of the UNE Board of Regents, walk into the station wearing a brown western suit, boots, and matching cowboy hat.

Conflict of interest?

"How can the president of the Board of Regents be Priscilla's attorney?" I asked, unable to control the incredulity in my voice.

"There is nothing in the charter which prevents him from continuing his private practice," Frank said softly.

"This ought to be fun," Jeanne said.

Is she going to request popcorn and a soda.

Priscilla and Cartwright were taken to the same room where Yano had interviewed Hatfield. Priscilla's slow pace was either the result of her stiletto heels or her lack of sobriety. She wore skin-tight black slacks with a red and white striped shirt that had a boatneck collar. Priscilla looked anything but comfortable.

Who wears heels on a ship?

"The same rules apply as when I interviewed Hatfield," Yano reminded us and left the room.

Cartwright stood up as soon as Yano entered the room, and walked over to introduce himself.

"Howdy," Cartwright said. "Let me introduce myself. Name's Earl Cartwright. My friends call me Earl. You can call me Mr. Cartwright." He reached over and shook Yano's hand.

"Nice to meet you, Mr. Cartwright," Yano replied. "I am Detective Yano Johnson, and you're welcome to call me Yano."

Yano sat in the chair next to Priscilla. Cartwright frowned, and said, "I'm sorry, Yano, but you've taken *ma* seat."

Yano got up and took the chair on the other side of Priscilla. Cartwright frowned again, and asked, "Would you mind sitting in *that* chair?"

He pointed to the one opposite Priscilla.

Yano moved yet again, and asked, "Is this better, Dr. Kennedy?"

Priscilla nodded.

"Let me begin by explaining that this interview is entirely voluntary," Yano said. "There are no charges against you at this time. It has been brought to my attention that you may have information which would shed light on the ongoing murder investigations."

"In that case," Cartwright said, "we'll be skedaddling, Priscilla."

Let the games begin!

"While you're welcome to leave the station," Yano clarified, "I cannot let you leave the state until the investigation is complete. Dr. Kennedy, you should consider whether or not you've told me *everything* you know about the murders of Hopper, Hernandez, Kim, and Bell. As your attorney can tell you, failure to disclose information in a murder investigation could result in a charge of obstruction of justice. Isn't that right, Mr. Cartwright?"

Cartwright nodded in agreement, and unbuttoned his jacket. He smiled at Priscilla and turned to Yano to ask, "Ya supposin' those murders are buckled together?"

"They are," Yano said. "Aren't they, Dr. Kennedy?"

"I can't," Priscilla finally spoke. "I mean, I *don't* see how."

Cartwright glared at her.

"Please, detective, call me Priscilla."

Yano smiled and said, "Do you need anything, Priscilla?"

"A cuppa joe would be most welcome," Cartwright suggested. "Wouldn't it, honey?"

She nodded her head like a scolded child. Yano tapped on his wearable, and a few moments later Officer Evans brought in a pot of coffee and three insulated metal mugs without handles. The officer served everyone their coffee and left the room.

"C. J. Hatfield has already confirmed much of what we suspected," Yano said. "Sara had Dr. Gregson kill Dr. Hopper at the Montreal conference in order to demonstrate her control over his exoskeleton."

"What does all that have to do with *me?*" Priscilla asked, as though Yano was talking about strangers.

"You were at the Montreal conference two years ago. My investigator found that you occupied the room above theirs," Yano said. "Or is my information incorrect?"

Cartwright shifted his position to be able to face Priscilla better. From his body language, I guessed these facts were new to him.

"I was at that asinine conference," Priscilla admitted.

"Yano," Cartwright said, "you'll have to do better than that. I bet a whole posse of people were at that conference."

Cartwright shifted uncomfortably in his soft chair "Priscilla, we should probably have a private confab."

"I'm fine, Earl," Priscilla said, and gently put her hand on the inside of his knee.

I am pretty sure Priscilla knows what color sheets the cowboy puts on his bed.

"You had tried to get a room on the same floor as Drs. Gregson and Hopper," Yano said, "Why?"

She stared straight ahead. "Sara had been bragging about getting the room next door and I wondered what she would do from that vantage point."

"Priscilla was not wondering, she was worried," I said to the AI.

"Why were you worried?" Yano asked.

Priscilla looked at her attorney, her lips pinched shut. She waited for him to speak.

"Yano," Cartwright said, "if Priscilla continues to provide you with evidence of Sara Sheppard's guilt in these crimes, will you forego charging her with obstruction of justice?"

"As long as she continues to cooperate," Yano promised, "she will not be charged with obstruction of justice."

Cartwright nodded to Priscilla, while making a sound like a snorting horse.

"Why were you worried?" Yano repeated.

"Sara and I kept a database of backdoor codes for around a hundred exoskeleton prototypes we made for the military," Priscilla said, her voice devoid of emotion. "Ten codes a week disappeared from our inventory before the conference. I asked Sara why she had taken them."

"What did she say?" Yano asked.

"She said those codes were ones that would demonstrate the value of our database," Priscilla answered.

"Demonstrate to who?" Yano asked.

"To our customers," Priscilla quickly replied.

"Who were your customers?"

"I don't know, Sara was in charge of sales." Priscilla sounded insulted that anyone would think she would stoop so low as to sell anything.

"What happened the night Dr. Hopper was murdered?" Yano asked.

"After my dinner," Priscilla began, "I sat on the balcony, listening to music, sipping a martini, in the comfortable Montreal night."

Sipping a martini from a pitcher, I bet.

"Priscilla, please tell me exactly what you saw from your balcony that night," Yano instructed.

"I only saw that poor woman fall from the balcony," Priscilla said. "At first, I thought she had jumped."

"Why is that?" Yano asked.

"Being above their balcony," Priscilla said, "I couldn't see anything *on* their balcony."

"Even I would know that," Cartwright added, a note of superiority to his voice.

"What caused you to look down?" Yano asked.

"The screams of the people in the café," she replied.

"Could you see onto Sara's balcony?" Yano asked.

"Not without being seen by her and anyone else looking around," Priscilla said.

Great self-preservation skills, blondie.

"When was the next time you talked to Sara?"

"Probably at lunch the next day," Priscilla said. "I didn't go to any of the morning sessions. I needed to catch up on my sleep."

Without a Canadian MOM, she probably drank herself to sleep.

"What did you and Sara talk about?" Yano asked.

"She said *we* had sold a slate of codes, but she still needed to work out the money transfer."

"Did she say *who* she sold the codes to?" Yano asked.

"No," Priscilla said, her volume and cadence increasing, "and I didn't ask. I only knew that the money transfer was complicated because the buyer was foreign."

Does she bleach her brain along with her hair?

Priscilla took several sips from her coffee. She seemed to be getting somewhat sober.

"Anything else, Yano?" Cartwright asked.

"I have a few more questions," Yano replied, "about the Hernandez murder."

Cartwright nodded to Priscilla. She shifted in her chair, and smoothed imaginary wrinkles out of her slacks.

"Priscilla, why did you leave your computer at Dr. Hernandez's home?"

"Well," Priscilla began, her tone softening, "Sara told me to leave it at Rollie's house."

Yano nodded for her to go on.

"Sara was always asking me to do shit that didn't make any sense," Priscilla said. "This didn't appear any *more* bizarre than her previous requests." As she leaned toward Yano, the neckline of her shirt fell open. "Like, how she would ask for my computer occasionally to perform an *upgrade.* I rarely saw any difference."

I said to the A. I., "Priscilla is not that dumb. She knew those so-called upgrades were how Sara was taking codes from their inventory."

She should take lessons from Hatfield in how to be a better liar.

"How many days before Dr. Hernandez was killed did you leave it there?" Yano asked.

"That was about four days before . . . Alisha killed Rollie," Priscilla said blinking back tears.

Bring out the crocodile tears!

"Is it possible that Dr. Sheppard used one of those backdoors to control Dr. Patel's cybernetic implant?" Yano asked.

Priscilla paused and then said softly, "Sara *might* have wanted revenge against Patel for when the dean denied her tenure."

If holding a grudge were an Olympic event, Sara could win a gold medal.

No one spoke for a few moments. Priscilla looked lost in her thoughts. She stood up and walked behind her chair. She placed her hands on its back.

"To hack into someone's cybernetic limb, as you propose," Priscilla said, "would require the puppetmaster to be in the room. Wouldn't it?"

Her question lingered in the air, unanswered. She slowly walked the rest of the way around the chair. After regaining her composure, she resumed her seat.

"Tell me about what happened on the Korean yacht the night Dr. Kim was killed," Yano requested.

"Sara insisted she come with me on the yacht," Priscilla said. "I wasn't exactly thrilled. You've gotta understand, she can be a real wet blanket when people start having fun."

Was Priscilla pouting?

"Did you tell General Westmore that you would be on board?" Yano asked.

"I did. He had asked me to let him know the next time I was invited for a boat party. I thought if I helped him out, he would feel better."

"Why did you need to make him feel better?" Yano asked in a friendly tone.

"Luke was a little angry when I broke off our affair."

Cartwright didn't even twitch at the word affair.

Ah, the cowboy knows about Priscilla's pillow hopping.

"Did you send Luke any gifts that night?"

"No. That would have given him the wrong impression." Priscilla made a pouty face. "I can't tell you much about that night, I remember there was an argument near the sky lounge. Sara told me to stay put in the entertainment room, and that she would investigate. I heard her scream and I hid behind the couch."

"Why did you hide?" Yano asked.

"I thought something had happened to Sara," Priscilla said, "and I would be next. When she came back to the room, she turned on a monitor. I could see Luke, unconscious in the lounge. I started to cry. She poured me a drink. I think she spiked it because I don't remember anything until the next day. When I woke up, Sara told me that Luke had killed Dr. Kim."

"Before Luke got on board the yacht," Yano began. "He drank some wine laced with Roby III. Wine that was delivered via drone, with a gift card signed by you."

"I didn't send that wine," Priscilla protested. "I had ended my affair with Luke."

"Shall I tell you what we think was supposed to happen?" Yano asked.

Ah, the royal we.

Priscilla nodded. Cartwright inched toward the front of his chair.

"Sara wanted to demonstrate her control over Luke's brain implant and his cybernetic limbs. She knew the brain implant was shielded, but hoped she could still control his limbs. There was no way to test that prior to the voyage. She planned to use a backdoor code to control Luke and force him to kill *you*."

Yano let that last sentence sink in.

"What a lot of hogwash," Cartwright said. "If Sara could control the general's cybernetic implants then Priscilla wouldn't still be alive."

"Right. But General Westmore's cybernetics were shielded as well." Yano explained.

Priscilla suddenly stood up. She shook her head and wrung her hands. Instead of fear, her face was red with rage. She began strolling around the room. Agitation filled her stride.

If you swim in the ocean, dearie, better expect a few sharks.

"That's a tall tale, if ever I heard one," Cartwright whinnied.

Priscilla shook her head.

Yano continued his narrative. "Meanwhile, Colonel Thae and Dr. Kim had an argument. The colonel confronted Kim with evidence that he had been selling research to people outside the Korean Empire. When Kim couldn't offer an explanation, the colonel shoved him overboard."

"Yong-Chun was killed because he sold research to Leonardo?" Priscilla asked, incredulously. She sat down again.

"Others as well," Yano replied.

"You *knew* Dr. Kim was selling UNE research, and didn't tell me?" There was more disappointment than anger in Cartwright's voice.

"Yong-Chun was always making deals with people," Priscilla said to her attorney. "I don't think Leonardo gave Yong-Chun *money*. At the same time, every year when the faculty senate voted on the IRB chair, Yong-Chun knew he would have Leonardo's support."

"If this yarn is true," Cartwright said, "Priscilla's life is in danger. Sara will want to kill her to prevent her testifying."

"That's not how she works," Yano explained. "The victims in these murders were the people who killed someone they loved. The person killed was only collateral damage."

"Sara's motive is all cattywampus," Cartwright declared. "You can't expect some highfalutin' judge will believe that yarn."

"Priscilla personally observed little," Yano said. "She will not make a convincing witness. A good lawyer, such as yourself, would be yelling *hearsay* until he was hoarse."

Cartwright grinned at Yano.

"Rather," Yano said with a smile, "Priscilla Kennedy, you are under arrest for conspiracy to commit espionage, conspiracy to commit theft of trade secrets, unlawful export, attempted export of DoD data, and circumventing the Medically Ordered Meals system."

Oh, that last charge is rich!

"Slow down there, cowpoke, we had a *deal!*" Cartwright blustered. "You can't go back on our agreement. I'll get the case tossed out faster than two shakes of a lamb's tail. It's only Friday, the judges will still be in their offices."

"We did have a deal," Yano said smiling, "which is why I'm *not* charging Dr. Kennedy with obstruction of justice."

"Don't worry honey," Cartwright hollered, "I will start filing motions within the hour."

Priscilla looked as dazed as if Yano had tased her.

Chapter 21
"Must Be the Truth"

When Yano returned to his office, we were all smiles. We had started updating the eDocs when I received a message from Ellie.

"Ellie wants to meet us for dinner," I announced. "Apparently what she wants to tell us should not be shared over wearables."

"In that case," Jeanne said, "the safest place would be the general's home."

I nodded, and Jeanne tapped a message on her wearable. A few moments later, she announced, "General Westmore says to ask her to come for dinner at seven. He wants to know if Malka will also be joining us."

I sent the invitation and asked if Malka was coming.

Ellie replied, "There will be three of us."

She was not usually so cryptic, so I assumed there was a good reason not to identify who else would be at dinner. If Malka was bringing her husband, there was no need to hide his identity. The third guest remained a mystery.

What is Ellie up to?

Jeanne let the general know that Ellie would be bringing two guests to dinner. As much as Luke loved to show off his cooking, I could only imagine the smile on his face when he was told he would have a full table of eight diners.

We all arrived at Luke's about 6:30 and sat in the kitchen telling him about the interviews while he finished cooking. Holmes and Sarge sat behind the doorway to the kitchen. Apparently Sarge had been trained not to enter, and Holmes was politely following suit.

Luke asked me to set the table with his heirloom china and crystal. Yano was directed to put several bottles of wine from Luke's wine cellar on the sideboard. Frank and Jeanne were chatting about how Luke appeared to be channeling Julia Child.

Around seven, Luke and I answered the knock at the door. Ellie, Malka, and a bearded man entered. The man was wearing ill-fitting clothes and had a haunted look. I stared at him for several moments, thinking he looked vaguely familiar. Suddenly I burst out, "Leonardo! You look like hell!"

Leonardo's smile appeared forced. He looked as though he had lost more weight than was healthy. "You are looking well," Leonardo said. "I'm glad you recovered from the attempt on your life."

Is that sincerity I hear in his voice?

Yano, Frank, and Jeanne came into the hallway. Unaware of the significance of Leonardo's presence, Jeanne suggested, "Let's eat before the food gets cold."

"Good ideer," Malka said.

We entered the dining room and everyone began remarking about the delicious aromas. Luke took his place at the head of the table. Malka seated Leonardo between herself and Ellie. Jeanne was at the other end of the table, which left me to sit between Frank and Yano. I fought the urge to stare at Leonardo. I felt as though I was sitting in front of a stranger.

The dishes started making their way around the table. I took some of the seared scallops with brown butter and lemon sauce; the smell was enchanting. Malka was dishing up some of the gorgonzola and pecan-stuffed cherry peppers, when Ellie passed her the spinach and artichoke bites. Leonardo declared the goat cheese pesto crostini to be a work of art. I could only imagine what we were going to be served for dessert.

I hope Luke opens a restaurant after he retires from the Army.

"Leonardo," I said between bites, "where have you been?

Malka answered for him. "Leonardo spent a few days hiding on auur sailboat in the cape." I found her tone of voice difficult to read.

"How did you find him?" I asked Malka, since she was acting as his mouthpiece.

"He sent me a message via the neighbor's six-year-old boy," Ellie answered. "The note was wrapped in his Venezuelan scarf. Leonardo asked me to meet him and bring him some food."

I cannot believe Leonardo parted with his scarf.

"Why did you run from the crime scene?" Yano asked Leonardo, ignoring how the women had been answering for him.

"I was scared," Leonardo said. "The machine stopped responding to my commands. I bloodied my hand trying to activate the kill switch. Then *it* killed my Josephine. In my nightmares, I can still see her face. She looked directly at me. I can hear her screams, over and over just as the claw . . .."

I could see tears moisten his eyes. For the first time, I noticed the dark circles and bags under his eyes. He had not been sleeping well. Malka put her hand on Leonardo's arm, and said something too soft for anyone else to hear.

Is this the same woman who would rather rearrange her lipsticks than have coffee with him?

Somewhere along the way, Leonardo had lost his air of self-importance. "I needed to figure out how I lost control, and why none of the three kill-switches worked," he continued. He swallowed hard and placed his hands on the table. "I thought Ellie could help me. After all, she wears an exoskeleton. There are more similarities than differences between her assistive device and the contraption I was wearing."

Ellie nodded in agreement. "Leonardo's account of what happened is nearly identical to what Alisha described when she lost control of her implant."

"Sara is behind all of this!" Leonardo exclaimed. "I saw her in the stands during the demonstration. She was smiling when everyone else was gasping in horror. What kind of person does that?"

"I told Leonardo about our working hypothesis," Ellie said.

"When the provost appointed me interim dean, I think Sara became obsessed with seeking revenge," Leonardo said, and then added, "Yano, could you cancel your wanted bulletin on me so I can walk around in public again?"

"Voice authentication is required for such an order," Yano explained and said over his wearable, "Dr. Leonardo Gonzales is no longer a fugitive. All officers are instructed to stand down."

"Now, I might even shave off my beard," Leonardo said.

Yano and Leonardo shared a chuckle.

"I have been wanting to ask you," Frank said, "what were you doing in Sara's lab?"

"That seems like such a long time ago," Leonardo said. "I was probably copying research notes. Sara began keeping handwritten notes like Cheryl, and for the same reasons. In many ways, they are more secure."

Honesty is the last thing I expect from Leonardo.

"Cheryl," Leonardo said, "I want to apologize for the way I treated you. I know you have no reason to believe me now, but I want you to know that I'm not the same egotistical jerk who stole your research and voted against your tenure."

I could not think what to say. If Malka had not changed her opinion of him, I would have considered his behavior an attempt at manipulation. Malka was an excellent judge of character.

"What has changed?" I finally asked.

"I killed my soulmate," Leonardo began. "Not only had I wronged her during our marriage, but I killed her. I hate sleeping. At night, when I am lying in bed, I try to figure out how I became such a pompous ass. Ellie helped me realize I didn't need to continue to be so arrogant."

His tone was one of appreciation, not seduction.

"Martin has been giving Leonardo medication to help him sleep," Malka said softly. "When he'll take it."

Luke broke the sober mood by inviting us into his great room. I hoped he would play the piano. Coffee was brewing at the bar and I selected the recliner which was the furthest away from it.

"Cheryl," Luke said, "can I get you something from the bar? I know you don't drink coffee."

"A 'circuit breaker' would be appreciated," I said, "easy on the scotch."

I wanted to believe Leonardo was a changed man, but it would take time.

Malka and Ellie continued to bookend Leonardo as he sat on the overstuffed couch. I soon realized their proximity was an effort to make him feel safe.

"Time to compare notes," I announced. "Yano interviewed Hatfield and Kennedy today."

"And arrested both of them," Jeanne added.

"Right," I said. "We can go over details later."

I turned to Ellie and asked, "What did you find out from Alisha?"

"Alisha had been away to a conference," Ellie began, "and she only returned the morning of her husband's death."

I nodded for her to continue.

"In hindsight, she realized that day was odd in a number of ways. First, Alisha forgot her lunch at home, so had to return to the house to eat. She said Sara was sitting in her car parked directly in front of her home. When Alisha asked what she was doing there, Sara told her she was hoping to get some advice."

If Sara asked for Alisha's advice, someone needs to check if Hell has become a deep freeze.

"Advice about what?" Frank asked.

"Alisha said she wanted advice about how to tell a friend that her husband had a mistress," Ellie said. "How crazy is that?"

"What did Alisha tell her?" Frank asked.

"To mind ha own business." Malka said, with a chuckle.

"Alisha also remembers that as she approached Sara's car," Ellie continued, "Sara was trying to cover up an object on the front seat of her SDV. Alisha said that below the sweater Sara had thrown over the object, she could make out that it was shaped like a pie pan. Does that mean anything to anyone?"

"Go on," Yano said, "that sounds familiar."

"Excuse me while I consult with my resident expert," I said, and stepped into the hallway.

"Emily, are you still up?" I said over my wearable.

"Mom, it's only a little after six here. What do you need?"

"Can you tell if Priscilla's computer has a program on the drive that could have been used to hack into a home's iDom?"

"I'll take a look," Emily said. "You realize that would require the computer to be in the iDom's home."

"That's what I was thinking," I said. "The only way an air-gapped computer could access the iDom would be through the house wiring."

I heard music from the piano and walked back into the great room. To my surprise, Yano was playing a swing jazz tune, to everyone's enjoyment. I went back to my chair and sipped on my circuit breaker.

"What did Squirrel say?" Frank asked.

"She will be getting back to me in a few minutes," I said, grinning.

"Your expert is a squirrel?" Jeanne asked.

Frank and I laughed. He leaned over and whispered something in her ear.

"Anything else Alisha thought was odd about that day?" I asked Ellie.

"Not that day exactly. Alisha said that Rollie had been acting nervous for a couple of days during their last conversations," Ellie reported. "That evening, Rollie seemed more relaxed. When she asked about his worries, he told her Bruce had done him a favor, and he felt better now."

"Your turn, Detective Yano," Malka said. "What have you been doing while we were aiding and abetting a fugitive?"

Yano told Malka and Ellie about the interviews with C.J. Hatfield and Priscilla. Malka laughed until tears were in her eyes as he described Priscilla's arrest.

Emily notified me that she had my answer. I adjusted my wearable to project her image in front of me.

"Impressive bit of programming," Emily said. "Priscilla's computer had been set to hack into the iDom at a specific time."

I nodded at her image.

"Mom," Emily continued, "I checked the error logs. The iDom was never activated. Either someone moved it out of the target location, or someone had put it in a shielded area."

"What was the computer programmed to do, once it accessed the iDom?"

"Broadcast the internal cameras to another device," Emily said. "But the plan didn't work. So how did the killer know when your former dean was close enough to her husband to kill him?"

Emily is one smart squirrel.

"The killer would have needed to resort to a Plan B at the last minute," I said. "More than one person has reported Sara having a device that is about the shape of a frisbee. Any guesses what that could be?"

"Sounds like a gamer's Circle of Hell," Emily said.

"Could you explain that to Frank, who has never played anything more advanced than Mario Universe?"

Frank winced.

"Most gamers don't use controllers like Frank did with "Shadows of the Assassins' Brotherhood"" Emily said. Patience saturated her words. "There are virtual reality interfaces which are far more responsive and totally illegal. These implants allow the player to feel as though they are *in* the game. Sorta like the holodeck on your favorite old sci-fi television show."

"Go on," I said. Frank looked bored.

"Gamers interface with the Circle of Hell through a brain implant. The circle allows the gamer to interface like an avatar. But there's a serious downside. Since the implant is placed near the cerebrum, the player runs the risk of impaired balance in real life if the implant is removed or made inoperable."

I looked around the room. Everyone was trying to understand the implications of Emily's description.

"If Sara had a brain implant, like the one you are describing," I said, "could she use it to control another person's cybernetic implant?"

"Easily," Emily said, "but she would still need to see how close they were to each other so she could operate the cybernetic limb at the right moment."

"Thank you, Emily. I think I can take it from here."

"Love you, Mom."

"Love you, too."

Emily's image disappeared from Luke's great room.

"Your daughter is every bit as pretty as her mother," Luke said.

I better not be blushing.

"Does Sara have a brain implant?" I asked.

"Bruce might know," Frank said, and sent an inquiry to the faculty implant peddler.

"Here is what I hypothesize," I said. "Sara told Priscilla to leave her computer at Rolando's house because she had installed the program which would allow her to see the proximity between the couple."

"But when she went to check on her interface," Ellie jumped in, "she discovered Priscilla's computer could not be accessed."

"Right," I said. "Rolando had given the computer to Bruce."

Holmes came into the room, with Sarge right behind. Holmes took up his post by my feet. Sarge nudged Luke for some petting.

"Suppose Sara was using this gamer device," I said. "How would she be able to see the couple's movements?"

"She could have used a drone," Luke suggested, "like the spy bug I used."

"Spy bugs are apparently commonplace among the faculty," Yano snorted.

"Bruce says Sara has an implant, but claims he didn't sell it to her," Frank shared.

"I'll call the district attorney tomorrow," Yano said. "I believe we have enough evidence to arrest Dr. Sheppard on first degree murder charges for Hopper, Hernandez, and Bell. She could be charged as an accessory to Dr. Kim's murder."

Ellie, Leonardo, and Malka were the first to leave. I was impressed by their compassion for someone who had been such an arrogant twit. I was fascinated by the transformation of the arrogant twit into the humble man who offered me a sincere apology. I was heartened by Leonardo's honesty.

Maybe there is hope for the assholes of the world after all.

Yano left next. I agreed to stay in Boston until after he had spoken to the D.A.

I said goodnight to Frank, Luke, and Jeanne, and while walking upstairs to go to bed, I could hear the three discussing whether or not the matter should be left in the hands of the justice system.

Anarchists.

Saturday morning, I awoke to the sounds of "The Holmes and Sarge Snoring Duet." No one barged into my room as I was about to take my shower. No one suggested I needed help getting dressed. No one let the two dogs out for their morning routine. I began to wonder if I were the only two-legged being in the house.

By the time I walked into the kitchen, Luke and Jeanne had returned from their morning run. Hot and sweaty, they retreated to showers and grooming. I shepherded Sarge and Holmes to the back door. The two dogs went to opposite ends of the yard to take care of business. Then Holmes walked to the center of the yard and waited. Sarge came over to him and performed an enthusiastic play bow. Holmes returned the bow, corgi-style. In a heartbeat, the two dogs engaged in a merry game of chase.

Sarge you are about to be outpaced by a corgi.

I enjoyed watching the dogs play and ended up sitting on the grass. Jeanne came and sat next to me. Her hair was still wet from the shower. Her gaze was on the playful pups.

"Sarge is going to be lost when you leave," she said.

"Holmes will miss his new friend," I said. "Maybe Luke should consider getting Sarge a companion."

"I'm not sure that Luke is ready to give his heart away again," Jeanne whispered.

"Breakfast is ready!" Luke yelled at us.

We ate in the kitchen and I appreciated the more casual atmosphere. I had not had a lazy Saturday in nearly a month.

"Has anyone heard from Yano?" I asked, between bites of scrambled eggs.

"You'd hear first," Luke said, and looked down at his wearable. "Frank is coming over to sit vigil as we wait for Yano's report."

No sooner had Frank arrived than Yano sent me a message. As he requested, I enabled his holograph to appear to the entire room.

"The district attorney will not prosecute Sara Sheppard for the murders," he said. "At first it seemed as though he didn't think I had enough evidence. He excused himself to make some calls. When he returned, he announced that *others* were in agreement with him. A public trial could result in mass hysteria."

Yano's face was red, and he had sweat on his brow. The detective looked angry.

"Let me guess," Frank said. "In order to charge her with the murders, the Cybernetics Overseers would have to acknowledge that medical implants can be controlled by hackers. Hence, the danger of furious crowds."

Frank paced around the room. Actually, he was stomping. His face was pinched. After all, Sara Sheppard had helped the Koreans injure his friend Luke.

Yano nodded.

"They are going to let Sara get away with murder! I mean murders!" My voice was filled with rage.

"We're not going to find justice in a court room," Yano lamented, "but maybe justice will find Sara Sheppard."

"There goes my hope of returning to Seattle with any sense of gratification."

"You'll need to wait until this evening to fly back," Luke said. "I'm sending a team this morning to retrieve Kennedy's computer. As long as it's in your home, you're at risk. We can't detain the Korean officers any longer. However, I have been assured they will be returning to the Korean Empire upon their release. I have been told the colonel will stand trial for murdering Dr. Kim."

What the Koreans call trials, we call skits.

I tapped a message on my wearable to let Emily know to expect someone to come for the computer. She replied that she would package it up for me, with a little gift for Yano.

What is my daughter up to?

"I think it's time I talk with Bruce," Frank said, and left.

"I wonder if there is a way to shield Sara's implant so she cannot continue to hack into other people's implants," I said.

Luke and Jeanne exchanged poignant looks.

"Lieutenant LeClerc," Luke said, "your assignment here is done. Please report back to the base for further orders."

Jeanne left the room and returned a few minutes later in her uniform with her duffle bag sitting just outside the door. I noticed her Black Ops badge, and wondered about her next assignment.

"Stay safe," Jeanne said, and gave me a hug.

"Thank you for all you did for me," I said.

About an hour later, Luke informed me that the computer had been picked up and the "little gift" would be delivered to his house in time for lunch.

"Since the gift is for Yano," Luke said, "I've invited the detective over here for lunch."

Yano arrived in jeans and a black t-shirt. After all, it was a lazy Saturday. Lunch was fruit salad, potato salad, coleslaw, and sandwiches. Luke made some fresh lemonade

We were eating our sandwiches when the military escort arrived. The sergeant reported the carrycase contained a computer and a gift wrapped in brown paper. Luke handed the package marked "Yano" to the detective.

To everyone's surprise inside the wrapping was Yano's book, "The 150th Anniversary of Superhero Comics."

"How . . . in the *world*?" I stuttered.

Emily had placed a note inside the cover:

> *Evidently, the general didn't appreciate the book Mom gave him and threw it in the trash at the Korean Embassy. A janitor thought the book might be worth some money and advertised it on one of the Internet auction sites. Now that it has been returned to its rightful owner, I hope my mom can get out of the dog house.*
> *Cheers!*
> *Emily*

"Am I?" I asked.

"Are you what?" Yano replied.

"Out of the dog house."

The smile on Yano's face was more than enough of an answer.

Yano insisted that he take me to the airport.

"The check's in the mail," Yano said, as he put my suitcase in the security screener.

"What check?" I asked.

"An old-fashioned figure of speech," Yano said, "I hired you and your daughter to help me solve Kim's murder. Remember?"

"You are forgetting Holmes," I said.

"I could never forget Holmes," Yano said. "I think he looks a little sad. Maybe you both should stay a little longer . . .with me."

"He will be fine once we get back home," I said. "Mori will be loving on him as soon as we walk in the door. I worry more about Sarge. I fear he will be lonely without Holmes."

"Don't forget me," Yano said.

"If you get lonely," I said, "you are welcome to visit me in Seattle. Police detectives get vacations, right?"

"They do," Yano said with a smile. "And I will."

As soon as I returned home, I sent messages to everybody letting them know I had safely returned. Malka and Ellie messaged me back immediately, expressing their own outrage with the D.A.'s decision. I was surprised when no one else responded before I went to bed. When I woke up the next morning, there were messages from all four on my wearable. Everyone was lamenting about the lack of justice for the victims of Sara Sheppard. At the same time, I thought it was odd that no one speculated about the identity of her next victim. I was worried that she might hold a grudge against Malka.

*   *   *

As I sat down for breakfast Sunday morning, I listened to my news stream. The death of Dr. Sara Sheppard was the top story.

Distinguished Professor Sara Sheppard was found dead this morning at her Roxbury home. Dr. Sheppard was recently the focus of an investigation into allegations of research misconduct. Those charges were dismissed. A source close to the case reported that her research assistant, Conrad Joe Hatfield, and a colleague, Dr. Priscilla Kennedy, are currently in custody on unrelated charges. In a press release received minutes ago, Detective Yano Johnson stated that Dr. Sheppard died from injuries she sustained when she fell down the stairs at her home. The police are satisfied that no foul play was involved.

"Watson," I said, "delete UNE from my newsfeed."

ABOUT THE AUTHOR

Ilana Lehmann is a high school drop-out who went on to earn a doctorate degree. After watching Neil Armstrong walk on the moon, she wanted to be an astronaut. After crawling inside a space capsule at the San Diego Aerospace Museum, she decided to wait until spacecraft were more like the USS Enterprise. Before the pandemic, she enjoyed comic-cons and used book sales. Now, when she isn't writing or imagining futuristic inventions everyone wants, she works her day job and watches sci-fi while rubbing her dog's belly. She is owned her cat, Hobbes, and bossed around by her coffee-obsessed Pembroke Welsh Corgi, Susie Derkins.

www.ingramcontent.com/pod-product-compliance
Lightning Source LLC
Chambersburg PA
CBHW051532020726
47506CB00008B/592